THE WIZARD AND THE WARRIOR KING

Joel Newlon

Silver Eel Publishing

Ebook ISBN: 978-1-7362211-8-1
Paperback ISBN: 978-1-7362211-9-8

Cover art by Kevin Sardinha
Cover design by Silver Eel Publishing

Printed in the United States of America

PRAISE FOR *THE CRAFTSMAN AND THE WIZARD*

What a great read. Newlon is an expert world-builder in this debut novel that wove fantasy elements with historical norse mythology seamlessly (there's even a bit of romance!!)

It was so refreshing to follow our unlikely heroes on their journey to conquer an evil demon who steals children. There were many interesting side-quests along their way and I was on the edge of my seat waiting for their paths to finally cross.

This was just what I needed: loveable heroes, realistic and strong female characters, the classic good vs evil struggle, love over hate, an epic journey, a touch of humor, magic aplenty! Five stars from me. I can't wait to read next from this author.

LEE COLGIN, AUTHOR OF *THE IMMORTAL JEWELS*

◆ ◆ ◆

This book is about heroes-- mythical, legendary, everyday, accidental, and all shades in between. It's a coming of age story for a young wizard. A last adventure for a venerable craftsman. A story about many different kinds of love. There are gods and goddesses. Ancient evils. Sentient animals. Good friends, tyrants, all kinds of magic and numerous interlocking stories of loss and redemption. It's hard to categorize everything this novel is, but it broke my heart and put it back together multiple times, and I'll definitely be thinking about it for some time to come.

BOOKSPROUT REVIEWS

◆ ◆ ◆

Joel Newlon brings us epic fantasy at its finest with The Craftsman and the Wizard! When an ancient evil rises again, a wizard, a dwarf, and a farmhand must team up to stop it. It sounds like your standard quest set up, but Newlon pours so much originality into each character and situation. I loved seeing the struggle of the wizard coping with disabilities, or the various (and often unexpected) forms of evil in the land! This was Dungeons and Dragons meets a more uplifting version of Game of Thrones, all wrapped around the central theme of love, and I loved every bit of it! If epic fantasy with dynamic characters and imaginative monsters is your meat pie, come questing with The Craftsman and the Wizard!

DIABOLIC SHRIMP REVIEWS

Available on Amazon!

BOOKS BY JOEL NEWLON

The Immortal Trilogy

Chasing Death
Chasing Ghosts
Chasing Victory

The Nordheim Sagas

The Craftsman and the Wizard

This book is dedicated to the memory of William Butler Yeats.

"Tread softly because you tread on my dreams."

CONTENTS

INTRODUCTION

The Wizard and the Warrior King is the followup to my novel *The Craftsman and the Wizard*. Right from the first book's debut, readers began asking for another book set in that world, but I had written *The Craftsman and the Wizard* as a standalone novel. It follows two separate stories that lead to one common goal in the end.

For the craftsman, it is his final adventure. Everyone he cares for is waiting for him across the rainbow bridge, so writing another book with him did not seem right. For the wizard, it is his first adventure, so it would make sense that his next book could be the continuing saga of the wizard and the woodcutter. But that idea didn't feel right either, and the only reason I can give for that is that the fairy-tale influence the story has means that writing another adventure for Asmund and Kolga would hurt the happily-ever-after ending I gave them.

This is why, even with the success of the first book and all of the readers asking for another book, I went and wrote the complete *Immortal* trilogy before returning and finally finding the path to writing the book you now hold in your hands.

The inspiration for this one came in much the same

way as the first book, and it solved the problem I had about writing for those characters again. The initial inspiration for *The Craftsman and the Wizard* came to me as I was reading Norse mythology and discovered the sons of Ivaldi, the family of dwarfs who forged the weapons of the gods. One of the things I have always loved is to focus on a minor character and dream up what their story might be. The craftsman is based on a few lines of text in the Scandinavian legends that were more interested in detailing the exploits of the gods and heroes instead of the dwarfs who made their gear. What I had done with the ancient text for the first book, I did for the second using my own novel. I found the character in *The Craftsman and the Wizard* who shows up for the space of just a handful of pages, plays his part in moving the story along, and then is gone before we can learn very much about him. That character was Rangvald the wizard.

In the first book, he is the aged master of the wizard school who plays the role of the wise mentor who must guide Asmund to the path of courage and self-discovery. His advanced age provided the answer to my main problem: if he were to become my adventurer and bring the reader along on his own hero's journey of learning and self-discovery, he would need to be younger and less wise. So now, I knew I was writing a prequel, and nothing need happen to the ending of the first novel. Now, even characters who went on to Valhalla in the first book could come back and entertain us once again. This has also proved to be an excellent way to write a novel that stands on its own without needing to have read the first. If that is you, I still suggest that you go and read the first book before this one, but if you don't, it will not hurt your enjoyment. There are a few references that are not integral to understanding the story that you won't get and some characters you will not have met before taking a hand in our tale.

So that is the story of how I came to write a followup at last. The only other thing I can think to tell you about it is that, as I mentioned before, it is written using inspiration from the actual Norse myths. This is how early modern fantasy books were first written, so if a dwarf or elf or dragon seem different than other recent depictions, this is why.

Also, I have to acknowledge William Butler Yeats' contributions to this book. I had been preparing to write a book using ancient Irish myth instead of Norse and had already conceived of how to weave in some of Yeats' profound imagery when the muse steered me back to Midgard. I brought these ideas with me and they worked perfectly here.

So that's it. I am leaving the door open to this mythical Norse world I am calling *The Nordheim Sagas* and will come back when I hear the call of the north.

JOEL NEWLON, SEPTEMBER 29, 2021

THE WIZARD AND THE WARRIOR KING

PROLOGUE

What sort of dream is that, Odin?
I dreamed I rose up before dawn to clear up Val-hall for slain people.
I aroused the Einheriar, bade them get up to strew the benches,
Clean the ale cups,
The Valkyries to serve wine
For the arrival of a Prince.

EIRIKSMAL, 10TH CENTURY

The king rose early on the first day of the feasts of Einherjar and led his army to the western sea.

Gorm was a warrior king, as had been all his fathers back to the time of Fjolnir and beyond. So would be his own son one day when Gorm was gone. Thus, when the rider had arrived from the farthest outpost and told of black sails arriving from afar, it was with an eager spirit that he took up his sword and shield once more.

For five days, no news came to the fortress of stone and oak. No word of victory or defeat. Then, on the morning of the sixth day, villagers with haunted eyes began arriving, carrying whatever possessions were left them, telling tales of death and destruction. It became clear that the invaders weren't satisfied with simply raiding and pillaging the towns and villages of the coasts and of the western hill country. They were, it seemed, determined to wipe them all from the face of the earth.

Late on the seventh morning, a lone warrior bearing the standard of the king stumbled into the keep. Before he died, he uttered a single word.

"Run."

CHAPTER ONE

Rangvald closed his spellbook and blew the candle out. The hour had grown late. He made his way to bed by the embers of the dying fire on the hearth.

He had only just closed his eyes when they shot back open and stared into the darkness. Had it been his imagination, or had something scraped along the outside of his windowsill? He lay still, listening closely, but all he could hear was the distant sound of the wind. Or was it the murmuring of voices? Rangvald was still straining to hear when sleep took him.

In an instant, he was dreaming a most peculiar dream wherein he watched himself as if from outside his body. From far away, he saw himself come galloping on a horse. This was a nice dream. Rangvald liked horses, though he was admittedly not much of a horseman—whenever he had traveled in the past, he had opted for a wagon's bench instead of a saddle. But he found horses to be noble and possessed of a simple wisdom. He enjoyed speaking to them, or rather, sharing thoughts with them. Wizards always referred to their strange ability as *speaking* to animals, but in truth, it didn't involve physical speech at all.

In the dream, he saw himself coursing ever nearer. He was pleased with what a heroic image it made. The horse was the color of bright yellow straw with dark-colored stockings on all four legs. It was not by any means lithe and graceful—it was a heavy horse, very stoutly built. Rangvald himself looked dashing with his long brown hair flying in the wind and a look of confident determination on his face.

This was exactly what he loved about a good dream. The subconscious could show oneself in ways that were so completely different from reality. Had he been awake, the idea of him charging valiantly across the fields on a mighty horse, looking so bold and strong, would have been laughable.

He watched his dream self dismount at a wide river. He expected that he would drink or lead the horse across on foot. But instead of either of those things—or anything at all practical—he watched himself simply stand, staring into the water, unmoving. He may have stood there a minute, a day, or an eternity. Dream time could not be trusted to make sense. Then Rangvald's eye was drawn to the water, where he watched a little silver fish crest the surface, then swiftly disappear again.

All at once, Rangvald felt a brief but intense sensation of falling. Now he was inhabiting his own body instead of watching it from afar. Looking up from the river, he found himself in a large tent of some kind. Men wearing armor were looking at a map spread out on a table and conversing in grave tones. He focused on a young man with rust-colored hair who stood listening to them with a look on his face that was trying desperately to conceal his fear. Rangvald wanted to help him, to comfort him somehow, but he didn't understand what was happening.

Without consciously deciding to, he walked past the table to the entrance of the tent. Stepping through the flap, he found himself in the center of a terrible battle. All around him, swords clashed and men died. Terror washed over him. He spun around, looking for an avenue of escape, but all was murder and carnage as far as the eye could see.

Feeling a sudden prickling at the back of his neck, he turned back around and beheld a creature hovering before him. It looked like the screaming corpse of a woman with midnight black hair. She rose a great cudgel, tipped with a massive sapphire, high above her head, then brought it crashing down on top of him once, twice, and a third time.

Boom! Boom! Boom!

Rangvald sat up in bed, seized with panic. His crazed mind grasped at consciousness, desperate to leave the nightmare behind. The faintly glowing embers reassured him that he was still safe in his own cottage. "Good," he gasped, getting a hold of himself. "It was only a—"

Boom! Boom! Boom!

The sound of the cudgel came crashing down on him again. He screamed, and throwing himself out of bed, tried to hide beneath it.

Boom! Boom! Boom! the sound repeated after a moment. But it became clear now that the pounding was coming from the door, and this time, it was accompanied by a voice. “Is that you screaming in there, Wizard? Open up, please—it's my son, Sven. He’s badly hurt. We need your help!”

Pulling himself together, Rangvald produced a candle flame from a shaking finger and lit a lantern. As soon as he unbarred the door, the widow Yrsa hurried in. Behind her, two of her burly sons helped a third, who was cradling an arm that was covered in blood and bent at an unnatural angle.

“What happened?” Rangvald asked as they lowered him into one of the chairs at the table.

“He was riding his horse back from the tavern, blind drunk again,” one of the sons explained.

“He broke it proper this time. Bones sticking out and everything,” the other one added helpfully.

“Can you heal him, wizard?” the widow asked, hope coloring her voice.

“Let me take a look,” Rangvald said, lighting two more lamps to brighten the cottage. “All right, let's see,” He leaned over and gently touched the mangled limb. The huge young man howled with pain and Rangvald flew back through the door, bodily ejected from his own home. Sitting up, he saw the widow Yrsa through the open door slap the moaning man in the back of his head. Rangvald rose and dusted himself off. Reentering the cottage, he skirted around the opposite side of the table, avoiding the injured man. Picking up his spellbook, he flipped to his healing spells. Memorizing the ones he needed, he rounded the table on the opposite side and came up behind the anguished youth. Filling his mind with magic, he whispered a single word in the old tongue close to his ear and touched him on his head. The widow and her two sons started with distress as the man closed his eyes and slumped in the chair.

"Fear not. It's nothing but a spell of deep sleep. Something to give him relief from his pain and allow me to get close enough to heal him," the wizard explained.

"How long does that last?" the widow inquired with concern.

"Usually only twenty minutes or so. More than long enough, typically, for a wizard to finish healing an injured person."

Rangvald examined the battered arm with a grim look on his face. Nodding to himself, he dragged a second chair around next to the first one, then fetched a short length of leather. "To heal him, I must first take the hurt into myself. Then I will use my magic to banish it. Some injuries must be done a little at a time, but I will attempt to heal this one all at once." He sat down and fitted the leather between his teeth. In preparation, he began to rock back and forth, bringing the spell to his mind, letting the magic fill his being. Reaching out, he laid his hand upon the broken arm. It began mending itself before their eyes.

Rangvald bit down on the leather as his arm began to twist out of shape. Once he had drawn the last of the injury from the young man, he released him. Desperately, he chanted the spell for healing in his mind. A cry of pain escaped from around the strip clenched in his teeth, and he felt himself begin to fall from his chair. He reached out and caught hold of the table with the arm that was still making itself whole again. He heard a gasp of amazement from behind him as the magic came to an end.

Removing the leather from his mouth, he breathed deeply. Then rising, from his chair, he turned and was greeted by the familiar looks of wonder and gratitude he had seen so many times before. He felt a twinge of something akin to guilt. He used to feel some pride or nobility at moments like this, but now... he felt nothing.

As he stood receiving their thanks, he gazed out his door and observed the youngest of the widow Yrsa's sons arriving on horseback. He dismounted excitedly and pulled the baskets from where they were slung on the horse's flanks.

"Mother, I brought what you told me. I came as fast as I could," he said, coming in and opening his cargo, a bounty of vegetables and herbs even a good-sized pot of honey. He piled them up on the table. "Thyra is all right, mother. Just shaken," the lad reported as he worked.

"Wait, what happened to Thyra?" Rangvald asked, concerned for the girl.

"She was walking home when Sven came riding out of control. His horse saw her and turned, throwing him from the saddle. If he hadn't, she would have been killed."

"That's good, son. Now be quiet," Yrsa said. Then, after an awkward pause, she asked, "Is this payment enough? If you would like, we could bring more."

"Thank you, no. It's too generous already," Rangvald replied, a little more woodenly than he had intended. Glancing at the payment, he couldn't stop himself from thinking about the years—his whole childhood, really, right up until manhood—that he had spent in Einarshofn studying at the school of magic. He had been the most promising student they had ever had. Most notable was that while all other students showed some greater aptitude in one of the disciplines, whether healing spells or battle magic or seeing things yet to come, Rangvald had mastered them all. It had been widely accepted that he would be the wizard to some great monarch, perhaps even the queen of Einarshofn herself.

So how was it that he found himself here five years later, healing the arms of drunken farmers? He knew the answer to that, of course. Barely an hour of the day went by that he did not think of her. He had loved Astrid with all of his heart, and she had pledged that she felt the same. But she had only loved his prominence at the school, the position he was destined to enjoy some time in the future. As soon as she had caught the eye of the princeling from Lundvar, she had had no further use for Rangvald. That was how he had landed here, heartbroken and hiding in the back of beyond.

"What are you doing here?" Yrsa asked suddenly.

Rangvald realized that he had spent the past minute staring listlessly at the vegetables on the table. "Oh, I apologize. I was just looking at the fine bounty you've brought me."

"No, I didn't mean that. I meant, what are you doing *here?* In Kalbaek."

"I was born in this valley. This is where I belong."

"No, it's not. If it were, then you wouldn't be standing there longing so to be quit of it."

"I wasn't. I was just..." He trailed off and fell silent at a look from her.

"I've passed fifty-two winters on this side of the ground. Two husbands and a son already await me on the other side, and four more have I raised. Here they are standing at your service in this very room. Well, three stand and one is sleeping in your chair. Even when he is awake, the best he can muster is to stagger at your service. But my point is, I need no magic to read a man's thoughts in his face."

"I'm sorry. It was wrong of me to deceive you. But really, they are only thoughts and nothing more. Just idle restlessness. This is where I have chosen to be. Besides, look at what I've just done. What would you have done if I hadn't been here to heal your son?"

"We would have taken him to the Willow sisters. You aren't the only healer in this village."

"But the sisters are getting very old," he argued.

"I know. That's why we came to you. So we could let them have their sleep."

"No, what I mean is, they won't always be here to help."

"I know what you meant. But it isn't a good reason for you to stay here and ignore your destiny. Yes, the sisters are old, but they are still here. And even if they weren't, that would be fine as well. Fewer and fewer villages have wizards these days, and do you know what? Their crops either grow, or they don't. The injured get well, or they don't. People are born and die every day. Life goes on. The Allfather decides, not you or I."

Rangvald couldn't think of a good rebuttal. He only knew that the thought of actually going out into the world still terrified him. He shrugged his shoulders. "Maybe you're right, but where would I even go?" Pointing at the vegetables, he added, "I can't remember the last time I was paid in anything but produce. It's not as though I have the silver to set off and see the world."

Yrsa shook her head, but before she could reply, her son sat up with a start and clutched at his arm. Finding it healed, he looked around at them in mild confusion.

"The wizard healed your arm," one of his brothers told him, to which he nodded his understanding.

"Do you have anything you would like to say?" his mother prompted.

"Yes. I'm thirsty," he replied.

Yrsa stepped forward, hand poised to strike, but Rangvald stopped her with a gentle hand on her shoulder. Then, crossing to his shelves, he filled a mug from a little cask. Sven licked his lips in anticipation and stared at the mug greedily. Even staring at it as he was, he missed Rangvald's simple prestidigitation. It wasn't actual magic, just plain sleight of hand. Receiving the mug, Sven tipped it back and guzzled with no knowledge of the vial of greenish liquid Rangvald had emptied into it. Rivulets of ale escaped down both cheeks as he swallowed. To his family's surprise, however, he stopped drinking before the mug was drained and pulled it away from his lips with a queer look on his face. After a brief pause, he took another pull, then set it down on the table with a clunk.

"Your ale has begun to sour," he said with a belch.

"That can't be. It's a new cask," Rangvald replied. "Here, a second mug might prove sweeter,"

Yrsa began to protest, but Rangvald gave her a look that caused her to hesitate. This time, his face revealed nothing of his thoughts, but she trusted him and remained silent.

"Here, try this one, my friend," Rangvald offered.

This time, Sven reached for the mug with less enthusiasm and raised it to his lips. His face scrunched up with disgust as the aroma of the beer reached his nostrils, and he moved to set it down on the table.

"Is my hospitality not good enough for you?" Rangvald demanded.

"No, I have simply drunk my fill," he stammered.

"When has that ever stopped you?" Rangvald spat.

"Please, I didn't mean to offend you—"

"But you have!" Rangvald interrupted. "Have one

sip more, or I will return your wounds to you."

"You can do that?" Sven asked in terror.

The answer to this question was that no, the magic did not actually work like that, but he was good at bluffing, so in reply, Rangvald raised his hands in the air, poised for spell-casting. The young man lifted the mug to his lips. A moment later, he lurched from his chair and bolted through the door. Sprawling on his hands and knees in the yard, he vomited with a great retch.

Turning to Yrsa, Rangvald said, "He will have no use for drink now. It is important that you keep him busy and help him find purpose in something useful. Nothing that has held a place in our hearts can go away without being replaced. It can be replaced with something healthful or something injurious, but it must be replaced."

"Yes, I understand," she said, but her face was wearing a sad, somehow sympathetic look.

"This will save his life, and possibly other peoples' lives as well. You don't approve?" Rangvald asked.

"Oh, no, I do approve. Sven will be all right. It's just..."

"Go on," Rangvald urged her.

"No, it's nothing. Thank you for everything you've done for us. We have kept you from your bed long enough. Come along boys," she said shooing them out.

When the door closed behind them, Rangvald slumped into a chair and stared at the wall. The whole affair had left him mentally and physically exhausted. And if he was honest, the well-meaning widow, between reading his thoughts and leaving with something so cryptically left unsaid, had exhausted him emotionally as well. "No, not just her," he muttered, looking back at his rumpled bedclothes and remembering the terrors of his vivid dreams. Now the thought of putting out the lamps and crawling back into bed seemed like the last thing he wanted to do.

He was still sitting there some time later when another knock came upon the door. It had none of the urgency of the earlier pounding. This knock was far more tentative. Opening the door, Rangvald was surprised to see Sven standing before him.

"I know that I am the last person you want to see, but I am thinking more clearly now, and I wanted to thank you for what you did for me. Everything you did for me."

"No need to thank me," Rangvald said, beginning to swing the door closed.

"Wait, please!"

Rangvald paused. "What?" he asked shortly.

"I didn't know I had almost killed Thyra. Not until they told me when we were riding home." Sven burst into tears. "I'm so sorry."

"You shouldn't be telling me that. You should tell Thyra, and your mother and brothers."

"I know. I just wanted to tell you that I'm going to change. I'm going to help people from now on."

"Good. That's good, Sven," Rangvald said, softening.

The young man wiped the back of his hand across his eyes. "I'm going to start with you."

"Well, that's very nice, but you don't need to help me."

"Yes, I do. Mother said that you want to go and seek your destiny, but that you use excuses like no money or opportunities to stay here where you feel safe."

"That's not true. And besides, it's hardly any of

your mother's affair," Rangvald said, bristling.

Sven ignored his protests and continued. "I'm giving you my horse, Plowbreaker. He is very strong and lucky. He is the one who saved Thyra from being killed."

"You can't give me your horse!"

"Yes, I can. Then you can go wherever you want."

"But you need him for the farm."

"No, we don't. You need him so you can go find what you need to fill your heart."

"What? What does that even mean?" Rangvald asked, growing angrier.

"My mother said that you told her that I would need to find something to take the place of drink. You said that nothing that has held a place in our hearts can go away without being replaced. She said it made her sad because you could say the words but could not hear them yourself." Rangvald was struck speechless. Seeing this, Sven pressed his advantage and said, "Wait here. I'll bring him up." Then he rushed off.

Finding his voice again, Rangvald called after him, "Look, I appreciate the gesture, but I can't take your hor—" Rangvald froze. The hair stood up on the back of his neck as a straw-colored stallion with dark stockings on each leg emerged from the darkness.

Hello, Rangvald thought to Plowbreaker, who approached slowly and nudged him with his muzzle a few times experimentally.

Are you real? Plowbreaker thought back to him.

Rangvald considered this strange question for a long moment, then replied, *I dreamed about you, too.*

CHAPTER TWO

"Tuck your elbow in and lower the point of your sword," Amazigh scolded.

Eirik did not respond to the corrections. He continued moving forward with his weapon held in a lazy guard. His attention had been diverted once again to the window which opened onto the courtyard.

"Prince Eirik," Amazigh snapped, trying to bring his pupil's concentration back to the lesson. When this failed, he crossed the floor with the speed of a shadow and struck. At last, Eirik's full attention was on his teacher as he stared up at the warrior from flat on his back.

There had never been a time that Eirik had not known Amazigh. The invincible swordsman had arrived with a band of warriors who had gone Viking in the southern lands long before Eirik was born. Having grown up with him, he tended to forget how truly massive he was. But right now, with the man towering above him, it was impossible not to remember. Having passed but seventeen winters himself, Eirik was actually very tall already. But no Northman he had ever seen was anywhere near as big as the giant from the faraway deserts.

"It is not like you to be so distracted at your lessons."

"I know. I'm sorry. It's just that it's been over a day since the standard-bearer returned and riders were sent forth in search of the army. How can I concentrate on training when there has been no news of my father yet?"

Amazigh helped the prince to his feet, and in a grave voice, replied, "Don't you see? You've never needed to concentrate on it more in your life."

"No, you don't understand me, Amazigh. War has come to the kingdom, and my father is not here. Why would I worry about fighting lessons on a day such as today?"

The giant took him by the shoulders and looked into his eyes. "Because, Eirik, war has come to the kingdom and your father is not here."

The prince's eyes filled with confusion, followed quickly by a look of panicked realization. "No. My father and his army will prevail."

"By all the gods, I hope they do. But you must accept that they may have already fallen." The giant's words landed like a slap.

"Don't say that! I don't want to think about that."

"But I must say it. And you must think about it. Now come, this may be my final chance to prepare you."

A dozen fresh protests sprang to Eirik's mind, but he did not voice them. Now that he had been made to face the truth of the situation, he was determined that he would not bring dishonor to his family. Long had they ruled in this land, and long had they protected it with sword and shield. His own mother had fallen, her quiver empty of arrows, when last foreign sails had trespassed on these shores. She could have stayed safe in the fortress of stone and oak—Eirik had been but ten and his sister only six. No one would have questioned her. But that was not their way. Now, if his father had also gone to the fields of the fallen or the halls of Valhalla, then Eirik would set his face to the western sea, and if the gods willed it so, he would follow them.

The prince nodded once, now wearing a determined expression. Amazigh released his shoulders. "Take up your sword and shield again," he commanded. Eirik complied and stood at the ready. "Now we must consider the realities of you engaging in battle as you are today. Not as you will one day be. The truth is that you do not yet possess the full strength of manhood. If you were to fight as the Northmen do, you would be killed at the outset of battle. Your kinsmen value nothing so much as strength. They live to smash their swords into each other's shields to measure who is the strongest.

"I have taught you to fight as I do, as my people did when empires went to war. This method uses your opponents' strength against them. It depends on traits that you, at seventeen, have in greater abundance than your elders: speed and boundless energy. You must remember always what I have taught you and not be drawn into their fight. Let them laugh at your thin and light sword, made like my own. Let them laugh at your small shield. Always remember to not simply hide behind your shield as they do. Dance with it, strike with it, never stop moving. Use the curve of your sword. This is a trick that is unknown here. They have no inkling of why your blade is shaped as it is, and by the time they learn the answer, it will be too late. Now, let us practice."

Amazigh took up a broad, straight sword and large wooden shield and came forward. Instantly, Eirik began moving evasively, attacking at odd angles and fading back before his opponent could launch counterattacks. With nearly every clash of swords, he rotated his hand and thrust, causing the spine of his blade to glide along the other sword. Amazigh pushed out defensively, but to no avail. The point of the light, swooping blade always touched the mail shirt on his chest before Eirik stopped and reset.

"Good. That's good," the giant praised. "Remember, in real battle, do not stop to admire your work. Strike and evade. Now, let's see your shield become more dynamic. It is small and light. Let it move with you and strike as its own weapon. It is not like a wooden shield that absorbs a blow. It is steel. It can be used to make swords glance in useful ways. Now, let us—"

Amazigh stopped speaking and the two of them stared at each other as the sound of clattering hooves came from the courtyard below. Eirik ran to the window and looked down. "One of the riders has returned."

"Very well, then. Our lesson is over," Amazigh said, exchanging his practice weapons for his own curved sword and diminutive shield.

"Perhaps it is good news!" Eirik exclaimed, unable to contain his excitement.

"I hope so. With all my heart, I do."

"But you don't believe it will be, do you?" the prince asked, deflating.

"It will be what it will be. You will rise to whatever challenge you are given. If it be battle, then heed what I have taught you. Always fight *your* fight. In your way, not your enemy's. If you do that, then you will prevail. Now hurry. Let us go and hear this news."

Eirik rushed to the throne room with Amazigh in tow. Arriving before the scout rider, he barged in and was startled to see a brown hen's egg floating through the air. At his intrusion, his sister looked up, and the egg splattered to the floor.

"Oh, come now, Prince Eirik. I must protest this disturbance. You have your lessons and Revna has hers. Don't you know it can be dangerous to distract a fledgling sorcerer while she is learning her spells?" complained the weathered old man in gray robes.

"We humbly beg your pardon, Val of Kattegat, but a rider has returned," Amazigh explained.

As if on cue, the messenger was admitted behind them. Eirik turned and looked into the rider's face. His heart was gripped by icy fingers. Such a hunted look could not portend good tidings. The man dropped to his knee. "I come bearing grave news, My King."

"Tell me, where is my father? Is he well?" Eirik inquired urgently. In reply, the rider gave him a sorrowful look. "Tell me!" Eirik demanded.

"He already has," Amazigh said gently. "He called you his king."

"But I'm not..." Eirik began. He fell silent as his bottom lip began to tremble.

Amazigh leaned over and whispered in his ear, "No. Be a king."

Eirik stood up straight and sniffed back the tears that were threatening. Focusing on the messenger, he finally noticed the sweat and dust coating the man's face. "Bring ale for the rider," he called in a firm voice, stepping forward and taking the man's hand. "Rise. Come to the table and tell us what you've learned. Val of Kattegat and Amazigh, sit with us and give me your counsel." Glancing at Amazigh, he drew strength from the look of approval on the big man's face.

Sitting at the table, the rider quaffed the ale brought to him and seemed much restored. "A half day's march from here, I found a remnant of the army moving back along the western road," he began.

"That is welcome news! How many are they?" Amazigh asked.

"A hundred and sixty. They had been held in reserve upon horseback when the armies met. They are under the command of Halfdan. They tried to advance when our lines broke, but King Gorm told them the battle was already lost. He ordered them to flee and to take his wounded standard-bearer so the flag of Vestmor would not fall. He charged Halfdan with defending the road to the fortress, and that is what they are doing."

" All that remains of an army of nearly seven hundred is a hundred and sixty men? How great were the enemy's numbers?" Eirik asked in horror.

"Less than half the size of our army, according to Halfdan."

"What about my apprentice, Ulfhild of the yellow hair? Where was the king's wizard?" Val of Kattegat demanded.

"It is said that she fell at the start of the battle."

"She's dead?" the old wizard asked in disbelief.

The messenger nodded, his eyes now glistening with tears. "The king, his wizard Ulfhild, and all his army, save those who were held in reserve, have fallen. As has every village, town, and even the tiny settlements. All of them are being burned to the ground as the enemy advances. The fleeing villagers say they burn the crops in the fields and slay the livestock in their pens. They kill everyone that cannot flee fast enough. They destroy everything in their path."

"They do?" Amazigh asked, brow wrinkled in confusion.

"Yes. The army has stopped and made camp where the road begins to rise. All the while I was there, survivors were passing us. They said that with each day, the enemy scours the country, moving inland and attacking every village they find. Every time, the story is the same. Total destruction."

Amazigh shook his head. "I do not understand. If a defending army destroyed all resources as they retreated, it would make sense, but not a conquering army. Raiding parties kill and burn after taking what they want so as to breed fear, but our villages will have no treasure to speak of, and the enemy does not appear to be taking slaves. Besides, they are coming too far away from their ships. They are not behaving like a raiding party."

"So it is conquest they seek," Eirik said.

"But that baffles me. Why kill and destroy everything in their path? Even if their army is smaller, as Captain Halfdan said, they still need food and other provisions to keep going. And why ruin everything they seek to rule? I am sorry, My King, but I can make no sense of it."

Eirik winced involuntarily when Amazigh called him "king." He did not want this. Any of this. It was all too fast. He wanted to mourn his father and become adjusted to the idea of being king, but he didn't have the time. "So the enemy is advancing toward us?"

"It appears so. What is left of the army is half a day

from here, and before I left them in the mid of night, their outriders had reported fires on the horizon. Halfdan believes they will see the enemy soon. He told me he does not believe they can defeat them. I have thought much of the standard-bearer as I rode back here, My King. Halfdan said the man had lost his senses and run off into the night. I believe he may have been right when he came and told us to run. Maybe we should heed his word and flee for our lives."

"Flee and go where, rider? This is the fortress of stone and oak. If we are threatened, we should remain here. I will have you ride back and tell Halfdan to bring his men here to aid us in our defense."

"My King," Amazigh said. "You asked for our counsel. Will you hear it?"

"Of course. What are your thoughts?"

"Over the last few days, the number of your homeless subjects arriving here at the fortress has increased to over a thousand people. They cannot all be housed inside the gates, and so hundreds of them are huddling outside the walls. The enemy's fire spared them nothing. We have been feeding them from our stores of food."

"Yes, I see," Eirik said, needing no further explanation. "But if we cannot stay here, where would we run?"

"The caves," Revna answered. All eyes turned to the princess, who until that moment had remained silent.

"Yes, the caves," Val said. "In the dawning of the kingdom, when the house of the king was little more than a hut on a mound, our kinfolk would sometimes flee to the Nordhule. No foe could ever breach its doors. It has been so long since the kings and queens of Vestmor have been truly challenged for this land that we have forgotten the Nordhule."

"Revna has not forgotten. She can find the wisdom in old stories where others cannot," Eirik said with pride.

"We have a fleet of wagons. We can take what provisions remain in the fortress and gather more as we pass the farms along our way," Revna said.

"Then it is settled," Val of Kattegat said, sounding almost cheerful for a change.

"Not so fast," Eirik said. "There is something else we must consider. Captain Halfdan believes he will be seeing the enemy very soon. They will hold them as long as they can, but now they are the smaller force, without a wizard or my father to lead them. So the enemy might push through their defenses with ease and come for us. Amazigh, how fast will the people be able to travel on foot alongside wagons filled with provisions?"

"I see your point, My King. The people will travel very slowly. If the enemy rips through Halfdan and his defenders, they will descend upon the people when they are out in the open. If they are not able to reach the caves, they will be defenseless."

The room was silent as the matter was considered. At last, Eirik drew a deep breath. "Hear the words of your king. Rider, go back to Halfdan and his men. Tell him that his king and every man who can hold a sword is riding to his side. Amazigh, have every last warrior in the fortress, no matter what age, gird themselves for war. Open the armory to every villager huddling at our gates. Tell them that they fight so that their loved ones might reach safety. Val of Kattegat, lead the people to the Nordhule. See that they reach it safely."

"No, My King. I ride to battle at your side."

"You have been wizard to three generations of my fathers. You have more than earned the right to speak so boldly. Out of the love I bear you, I will answer you just as boldly. You are too old to ride to battle. Your mind is yet keen, but your body has grown frail. Go to the caves. Watch over our people and continue my sister's training."

"I have earned more than my bold tongue. I have earned my vengeance. This scourge has killed my apprentice, she who carried my legacy. They have killed a king, your father, whom I loved as a son. You can command me to not go to battle, but to enforce it, you will have to kill me."

Eirik was silent for a long moment, then said "Very well, then. Amazigh, you will lead the people to—"

"Enough!" Revna interrupted. "You will need a wizard and the best swordsman in the kingdom if you are to hold the enemy at bay. The person who will lead the people to the caves is me. Yes, me, who has only seen thirteen winters, but who is also an apprentice wizard and a princess of Vestmor. Now don't argue with me, Eirik, I can —"

"I won't," he said, cutting her off.

"You won't?" she repeated in surprise.

"No, I won't. Today is a day of destiny for us all. We have already lost so much, without even being given a chance to feel its loss. We will lose more before we are done. If we must die, then we will die well, and meet again across the rainbow bridge. Now, away, all of us. There is much to be done."

CHAPTER THREE

Rangvald lay on his bed and stared at the ceiling beams. The morning sun had been up for some time, beckoning him to rise, but he couldn't find the will.

After Sven had left and he had made a place for Plowbreaker in the old barn, he had lain restlessly in bed, sleep eluding him. The events of the night played over and over again in his head, causing his stomach to tie itself in knots. The widow Yrsa reading his restlessness with such ease, forcing him to face the fact that he was here hiding from the world. Hiding from the hurt he was still carrying inside.

That would have been enough to make him miserable, but it was nothing compared to dreaming of the horse then having him come into his life in reality. Rangvald was a student of the magic arts. He had knowledge of the arcane secrets. Someone else might be able to convince themselves that dreaming of riding a horse and then being given that same horse a few hours later was some kind of coincidence. But Rangvald knew better.

Worse yet, if his dream about the horse had been a vision destined to come to pass, then what of the other things he had seen? Were these things also his destiny? What did they mean? A silver fish jumping in the stream, a young warrior with a troubled brow? Worst of all, the evil looking woman smashing him with crushing blows? Was this, too, something fated to occur?

Rangvald pulled the blanket up over his head. *No! None of that is going to happen, because I'm simply not getting out of bed... Ever!* Rangvald lay there with his eyes shut, blocking out the world, until the air grew stale beneath the heavy blanket. He obstinately lingered another minute, until the desire for a fresh breath of air won out and he threw the covers off in exasperation. *All right, things are never as helpless as they appear. What can I do?* Rangvald asked himself. The answer presented itself at once. Sitting up in bed, he exclaimed, "I've got it!"

He got up, hurried to his shelves, and took down his distaff and some flax. It was not hopeless at all! He was frightened by what his future would bring, but he was skilled in seeing the future. All he need do was peer at what would be; then he could choose his path.

Rangvald sat down and began to spin the flax with the distaff until the trance took hold and his mind floated gently away from him. "What will the future bring me?" he called into the limitless void unfolding before his mind's eye. In an instant, his vision went hurtling through space and time toward a distant point that shone with the beckoning light of a blue star. Rangvald reached out with his mind, eager to see, but then something went wrong. Out of nowhere, his vision jerked to a halt. He hung in the boundless nothing for a second, then he felt himself plummeting through darkness. A cold fear gripped his mind. He shut his eyes and tried to stop spinning the flax. He willed himself to cease his spell-casting, but to no avail. His movements were no longer his own. A scream escaped his lips, but then was silenced at the touch of a hand resting gently upon his cheek.

Rangvald opened his eyes and squinted in the bright sunlight. He was no longer falling through space, but instead standing in a place filled with trees and birdsong. A woman in a long white dress removed her hand from his cheek, and turning, glided down the gentle hill toward a cascading waterfall which fed into a crystal pool. Rangvald followed her, marveling at the magical surroundings. Everything seemed so real. He could feel the warmth of the sun and smell the blossoms in the air.

"Is this my future?" Rangvald asked in a daze.

"No, it is your present," the woman replied.

"Oh. I was trying to see my future."

"I know. I stopped you. You've already been shown what you need to see."

Rangvald considered her words for a moment. "Do you mean the dream?"

"Yes, the dream."

"But what have I seen? A horse, a fish, a young man, and a monster? What does it all mean?"

"It means that people are in danger and you are needed."

"For what?" Rangvald asked, a tinge of panic entering his voice. "What will happen to me if I go?"

"You will find glory. Or you will find death. But you will find," she answered serenely.

"It must be death that I will find then," he reasoned.

"If what you want is for me to go, and it were glory that awaited me, then you would let me see."

"Very well, then, it's death," she agreed.

"All right, so I won't go!" he declared triumphantly.

"Only you can decide that," she said in a tone so sympathetic that it robbed him of his defiance.

"Can't you just tell me what it's about? If I only understood," he pleaded.

"Be at peace, Rangvald," she said, turning back to face him and taking his hand in hers. "It really is all right whether you choose to go or not. Everyone is called to something in life, even if only once. For wizards and warriors, that might be to save kingdoms in peril. For others, it might be something less daring. But each of them must decide to answer the call or not, and then live with the decision they have made. In your case, you have been given gifts greater than all those around you, but you have also been broken in the heart. First when the fever took your parents, and then again when Astrid did not love you back."

Even though Rangvald's mind was far far away from his body, tears began to roll down his cheeks as he sat casting in the cottage. In the magical garden, the lady reached up and he felt her hand brushing his tears away. "I wish that I could let you see what would happen, but then what you chose would have no meaning. I will let you know that if you do not answer this call, you will live a long, peaceful life in the Valley of the Two Rivers, healing injured farmers and helping their crops to grow."

"And if I do answer the call?"

"As you surmised. You may meet your doom, but not before living. I mean truly *living.* Only out there can you replace what your heart is missing. Only out there will you taste the silver apples of the moon, the golden apples of the sun."

Rangvald looked around himself again and felt the current of magic surrounding him. "You are the maiden of the gods, aren't you?" he asked in wonder.

She smiled gently and replied, "I am just me, Idunn, last of the daughters of Ivaldi."

She kissed him on the cheek, and then all was darkness.

◆ ◆ ◆

Rangvald's mind floated in the darkness. For how long, he did not know, but when he finally opened his eyes, he found that he had spun the flax into a massive coil of thread. He walked sluggishly to his wooden chest, then opened it and found one of his mother's old spools that his father had carved for her long, long ago. He wound the thread around it, removing it from the spindle. He laid his distaff back on the shelf, then paused and stared at it for a long moment. Taking it back down, he placed it in his large leather traveling purse, the one he had been gifted by Astrid when they were still at school. Next, he put in two small books, followed by some potions, then some small charmed items, each of which was used for different assorted magics. Thinking for a moment, he went to his shelf and selected some useful herbs and plenty of seeds and placed them in the bag as well.

"What else?" he asked himself aloud. Spying his gray wizard's robe hanging by his bed, he walked to it and regarded it for a long moment before shaking his head dismissively. It just didn't feel like *him* anymore. He did, however, take down a short iron rod, charmed with a glowing spell, that hung from its cord on the same peg as his robe. He tied it to his belt, then turned and scanned the cottage for anything else that might be useful.

He paused as a thought occurred to him. Did this mean he'd made up his mind to go? An uneasy feeling crawled up his spine and he shook his head. "No, it doesn't mean anything of the sort," he muttered out loud. Rangvald put it out of his mind, but still, he continued to gather supplies. On a whim, he grabbed the spool of new thread. He lifted the bag from his table to put it in, but then stopped and stood unmoving.

Holding both the purse Astrid had given him and the spool his father had carved for his mother, he felt a heavy stone of loneliness roll onto his heart and settle there. He looked to his bed and longed to be beneath his blanket once more. He put the spool into the bag and put it down. As he reached his bed, he heard a whinny from outside and he stopped. A horse? *My horse,* he realized, remembering Plowbreaker. Abandoning the thought of hiding under the covers again, Rangvald dressed quickly, slung the bag over his shoulder, and hurried out to the barn.

◆ ◆ ◆

Plowbreaker trotted merrily down the lane, first past the blacksmith and then past the tavern to the main road leading out of the valley. The sun was high, the summer air fresh and sweet, and they chased away any thoughts of loneliness. Rangvald waved cheerily as he passed the last farm in the village. The old farmer stopped tending the crops that grew around the large white stone with the faded runes carved on it and waved back.

Finally, they came to the place where the two rivers converged. Plowbreaker stopped along the bank of the waters that coursed northward. *Why are we stopping?* Rangvald thought to him.

This is the place. Don't you recognize it? Plowbreaker thought in reply.

Rangvald looked around in confusion, then realized that he did indeed recognize it. He felt the same tingle of gooseflesh he felt when Sven had led Plowbreaker from the darkness. Rangvald dismounted and stood staring into the waters, just as he had watched himself do in the dream. Gazing transfixed at the surface of the water, he was surprised to realize that he was in terror of seeing the silver fish. His mind was on fire, desperately begging it not to appear. He didn't quite know why he should fear it. He did not know what would happen if it appeared.

Perhaps that was just it, he realized. He did not know what would happen when another vision fulfilled itself. Somehow, it would call him to glory or doom—most likely doom—and he would have to make a decision. Rangvald's entire body jolted as the little silver fish crested the surface of the water, just as he had seen, and just as he had known it would. He stood, stiff and tense, waiting for what would come next. He would not even allow his eyes to blink. Ten minutes passed as he stared at the spot where the fish had appeared and then swiftly disappeared again. Then another ten minutes passed. Slowly, he relaxed, letting his cramping muscles uncoil. When ten more minutes had elapsed, he glanced over at Plowbreaker, and they shared a look.

What happened? Plowbreaker asked.

Nothing.

Nothing?

Nothing. I was in mortal dread of seeing that fish, and then when we saw it, it didn't mean a thing, Rangvald replied.

They continued staring at the river until finally, Rangvald felt a huge wave of embarrassment. *This is foolishness! We knew that we would see a fish jumping in the water, and we saw one, so now we think it means something, but it doesn't. Fish jump in water. They do it all the time. It doesn't mean anything!*

This was confusing to Plowbreaker, who simply replied, *But we dreamed it.*

I know, but maybe we dreamed it for no reason. Or maybe some Vettir is toying with us for their amusement. Either way, it doesn't matter. You know, I'm actually relieved it means nothing. I was very frightened before. Now let's leave.

No sooner had he thought this to Plowbreaker than the little silver fish reappeared and splashed back again, just as it had before. Rangvald stared again, hardly permitting himself to breathe. After another ten minutes passed, Plowbreaker asked again, *What happened?*

"Nothing!" Rangvald shouted, his anger flaring and taking them both by surprise. "What?" He shouted at the river. "What do you want?" When there was no answer, he said, "You see? We are being made fools of!"

Plowbreaker snorted, and Rangvald turned to mount the saddle. Then an idea struck him and he hesitated. *Wait here,* he thought to Plowbreaker, then strode off across the road.

Entering the hazel wood beside the road, he found a nice straight branch, not too thick and not too thin. Just right. Drawing his belt knife, he cut and peeled it into a long wand. Next, he found a dry twig upon the ground with just the right offshoot jutting from the main branch. In it, he imagined the shape he would need, and whittled it carefully until it matched his vision. Satisfied with his work, he walked up the road until he found a bush he had glimpsed on their way out of the village. From it, he gathered a handful of berries before hurrying back to Plowbreaker.

"Now to put it all together," he said, removing the spool of new-spun thread he had made while scrying for the future. He cut a length of it, attached it at one end to the hazel wand and at the other to the hook he had whittled. Lastly, he placed one of the bright red berries onto the hook and lowered it into the river.

"Now we wai—" he began, but was interrupted by the flexing of the hazel wand. He lifted it up, and the little silver fish appeared on the end. Rangvald caught hold of it, and it spat the hook out, berry intact. A shadow of doubt tugged at his certainty. "Do you have a message for us?" he asked. There was no reply. He tried to communicate the question to the fish with his wizard thoughts, but to no avail. There were some creatures in the deep seas who could speak to wizards, but fish such as this one always repeated the same three things: *Swim, eat, breed.* Rangvald shrugged and said, "Oh well, I suppose you'll go quite nicely with some of the widow Yrsa's turnips."

As they trotted back home, Rangvald's mood began to lighten once more. *Perhaps everything is fine,* he thought to himself. So far, the visions in his dream coming true had only brought him good things. First he had gained companionship and transportation when Plowbreaker had come to him, and now he had a delicious dinner in store. The thought made Rangvald smile happily as they trotted past the large white stone in the little farm again. Then a frown stole across his face as he remembered the rest of the dream. The red-haired youth trying to hide a troubled and fearful mind didn't automatically portend unfavorable happenings. Perhaps Rangvald would help him somehow and bring him comfort. *And the hideous screeching woman smashing you with a great jeweled cudgel?* he asked himself. *That one is a little more difficult to cast in a positive light, I'll admit.*

Plowbreaker, what do you make of the young warrior with the worried face and the evil woman that smashes me with a club?

Plowbreaker was silent for a few moments, then answered, *All right, I give up. What do you make of the young warrior with the worried face and the evil woman that smashes me with a club?*

What? No, I'm asking you what you think they mean, Rangvald thought back in exasperation.

Plowbreaker was silent again, then thought, *That's the worst jest I've ever heard. It doesn't even make sense.*

Rangvald laid his palm over his face and sighed. *It's not a jest. I'm asking you about the young warrior and the frightening hag that we see in the dream after we see the fish.*

But we don't see a warrior and a hag after the fish. We see a naked woman with a book and we see a cave high up.

"We see what?" Rangvald blurted out loud. He considered this strange inconsistency as they turned onto the side lane and passed the tavern. He remembered something that had struck him as strange even as he dreamed it. He had seen himself and Plowbreaker as they rode together and as they had stood by the river, then his perspective had changed. *Plowbreaker, when you saw the woman with the book and the cave did you see yourself seeing those things, or did you see them through your own eyes in the more natural way?*

Plowbreaker considered his question, then confirmed Rangvald's theory with, *The second one.*

Okay so we had the same visions until after the river, then we saw different things.

I see, Plowbreaker said. *So what does that mean?*

Rangvald thought about it as they passed the blacksmith's shop and drew closer to home. *It still means nothing,* he said exasperatedly. *Or it means something, but I know not what. I do have to admit that I prefer your dream over mine. I would much rather have a naked woman read me a book in a cave then be bludgeoned to death by a hideous crone in the company of a sullen youth.*

Plowbreaker whinnied with delight and said, *There! Now that was a much funnier jest!*

CHAPTER FOUR

Revna was hastily packing what she would need into her satchel when a knock came upon her chamber door. She opened it to reveal her teacher Val of Kattegat wearing his old battle robes, colored iron gray and hemmed with crimson ribbon. She knew that once, long ago the garment would have helped him cut quite an imposing figure, but today, with his stooped, narrow shoulders and wizened face, it served only to accentuate how feeble he appeared.

"I brought you some things to help you on your way," he said shuffling in quickly. "They belonged to my apprentice Ulfhild when she was around your age." He handed her a faded brown apprentice's robe. Revna held it up against herself and they both took note of the extra foot of fabric that spilled down past her feet.

"Well, she may have been a few years older than you, come to think of it."

"I have some shears, shall I cut some off of the bottom?"

"No. That would be a most difficult task. You see, that is just the point of it. This robe has been charmed for battle. It can turn blades and arrows much of the time. It will even ward fire. Do not let it embolden you, however; it has its limits."

"I can belt it at the waist so that it doesn't hang so low and tie up the sleeves so they are not too much in the way," she said, donning the hand-me-down garment.

Now it was Val's turn to think how the ill-fitting robes only accentuated how small and weak the princess appeared. "Here, this was Ulfhild's as well," he said, holding up a short sword. "It has a number of charms with which you will be familiar, such as eversharp, glow, and true north. But it also has an enchantment."

"An enchanted sword?" Revna said in wonder. "What is its enchantment?"

"You tell me," Val replied, handing it to her.

Revna braced herself to bear the weight of the weapon and was shocked when she found that there wasn't any. "It's like a handful of feathers!" she gasped in astonishment.

"Yes, a most difficult enchantment. But do not let it embolden you, either. Yes, it is a sword light enough for a child to wield, but it will not make you know how to wield it. And with no weight, its chop is weak. If you are forced to call upon it, use its point to pierce and its eversharp edge to slice."

"I understand," Revna said, belting it on over the robe. "You had to give it a name while enchanting it, didn't you?"

"That's right. Its name is Deathwhisper, and it

belongs to you now,"

"Deathwhisper," Revna repeated reaching down and stroking its hilt reverently.

"May it keep you safe, Princess. Think of Ulfhild when you use it. She would be very proud to know it serves you now."

At that, Revna stood up straight and proud, but with her floppy, oversized robe and magic sword sagging from her hip, it did nothing to make her appear like anything other than a girl of thirteen playing at dress-up. Val of Kattegat regarded her for a long moment. Inside him, a heated debate was raging. Finally, the debate was settled by Revna when she asked, "And what about the final item?"

"What? What's that you say?"

"The last item that you brought. The one you are now holding behind yourself, hoping I will not notice."

"Very observant, Revna. There is another item that I brought, but I have decided that I shall take it away with me once more and lock it back where it belongs."

"As you wish, Master. But can I ask what it was that made you first think to bring it?"

The wizard smiled sadly and said, "Very wise, my apprentice. You make me remember my motives and reconsider once more." Val hesitated again, and the sadness deepened on his face. "You had a very short childhood indeed. It ended the day your mother's body arrived at the gates, bloodied and broken from the battle. Ever since that time I have never seen you at play, never heard you in song. It is a rare occasion when I've even seen your face softened with a smile. Every day you strive tirelessly at your lessons, hungry to know every magic I can teach you."

"I can see that this saddens you, but I can only be that which I am."

"Yes, it saddens me, but that is only my own foolishness. It was right that you grew up and prepared yourself to act as a wizard and as a princess. Today is the proof of that. Many lives are depending on you now."

"So the final object?" she asked.

Val seemed to remember it and almost pulled it forward from where it hid behind his thigh, but stopped, seeming still reluctant. "All right, I will show you, and we will discuss it together and decide." With that, he finally lifted his hand, revealing what was concealed there.

At first, Revna saw nothing but a lump of blackened leather, but then she was able to distinguish the clump of bony human fingers and realized that the petrified mass was a severed human hand. "Someone's hand?" she asked with distaste.

"Yes. The hand of a condemned man," he replied.

"What is it? What does it do?"

"It is a Hand of Fate. Made by my master, Skarde The Conjurer, long, long ago. With a few words spoken, it separates a soul from a body."

"What? So you point the hand at somebody, say the words, and what? They fall dead?"

"Yes, precisely. To be honest, a charmed robe and enchanted sword will only do so much. Even as grown-up as your mind is, you still have the body of a child, and it isn't likely that you could best grown warriors in combat."

"Yes, I agree. So then why do you hesitate to give me the Hand of Fate?" she asked, perplexed.

"You do not understand, Revna. This is not wizard's magic. It is the magic of the gods. This hand is a talisman of the goddess Hel. Its use will ask a heavy price of you. Every time you send a soul to her in her underworld realm of Helheim, she will take a piece of your soul in the bargain. Its use will actually hasten your own demise. It will literally take years from the span of your days. I reasoned with myself that you, being so young, could perhaps use it once or twice when in dire need and still have plenty of life left to you. But now I feel that was foolish of me. I know you. If your people are in danger, you will call on it, again and again, paying the toll and aging until the goddess takes you too."

Revna regarded the black lump with disgust. "Why would your master make such a wicked thing?"

"Like so many things in this life, the object itself is not wicked. It's what we choose to use it for that decides that. I brought this to you today as something wicked, as a weapon of death, but such was not its purpose when Skarde The Conjurer asked the goddess to imbue it with her power. Its purpose then was one of good. You see, in our world, sometimes there are souls who become lost and unable to pass over to their rest. They wander the land of the living. Sometimes, there are undying hatreds so vile that they slip the bonds of their graves to revisit our world and bring harm. Also, there are spirits of ancient things that belong nowhere. There have even been those who practice dark magics, necromancers, if you will, who put the tainted little souls of these ancient things into the bodies of the dead."

"Ancient things?" Revna repeated with uncertainty.

"Yes. There are spirits as old as Midgard, maybe older. They are the shadows in the cavern, the specters in the desert. The forgotten gods under the deep blue sea. The dark and evil wizard who can learn to call their names again will have them do their bidding. For all of these types of souls was the Hand of Fate conjured; for every wayward ghost or hateful Dragr. For every spirit possessing the dead or ghost trapped where it did not belong that was sent to the goddess, my master was blessed and given an even longer life than wizards usually enjoy, which, as you know, can already be quite long indeed. But in a moment of desperation, when he had fought the evil wizard Fenric to a standstill and neither could prevail, Skarde knew that if he could not defeat him, our army would be lost. He pointed the Hand of Fate at a living man and spoke the words. The goddess accepted Fenric's soul, but that was the end of Skarde's borrowed time. Three hours later, she called him to her side as well.

"The hand passed then to Sten Stonheart, my master's older apprentice. In the reign of your great-grandfather, Njal the Small, Sten saved the kingdom by calling on the Hand of Fate. Right in the throne room where you take your lessons, he stood between the king and queen and a band of assassins sent from the land of the Geats. Those four killers wore talismans so powerful that wizards' magic could barely harm them. Sten turned to the magic of the gods, pointing the hand and speaking the words four times. Each time, his face grew older, his hair grayer. When the fourth and final assassin's soul departed, Sten fell. He lived but one day more, and when he passed away, the Hand of Fate came to me. I would not carry it as those who came before me. Twice it had broken my heart, so it remained locked away. I took it out once, to the village near the great mere of the south, and set free the ghost of a little boy lost down at the bottom of a well. But that is the only time I have held it in many years, until today. Now that you know what it is and its history, I think you will see why I hesitate."

When Val of Kattegat finished speaking, Revna nodded gravely, then stepped forward and took the hand from him. "The words?" she asked quietly. He produced a small parchment and handed it to her. Revna studied it for a moment, then placed both it and the Hand of Fate into her purse.

"I bowed just now to the certainty I saw in your face and gave you no argument. Will you share with me, however, from whence such a certainty came?" Val asked.

"I do not know what will happen, and I admit, that terrifies me, but I was born to fight—and to die if I must—for the people of Vestmor, just like my mother and father before me. Just like Skarde the Conjurer and Sten Stoneheart. If there comes a time that I must use the Hand of Fate and sacrifice myself, then I will do just that without question." Val did not speak. Revna searched his features, trying to read his thoughts, but his face revealed nothing. "Do you understand what I mean, Master?"

"Better than you know, Revna. You see, before I came to you, I cast my seeing into the mirror of scrying, hoping to learn what would be. I was allowed only glimpses of a strange dream. I saw a man on a straw-colored horse. I saw a silver fish. I saw fires at night, and lastly, I saw..." Val of Kattegat stopped talking and bit his lip, then continued. "I did not see everything that was to be, but I saw that you and I will never meet again in this lifetime. Whatever hand I have to play in this, I know that it ends in my death. So, yes, I do understand being ready to sacrifice yourself for those who are counting on you."

Revna rushed forward and hugged him. Tears

welled up in her eyes and she fought them with all of her might. Releasing him, she stepped back with a lump in her throat, but dry eyes.

"Goodbye, Princess Revna of Vestmor, Apprentice Wizard," he said with a bow.

"Goodbye to you, Val of Kattegat, Master Wizard," she replied, at last losing her battle and openly weeping. Then he smiled at her one last time and was gone.

◆ ◆ ◆

Revna wiped the tears from her face. "No crying until the kingdom is safe," she chastised herself. Then she gathered the last of her provisions and hurried down to the courtyard. The place was astir with the frenzied activity of people arming themselves to follow her brother or hurrying with provisions to the train of wagons that would be fleeing to the north. Spying her father's huntsman and his son coming from the armory, she called out, "Master Trygve."

"Yes, Princess," the hunter replied, hurrying through the crowd toward her with his son in tow. Her father, the king, had thought very highly of Trygve, saying that he was the bravest and most resourceful man in the kingdom. It was based on this high esteem she instantly made her decision. The huntsman's son, Leif, was only a year or two older than she, but already he took after his father, being strongly built and having a very sure step. Over the past year or so, Revna had found herself daydreaming about the boy on more than one occasion. With a flush of embarrassment, she banished that thought. "You will not be going to the battle with my brother. You will come with me as I lead the people to the Nordhule."

"Yes, My Princess," the huntsman replied.

"But we are needed at the battle," his son objected. Trygve gave the boy a withering look and seemed on the verge of boxing his ears when Revna held up a hand to forestall him.

"Leif, you and your father are the best archers in all the kingdom. In a battle between two armies, the side with the best archers does not win. The army with the *most* archers wins. For our task, where only three must protect hundreds, I will need archers who shoot fast and always hit their mark. Do you understand?"

The boy looked at her with a touch of sullen defiance in the blue eyes she found so irritatingly beautiful right now. Though he was only a little bit her elder, he was almost twice as tall and he towered over her. His father cleared his throat menacingly. Remembering himself, Leif mumbled, "Yes, My Princess."

"Very good," she said, turning to go. "Oh, and Leif?" she added, turning back.

"Yes?" he replied, this time before needing to be prodded by his father.

"This is the last time I will explain myself to you. Question me while we are out there and I will slay you myself and leave you for the crows." The boy's eyebrows rose in shock, but Revna had already spun and began to stride away. "Saddle your horses and meet me outside the keep. We leave at once," she called over her shoulder.

◆ ◆ ◆

Riding out of the fortress, Revna found that men were already marching west to meet the invaders and put themselves between them and the fleeing villagers.

On the north side of the walls, she found the ragged

column of people and wagons loaded with provisions and ready to depart. The last of the sons and fathers, and even grandfathers, who had been equipped with spears and swords from the armory or were carrying their own axes and farm tools were hugging their families goodbye, then joining the westward march behind the boy king.

Seeing Trygve and Leif riding out to join them, she wheeled her horse, and loping to the front of the host, called out, "Forward, my people. Forward to the Nordhule!"

CHAPTER FIVE

Rangvald placed the fish upon the floor of the cottage and went to blow the fire aflame. His mouth began to water at the thought of the coming feast, and all thoughts of omens, either ill or benign, were banished from his mind. Even when a rustling from behind distracted him from his task, he thought nothing of it. He simply stood, turned, and upon seeing nothing out of the ordinary, resumed his preparations. However, a minute later, when the rustling sounded again, this time accompanied by a voice calling his name, all of his previous portentous dread came rushing back upon him in an instant. It was with the greatest reluctance that Rangvald slowly turned and faced who was there.

Rangvald had only ever known one lover, and as such, he was not accustomed to seeing women standing boldly nude before him. No, not boldly, that wasn't it. Innocently and not at all self-consciously would describe it better. Her hair was black as night and sprinkled with apple blossoms, her eyes the green of storm-tossed seas. Her body redefined for him the perfection the human form could attain. Pale and pink, but also shimmering, as if somehow faintly silver too.

Rangvald's mind snapped back to attention and he searched the floor for the fish he had caught. Finding it absent, realization struck him, and he turned his astonished gaze back to her. This caused her to laugh with delight. The sound of her laughter was a chorus of birdsong mingled with the sort of thunder that distant waves made along a rocky shore. Rangvald's eyes closed, and the laughter filled his heart. He opened his eyes when again she spoke his name, and he saw her scoop his spellbook from the table and scamper out of the door.

"Wait!" he shouted in a panic, giving chase. "Please don't take my spellbook, it's my whole life!" Bursting through the door, he stopped and searched desperately for any sign of her. "Plowbreaker, the fish!" he cried, almost incoherently. Plowbreaker was facing away from him, gazing out across the field. Rangvald followed his gaze and spied the woman standing among the long, dappled grass with sun splashing off the silver glimmer of her. When she saw that he could see her she lifted the book of magic above her head and waved it tauntingly. "There she is! We must get my book back!" he shouted, running to the horse.

Halfway into the saddle, Plowbreaker thought him to him, *This is it.*

What? Rangvald thought back.

This is it, the horse repeated.

Rangvald stepped back down to the ground and looked out across the field once again. "Naked woman with a book," he whispered. He stood frozen with trepidation until he saw her turn and skip away playfully. He hurried back into the cottage and slung his satchel over his shoulder. Grabbing up another sack, he stuffed some food, a flask of water, and a blanket inside. He pulled the door closed behind him, then mounted. As they galloped off across the field, he repeated what Plowbreaker had said once more. "This is it."

◆ ◆ ◆

Galloping across the field and meadow, they left the Valley of the Two Rivers and plunged into the wilds beyond, never losing sight of the strange and frolicsome woman, but never catching up with her, either.

Sometimes she would stop, perched on a stone or hillock, and wait for them to draw near—almost within shouting distance. Sometimes Rangvald would open his mouth to call out, to plead with her, but always she would turn and fly from them before he could.

When a few hours had passed, the shadows began to grow longer and the western sky glowed with a gentle orange fire. *It will be dark soon, and too dangerous for me to run so fast,* Plowbreaker thought.

Rangvald brought them to a halt and stared despondently at the shimmering figure who was now dancing on the ridge ahead of them. When she disappeared down the other side, they followed, but now only at a walk. All hope of recovering the book was fading with the setting sun. When at last they crested the ridge themselves, they halted again and gaped at what lay before them. Down a small slope by a gently babbling brook lay the stump of a mighty oak, felled long ago by some unknown hand. There, on the wooden pedestal it created, lay his book of magic. Of the woman, no sign could now be seen.

Picking up their pace, they hurried toward the stump. With every step, Rangvald became convinced that the woman would reappear, scoop up the book, and caper away once more. He eyed the brook suspiciously, imagining that she had transformed herself into a fish again and was hiding just below the surface of the water. To his relief, however, they reached the stump without mishap. He dismounted and stood holding the book to his chest.

Plowbreaker walked over to the brook and had a drink. *Well, now what?* he thought.

Rangvald pondered for a moment, then replied, *We could turn around and head right back home.*

So do you think our adventure is over? Was this all we were meant to do—chase a book-stealing fish woman across the countryside all evening, then go home?

No, this isn't all of it. What about the other things we saw? Everything hasn't happened yet. I think she led us here for a reason. Maybe if we stay here, something will happen, Rangvald thought back.

Neither one of them moved or spoke as a couple of long minutes crept slowly by. At last, Plowbreaker broke the silence. *So, I can't help but notice that we're still not moving.*

Yes, I noticed that, too, Rangvald agreed.

Why do you think that is? the horse asked.

Maybe this is the actual moment of decision, thought Rangvald. *Right here and now. The strange lady got us moving and away from the comfort and shelter of home. Maybe she wasn't really trying to steal my spellbook. Something tells me she can wield magics far beyond what can be found in my humble book of spells. Maybe she was bringing us out here to this quiet, peaceful place, hovering at the cusp of nightfall, so we could decide. Truly decide.*

You decide for us, Plowbreaker replied. *I can be happy on the open trail, moving forward, not knowing what tomorrow will bring. But I would also be happy staying home and knowing that each day will be like the last.*

I wish I felt at peace with either decision as well. But I am torn. The road ahead fills me with dread. If I am right about their motives, then I understand why we were led from home to decide, because I don't think I would ever choose to leave the safety and familiarity of the cottage for the unknown.

Well, we're out here now, so does that mean we stay and see what happens? Plowbreaker asked.

Rangvald hesitated. Turning, he started back toward home. *The goddess Idunn told me that it truly did not matter which way I chose. The universe would carry on regardless of what I did. She said that if I stayed home I would live a long life, healing farmers and helping their crops grow. She said if I went I may die, but I would finally live. Truly live.*

Well, if the choices are between a long life or a possible death, we should go home, Plowbreaker replied helpfully.

That sounded perfectly reasonable to Rangvald, but still, he stood motionless.

I don't understand. Why do you hesitate? Plowbreaker asked.

I don't know. I'm still thinking. It's all so simple, really, when I say it out loud. I can go home and live a long life, feeling restless and brokenhearted, or I can go live a short life where I can grow and find what my heart needs.

Good. You've decided, then?

Rangvald nodded and began to answer, then stopped. "No! I can't! It's impossible to decide. I want to live a long, peaceful life, and I *also* want to have adventure and be fulfilled. I don't know what to choose. You decide for us, Plowbreaker. I cannot!"

Plowbreaker turned and took another drink from the brook. *Do you know why I liked being a farm horse?*

Rangvald was surprised by the seeming change of topic, but replied, No.

I always knew what my purpose was. I liked plowing so much that I would often get carried away and wreck the plow. I loved to be hitched to the wagon when it was laden so heavily that I was the only horse that could shift it. I got to be what I am, and the people got to grow crops and eat. I never doubted who I was or what my place in the world was. You are nothing like a horse, Rangvald. You never stop asking yourself who you are, or who you should be. And you never stop doubting yourself, even when you know the answers. You remind me of young Sven.

Sven? repeated Rangvald. *The drunken farmer you had to stop from running over a little girl? That is hardly complimentary, Plowbreaker.*

No, you don't understand how much alike you are. He hates being a farmer, and so he is very bad at it. He wants to draw pictures of the things we would see wandering around the countryside. He had an amazing gift for it. But then he feels guilt for wanting to do that instead of working hard on the farm as his brothers do. He does not know, or rather, does not accept who he is and what his purpose in life is. That is why he is a drunkard, and that is also why you cannot decide what to do.

Rangvald sat down hard on the stump of the oak tree. Plowbreaker was just an outline now, barely visible in the gathering gloom. But he stared toward him as the thoughts still echoed in his mind. At last, he said, "Thank you, Plowbreaker. Thank you for your wisdom. I see now what part you had to play in all this. I think I may see everything now. I have spent far too long trying to escape from who and what I am. Too long ignoring my purpose. I am not needed in the Village of the Two Rivers. The Willow sisters do the healing and the farm magic. I asked the goddess Idunn why I was being called, and she told me it was because people were in danger and needed my help. I hardly heard her. My only concern was what would be the safest and most comfortable choice for me. I have made my decision!"

He leaped to his feet and stood on the wooden pedestal. A wind blew up, seemingly out of nowhere. Holding his arms out to it, he declared, "I am reborn. Henceforth, I will be Rangvald, Wizard of the Oaken Stump. I will not forget who I am or turn aside from my purpose. And in however many days I have left, I will remember this moment, and remember the wisdom you have given to me." Rangvald lifted his face to the sky and called out in a loud voice, "I say *yes* to the call. I am ready."

At that moment, the wind died back down and both of them stood silently, waiting.

What happened? Plowbreaker asked after a few minutes had passed.

Nothing, Rangvald replied, climbing down from the stump and feeling extremely foolish.

So what do we do now?

I guess we eat supper and go to sleep.

◆ ◆ ◆

Rangvald and Plowbreaker lay beside a small fire as the sound of the murmuring waters lulled them to sleep. Rangvald had worried that rest might be just as elusive as it had been the night before, when at last his nighttime visitors had all departed and the strange futures that had been hinted at were swirling in his mind. But to his great surprise, lying out here in this dark and alien wilderness, waiting for fate to drag him out into whatever danger and turmoil it had selected for him, he felt incredibly at peace. His fear and indecision were gone, replaced now with a sense of peaceful resolve. He heard Plowbreaker's deep, steady breathing mingle with the sound of the brook, and he floated into a deep, dreamless slumber.

"Rangvald."

His sleeping mind roused a little as it heard a familiar voice calling his name. It was a feminine voice, so gentle and sweet, so a part of nature, that he could scarcely distinguish it from the tinkling waters of the burbling brook. "Rangvald," the voice called out once more, and he opened his eyes. Sitting up, he saw the woman who had led them to this place standing by the water.

"Oh, it's you," he said, surprised. In reply, she gave a single nod blinking her big, sea-green eyes, her long lashes fanning her pale cheeks. Rangvald's heart instantly began to ache.

Stepping forward, she stretched out her hand, and in a voice like soft rain, said, "Come away, oh human child, to the waters and the wild."

Rangvald's conscious mind took no part in what happened next as he stood and grasped her small, white-silver hand. They left the small fire, the sleeping Plowbreaker, and the oaken stump behind. Hand in hand, they walked out into the whispering dark of midnight.

They followed the winding path of the waters, mingling hands and mingling glances, the ache in Rangvald's heart doubling each time her eyes sought out his. As they strolled, the brook became a stream, which in turn became a small river that eventually emptied itself into a still and tranquil pool.

She released his hand and waded into the pool up to her knees, then turned back to face him. As he watched the ripples disappear from the surface of the water, the pool became a mirror reflecting the night sky above. Rangvald's eyes glistened with tears as he beheld her standing among the shimmering stars of heaven, the moon-glow casting sparks across her silvery skin and tracing shadows around the curves and muscles of her perfect form.

"The silver apples of the moon," he whispered to himself. Rangvald understood now that the ache in his heart was just the emptiness that was there being filled again. Idunn's promise was fulfilled. He had answered the call and truly lived again. If he died right now, it would be with a fuller heart than he could ever have imagined.

"Why did you not return home when you had your book of magic back?" she asked, waking him from his trance.

Rangvald thought for a moment before replying. "The maiden of the gods told me that people were in danger and that I could help them. It wasn't until my friend gave me his wisdom that I finally realized that I have to face outward, not inward."

The woman smiled, and tilting her head, asked, "What does that mean?"

"I think what I'm trying to say is that I was only focusing on myself. What I wanted. What made me comfortable. What had hurt my feelings in the past. I thought that was the way to find happiness, but I know now that I was wrong. I was miserable."

"But now you are not miserable anymore?"

"No. I feel at peace with life. I am facing outward. People need my help. I have been given gifts in this life. I have to use them—it's my true purpose, my calling."

The woman's face bloomed with pure joy. "I love you, Rangvald the Reborn, Wizard of the Oaken Stump. Will you come join me here where the waters grow deep?" She stretched out her arms toward him. Rangvald made to hurry to her, but then he hesitated.

"Wait. Who are you? I don't even know who you are, or what your part in all of this is."

"I am Hefring, the ninth daughter of the goddess Ran. I am the lifting wave. I am the mother of Heimdal, who watches for the coming of Ragnarok, and my part in all of this was to lead you to yourself."

Rangvald's mind spun as he beheld the glowing goddess standing in the waters before him, her arms outstretched. "You are one of the wave daughters of the goddess Ran, she who keeps the souls of drowned men at the bottom of the seas. You asked me to join your embrace where the waters grow deep. Do you mean to drag me down to your mother's realm and kill me?"

"Do not ask me that question. Ask your own heart," she replied, her arms still inviting him to the water.

Rangvald did as he was told, and his heart answered him in an instant. A moment later, they wrapped their arms around each other and stood together in the crystal pool.

"Do you want to kiss me?" she asked, pulling back and looking into his eyes.

"You know that I do," he answered desperately.

"But you must tell me, Rangvald," she replied solemnly.

"Yes, I want to kiss you, and love you, and never leave you," he vowed. As soon as the words left his lips, Hefring covered them with her own in a passionate kiss that made his head swim drunkenly.

As the kiss lingered and grew even deeper, Rangvald felt a subtle tingle develop in his chest. Then probing tendrils of warmth began to spread out, until finally, his lungs were filled with a fiery wetness. He did not fight it when she started to rock backward and they plunged off the ledge and plummeted toward the briny depths. Not one hint of panic intruded upon his ecstasy as they glided down through the cool, clean waters. He had asked his heart what he should do, and it had answered. He would not doubt that answer now.

They came to rest on the pool's floor, and only then did she break the kiss. She watched with amusement as Rangvald tilted his head this way and that, trying to analyze his condition. It did not seem that he was breathing underwater exactly, it was more like he had drowned and that it was no cause for any concern. Satisfied that all was well, he cast his glance about him and found that light was being provided by a circle of crystals surrounding them, each the size of a man's head. It seemed as though they were somehow channeling the moon's glow through themselves. Strewn across the sandy floor at their feet, he saw a carpet of swords. For a moment, this struck him as even stranger than the magic crystals. But then he recalled that sometimes, the victors of a battle would cast the weapons of their vanquished foes into a mere. Hefring followed his gaze toward the blades. With a look of delight, she swam off. She seemed to search all over for a minute before reaching down, moving some of the weapons, and lifting one from their midst. Holding it reverently across her open palms, she returned and presented it to him.

"For me?" he asked, surprised by the muffled sound of his own voice.

"Yes. It is special. Do not lose it. It will serve you well when you most need it to."

Rangvald accepted the sword and marveled at the beautiful chasing which had been wrought masterfully across its hilt. Unlike many of the swords around them, this one showed no hint of rust or decay.

"Come with me," she said, taking his hand, and together they swam past the tumbled columns of a marble temple into a sunken grotto then on to the broken prow of a longship, its craven dragon's head still staring proudly forward. On a remnant of deck draped in tattered sailcloth striped in crimson and white, they made their bed. Again, she took on a solemn demeanor, and looking deep into his eyes, asked, "Will you take me as your lover? Just as before, I must ask, and you must answer."

Tears again sprang to his eyes, but this time, they simply mingled with the drifting waters around him. "Yes. A thousand times, yes. With every bit of my now-mended heart, yes," Rangvald swore to her, and goddess and wizard became one.

CHAPTER SIX

Plowbreaker snorted and nudged Rangvald a little harder. The wizard let out a defiant snore and rolled over, pulling his blanket around himself tighter.

Wake up! Plowbreaker shouted in his brain and nipped him in the behind.

"OUCH!" Rangvald yowled, rubbing at his buttocks. "Plowbreaker, that hurt! Why do you wake me? I am having the most wonderful of dreams!"

Look around us, Rangvald. Something strange has happened, Plowbreaker said urgently.

Rangvald rolled onto his back. Looking up, he saw the boughs of a tall tree stretching out above them. *Where did that come from?* Turning his head first one way, then the other, he blurted "Where are the brook and the stump?"

We are somewhere else now, Plowbreaker said gravely.

How can that be? Rangvald asked, sitting up. *We went to sleep by the stump, and I dreamed that...* Rangvald trailed off as his hand came to rest on the ground by his side. He lifted what it found there and gazed at the exquisite sword. In a flash, the sleep left his mind, and he remembered all. All but the end, and how they came to be here, wherever *here* was.

I woke you because I think we may be in danger, Plowbreaker said.

Danger? Rangvald repeated, scrambling to his feet and taking in their surroundings. He found that they were standing at the side of a broad road on top of a hill. It was no longer morning, as he had believed, but somewhere past midday, perhaps even approaching evening. The most distressing feature of their new surroundings, however, had to be the army of warriors armed for battle marching up the road straight for them.

Should we run away? Plowbreaker asked.

Rangvald considered for a minute, then finally replied, *No. I think that is our fate marching toward us now.* As quickly as he could, he saddled Plowbreaker and swung his satchel over his shoulder. Having no scabbard, he tucked the new sword into his belt and made to mount, but then he saw two riders detach from the front of the advancing host and come galloping toward him. *Here comes the welcoming party,* he thought to Plowbreaker, stepping forward and waving at the riders as they bounded up the hill and reigned up before him. "Good day, noble warriors," he called. At his words, the two horsemen traded a leery glance with one another, then, dismounting, they drew their swords and approached him.

"Who are you, and what is your business in Vestmor?" one of the warriors demanded, pointing his sword at him.

"Where am I?" Rangvald asked, switching to the northern dialect the man had used. Having lived and studied in the great port city of Einarshofn, Rangvald was fortunate to have learned the tongues of many travelers, but he couldn't recall having heard of a place named Vestmor.

"You don't even know what land it is you have invaded, you murdering dog?" the warrior yelled venomously.

"I haven't invaded any land, and I am no murderer," Rangvald protested.

The man hesitated, then glancing at the imposing sword at Rangvald's side, shouted, "Save your lies, foreign marauder. I will avenge my king!"

Rangvald staggered back as the warrior lifted his sword and advanced to strike. His panicked mind sought a way out. He had prepared no battle spells. Why? Why had he prepared no battle spells? He knew that great forces had begun to call him toward danger, yet still, all he had prepared were some simple mundane spells such as...

That's it! he realized. He had the spell of the Unseen Hand prepared. It wasn't much. At its strongest, it could push open his cottage door when his arms were full of firewood. But maybe it would push the warrior and strike fear into his heart. Rangvald lifted his hand. "Stay back!" he cried as he cast the magic. An alien throb gripped his heart. He gaped in wonder as the man went hurtling through the air and came crashing down dozens of yards away.

Rangvald stared in horror at the man's motionless figure at the side of the road, fearing that his neck must have snapped like a twig upon impact. He let out a loud sigh of relief a moment later when the warrior slowly came to his hands and knees. Rangvald turned his attention to the second man but found him backing away down the hill with terror in his eyes.

How did I do that? he asked himself in a daze. The flesh was still tingling over his heart, and he pulled the fabric of his tunic aside to examine his chest. To his great surprise, he saw a spot shimmering with silver. His eyes closed of their own accord. He could see his goddess, Hefring, kissing him above his heart as they floated in the deep blue realm of a dream.

"Archers at the ready," he heard a voice command. Reluctantly, he opened his eyes to see the bowmen fanning out at the foot of the hill, preparing to fire.

"Stop! Hold your arrows!" another voice ordered. It was an old and shrill voice. "Hold, I say. Let me through." Rangvald saw the soldiers part and a small cart pulled up to the foot of the hill driven by a bent old man. He stopped the cart and stood wearing the battle robes of a master wizard.

"What is your name, Wizard?" the old man called up to him.

"I am called Rangvald," he answered.

"What is the name of your horse?"

"He is called Plowbreaker."

"Have you seen the silver fish yet?"

Rangvald knew that he should be shocked by this question, but in light of everything that had happened thus far, he found that he was not. "Yes, she sent us here," he replied.

The old man nodded, then turned to the man who was mounted on the big chestnut charger beside him. "I have seen this wizard and this horse in my visions. I believe they are here to help us, My King."

The man lifted his helmet and Rangvald beheld the youth from his dream, the youth with rusty hair and a troubled face, struggling to hide his fear.

◆ ◆ ◆

Rangvald rode alongside Val of Kattegat and heard his tale of woe, how in but a few short days, their prosperous kingdom had come to the brink of complete and final devastation. In spite of these grim tidings, Rangvald found himself feeling rather optimistic. Reading this on his face, Val remarked, "You don't seem very concerned, Wizard Rangvald,"

"Oh, I am duly concerned. But I believe that perhaps the fortunes have changed," he replied.

"How is that?"

"I see a grim determination in the faces of the warriors at our side, and here are we two wizards who can perform battle magic. I can't help but feel encouraged by the fact that I was selected to come here, singled out by the gods. That means that the plight of Vestmor has not escaped their notice, and they must know that I can aid her." As he finished speaking, he noticed the set of the wizard's bushy gray eyebrows as he gave him a look that could only be described as sympathetic. "What? You don't agree?"

"I will say nothing to mar your high spirits. No, not for the world. If you say we can prevail, then we can prevail."

The two rode on in silence for a while as the army advanced along the road. With each step, Rangvald felt his youthful exuberance being left behind. Yes, no fewer than two goddesses had bidden him come on this quest, but neither one would assure him of his safety. In fact, he had been assured that death may very well await him along this path. He let out a deep sigh and looked back at Val of Kattegat, encountering once again that look of sympathy. "It occurs to me now that the sagas are filled with doomed men who were singled out for adventure by the gods."

"I'm afraid so," Val agreed with a laugh.

"Then does our mission come with naught but a grim ending?"

"No, there is hope. There is always hope. I see around me a collection of the truest hearts I have ever encountered. You may have missed the fact that the warriors marching at our side are mostly aging guardsmen and unseasoned farmers, but you were right when you said they were grimly determined to defend their families. They are led by a boy king and a girl princess, but this boy and girl embody the meaning of true nobility and this fight will require that. Their youth will be their ally not their enemy in this regard. The ideals of sacrifice and true nobility live strongest in the hearts of those who have not yet tasted the constant compromise and disillusionment of life. And then there is you." Val trailed off.

"What about me?"

"Well, you are, without a doubt, the most powerful wizard I have ever met. Power virtually drips from your fingertips."

"Yes, well, the dripping is all rather new, I assure you."

"Yes, perhaps. But even before that, you would have always been the most gifted in any room of wizards, wouldn't you?"

"And the most cowardly," Rangvald said quietly.

"I don't believe that. I don't think you were ever a coward. You are simply more sensitive, more easily bruised. You know it was your open and sensitive spirit that allowed you to master magics with ease. It is that same heart that will give you great courage and conviction when you need it."

Rangvald felt uncomfortable listening to Val's words of praise. "I can't tell how much of that is your great wisdom and how much is just encouragement."

"Oh, I will offer you no empty encouragements now. I will tell you plainly that I think we may be marching towards our defeat. I tried to see what will be, but a veil is thrown over the near future, and only glimpses could be seen. It is important to someone that we act according to our true hearts with no foreknowledge."

"Then why do you fear our defeat? What I said before is still true. We are two wizards amongst a band of stout-hearted warriors. You told me that the captain of the horsemen told you that the invaders are not that vast an army. Maybe we will prevail."

"Maybe," Val of Kattegat agreed unconvincingly.

"Maybe, but you don't believe so."

Val shook his head sadly. "No, I don't. I sense a great and terrible magic. Or rather, I suspect it. I sense nothing, to tell the truth. Nothing beyond what my vision showed me: a mass of fires approaching in the dark and death. King Gorm and Ulfhild the wizard along with an army twice the size of the enemy fell with ease. Then the villages throughout the west were destroyed. Not just the ones that fell in the enemy's path, but all of them, methodically destroyed. Not taken, not plundered, but burned and wiped away from the earth."

"I don't understand."

"Nor do I. They are not conquering the land, they are killing it. They are not feeding off the crops or enjoying its riches. They appear to be doing evil for evil's sake, for all that I can reckon, and it speaks to me of dark magics."

Rangvald considered these words gravely as a large tent with a force of soldiers around it hove into view up ahead.

"Ah, at last," Val said with relief. "We have at best another two hours until dark. My visions yet unfulfilled all take place at night. So I would advise us both to use the time to prepare what warlike spells our heads can contain."

"I, too, have visions yet to be fulfilled. One is of our boy king in a tent. That one there, I'll wager. I saw him with a face struggling to conceal a world of uncertainty. The other is of a battlefield at night. I saw what I fear may be the source of this evil magic you so dread, a thin and wretched figure of a woman with tangled black hair and skin as pale as that of a corpse. She wields a dark and twisted wand topped with some giant sapphire with which she strikes me. That, I fear, is how I shall die."

Val of Kattegat grunted and stroked his long gray beard with thought. "She strikes you and you fall before her?"

"Well, no. She strikes me three times with it."

"Does she now?"

"Yes, it was terrifying when I dreamed it. I can't get it out of my mind."

"Yes, it sounds it," the old wizard said, sounding almost cheerful.

"You don't sound too impressed," Rangvald noted.

"I am most certain you are correct and that this wicked-looking creature must be our magical nemesis. As for her killing you, well, I don't know any more about it than you do. But it seems that a powerful weapon such as you describe would fell a man with a single blow. Now, if I hear that he could sustain three in a row without losing his feet, well then, I might just be inclined to believe he could receive ten or twenty, or maybe even a thousand such blows without dying."

Rangvald's mood brightened a bit at that reasoning, and a small measure of his optimism returned in spite of all the sobering revelations Val of Kattegat had given him.

As they arrived at the camp, King Eirik called out, "Where is Halfdan? Where is your captain?" In answer, a dozen fingers pointed to the large tent. "Amazigh, Val, and Rangvald, attend me, please," the young king called. They all dismounted and hurried to the large pavilion that had been set up to the side of the road. As they entered, Rangvald saw that his suspicion had been correct. This was indeed the tent he had seen in his dream, complete with the warriors who had been leaning over a map but were now kneeling to their new king.

"Rise and report, Halfdan," Eirik commanded.

"Last night, the enemy attacked and burned the last of the villages in the west country. It was really no more than a collection of three farms here," Halfdan said, pointing a finger at the map as they all clustered around the table. "The enemy's raiding parties consolidated here with the main force in the early morning hours." Halfdan indicated a point further down the road. "We expect them to attack us a few hours after dark."

"So they prefer surprise attack under the cover of

darkness?" Amazigh inquired.

"No. They use no stealth. Everywhere they go, they can be seen by the torches they carry. This is why there tend to be survivors whenever they strike."

"I don't understand what advantage they see in moving by night then," Amazigh said.

"They have only ever moved by night. From the first battle to each and every village they have struck, it has always been in the dark," Halfdan explained.

"What does this mean, Val?" Eirik asked the elderly wizard.

Val of Kattegat stroked his long beard. "Trolls or some such nighttime creature, perhaps?" Halfdan shared a look with his lieutenants, who all shook their heads. "Some trolls are big and misshapen, but some are the size and shape of men," the wizard added.

"Yes, Val of Kattegat, but we could see the enemy clearly before good King Gorm ordered our retreat. They were only men. They were grim-faced and blood-soaked, but men. I swear it on my sword."

"Very well, if they are but men, then we will kill them, no matter what hour they choose," the king declared. "If we cannot defeat them outright, then it is imperative that we at least hold them as long as we are able while our people escape to the caves. Captain Halfdan, ready your men for battle."

Again, Halfdan and his lieutenants shared a glance. "My King, what provisions have you brought?"

"Provisions?" Eirik asked.

"Yes, My Lord. My men are going on ten days since they have had a proper meal. Have you brought wagons with camp provisions?"

"No, we marched at once, sending all the wagons

loaded with food to the caves. The men with us are carrying only marching provisions, nothing more. Have you sent parties to forage for food? If the enemy never moves at day, your riders could be scouring the countryside."

"Yes, My King, we have riders foraging every hour of the day. But all of the crops have been burned, and the game animals have fled in terror from the evil which plagues our land. The only thing we have in good supply is water from the rivers. We've gotten some fish there, but not nearly enough."

"This is an error my father never would have made," Eirik said miserably. Rangvald saw the men around him stare silently at the ground. Then the giant man with dark skin who seemed to never leave the young king's side placed a fatherly hand on the youth's arm and shook his head gravely. The boy seem to remember himself and said, "Amazigh, have the men who came with us give their marching provisions to Halfdan's defenders. Then they themselves will take over the front lines."

"Very wise, My King," the giant answered.

"Come now, everyone, let's prepare for battle," the king ordered in a clear, strong voice.

Rangvald saw some confidence returning to the assembly. The men began to busy themselves once more as the big man hurried from the tent to carry out the king's orders. Rangvald saw Eirik turn and step away from the table. It was then, when the king thought himself unobserved, that Rangvald's vision was fulfilled. He glimpsed the boy's face struggling to mask all the fear and uncertainty that was raging inside of him. Just as in the dream, Rangvald felt helplessness assailing his heart.

"Come now, Rangvald, let's prepare our spells for battle," Val said, taking his arm and leading him out into the evening's waning sunlight. Val walked to his cart, then sat and opened his ancient book of magic. After a brief search, Rangvald located Plowbreaker lazily eating grass in the field behind the tent.

I wish the soldiers could eat grass as you do. Then maybe they could draw strength for the coming fight.

Well, why don't you grow them something they can eat? Plowbreaker replied.

Rangvald considered this idea. *No, I wish there were time for that, but there just isn't. There are some things that love to grow. Those, I can make spring up in an instant, things like vines and wildflowers. But more complex crops —things that could feed an army—they take far too much time.* Rangvald knew that what he was saying was a fact, but still, something was tugging at his mind. It was the image of the armored warrior flying off of the hill at Rangvald's command.

Almost without realizing it, he found himself opening his purse and searching through it until he found the seeds he had packed therein before leaving home. He selected one and knelt; then, digging with his hands, he planted it in the soil. His spellbook fairly opened itself to the page he needed. It had been the spell he had used the most over the last couple of years, living in a farm community and boosting the farmers' labors, ensuring large and bounteous harvests.

Rangvald concentrated on the magic, letting it fill him and hum through his veins until he was rocking back and forth on his knees. When his body would no longer contain it, he cast the crackling power into the seed.

"Well, I have to admit I've never grown such a complex plant this quickly," he said, peering at the barely-visible sprig of green that had just pushed its way through the dirt. "In a couple of years, that will really be something." Rangvald rose and rejoined Plowbreaker. "Well, so much for 'dripping with power,' I guess."

"Oh, you're dripping with power, all right. What you lack is conviction."

Rangvald spun to find Val of Kattegat watching him. "What do you mean?"

"That seed grew just as well as you really expected it to. Just as well as you believed possible."

"I still don't understand."

"Let me see if I can explain it better. Oh, yes. When you were on that hill and the warrior raised his sword to kill you, was it merely a casual affair when you cast the Unseen Hand?"

"No, I cast it in a terror. I just wanted him away from me at all costs."

"Good, then take up your book and cast your spell on the seed once more."

Rangvald obeyed, kneeling down and reading the spell. Again, he let the magic fill him to the brim. Again, he began rocking, preparing to release the magic.

"Not yet! You don't want it. Not truly. You need to want it desperately and passionately, like you did when that sword was coming down at your head. Just think, Rangvald. These men will be facing the battle of their lives while faint from hunger. Don't you care about them? Won't you feed them?"

Rangvald's eyes fell shut as the old wizard's words stirred something inside of him, he felt the throbbing kiss of the goddess touch his heart again. The magic flowed from him, and his ears filled with a groaning and creaking noise that grew almost deafening for one brief moment before falling silent all at once. When Rangvald opened his eyes, he was kneeling at the foot of the largest apple tree he had ever seen, its boughs heavy with pale yellow apples each one the size of a fist. "The golden apples of the sun," Rangvald whispered, feeling breathless.

"Do it again. Make sure you are the master of it now," Val of Kattegat said from behind him. "Make sure that when you do anything from now on, you know why it must be done and believe in its doing."

Rangvald selected another seed. A minute later, a second apple tree stood by the first one, this one bearing apples of pale red. "I harnessed the power much more quickly that time," he told Val in wonder. Another minute and a third tree stood heavy with deep crimson apples. Rangvald plucked one of the red apples, and turning back to Val, said, "That one was almost effortless. I did it with conviction."

"And so you did," the old wizard agreed.

Rangvald went and fed the apple to Plowbreaker as hungry warriors hurried over and began to harvest the fruit.

Excited shouts and hurrying feet summoned the king from the tent and he followed the commotion around to the back, where he stood amazed by the three new apple trees. Rangvald looked up just as the look of fear and worry left his young face. "I did it. I soothed that worried brow... At least for the moment," Rangvald told himself, and it warmed his heart.

CHAPTER SEVEN

It was almost midnight when another of Val of Kattegat's visions came to pass. After the scout riders had returned to warn of the enemy's approach, King Eirik's ragtag army of defenders had moved to the rise where the road began to descend gently towards the low lands of the coast. Their position could not be called a commanding high ground, but it was high ground nonetheless, and they would make the enemy come to them. As they watched the enemy spilling into view in the distance, Val leaned over to Rangvald. "This is it—the fire in the night. I saw this in my vision, but I did not realize how many there were." Ten minutes later, there were still fires coming over the horizon and joining the oncoming army. Now a vast sea of torches was approaching them from out of the gloom.

"By my reckoning, there are at least a thousand," Amazigh announced, causing Rangvald's knees to turn to wet barley meal.

"How can that be? I swear they were less than half that number when we first faced them," said Halfdan.

"Perhaps they have been remaining in the west while more of their kinsmen sailed to join them," Val of Kattegat suggested.

"Can we spread out more? Look how they extend past our flanks on both sides," the king said.

"I'm afraid we dare not spread any more, My King. We simply do not have the numbers," Amazigh answered.

"Very well. When they come, they will surround us with ease. We stay together and fight as brothers to the end. We must buy Revna and the people time," the king said, struggling to keep his voice from wavering.

Rangvald's stomach clenched and a bile of acid crawled up his throat. *We can't win this. This is suicide,* he thought to himself. *Why have I come here to die among strangers? Plowbreaker is behind me back at the tent. I have to get to him and fly from here.*

"I'm very proud of you, Rangvald."

"What?" Rangvald demanded, turning to the old wizard.

"I said I'm very proud of you. Am I allowed to say that even though I've only known you for less than a day?"

Rangvald sighed uncomfortably and whispered, "You wouldn't be saying that if you knew what I was just thinking."

"But I do know what you were just thinking. It was written all over your face. But I also know that you will not run. You will stay and fight. This is your moment of destiny, and you will shake the very boughs of Yggdrasil with your magic."

"I will?"

"You most certainly will."

Rangvald took a deep breath and felt strength come back into his knees. "Thank you, Master Val. Thank you for everything you've done for me. I know that it's been less than a day that we've known each other but... Well, I just want to..."

The old man reached out and grasped his hand. "Me too, son. Me too."

"Oh, dark and treacherous days!" the giant Amazigh lamented, drawing their attention.

"What is it?" Val asked him.

"It is not their wretched kinsmen that swell the enemy's ranks. It is our own."

"What?" gasped the king.

"There, in the light of their torches. I see farmers carrying their pitchforks and pruning hooks. They are soaked in gore, no doubt from some unholy deeds."

"He speaks the truth, My King. I, too, see farmers with my own eyes," Halfdan confirmed.

"That is not the worst of it," Amazigh said gravely.

"What, Amazigh? Speak!" Eirik pleaded when the big man hesitated.

"I see our own soldiers among them. I see the armor. I see the crest of Vestmor upon their shields."

"Oh, black betrayal! Is this how my father was undone by a smaller force? Did his own army turn against him?" Eirik asked, close to tears.

"Steady, My King," Amazigh cautioned.

"Yes. Yes, right," the boy answered. Drawing his sword, he shouted, "Ready yourselves, my brothers. Tonight we drink in Valhalla!" All around him, men drew their weapons and cheered.

Beside him, Rangvald saw Val of Kattegat pull up the left sleeve of his robe and begin to unlace a strange vambrace that covered his forearm. "Here, I want you to have this," he said pulling it off and shoving it at Rangvald.

"Now? You are giving me something *now*?" he protested.

"It only just occurred to me. Quickly, now. Put it on."

Rangvald obeyed him, but he couldn't see the point. Made of flimsy buff leather, the vambrace didn't appear to be of much use as armor. Securing the laces, it occurred to him that for the old wizard to have given it to him, it must have magical properties. "Is it charmed?" he asked.

"Yes, here," Val said, waving a hand over its surface. Rangvald could now see a line of runes faintly glowing along its surface.

"All right, what's it do?" he asked eagerly.

"That. It's doing it," Val answered with a definitive point of his finger.

"It does this? It has runes that glow, that's it? They don't even glow that brightly."

"Have you read what they say yet?" Val asked patiently.

Rangvald studied the runes, finding instantly that they could be read easily in spite of the darkness. "Oh, it's a fire spell. But I've already memorized it for the battle."

"Right. And once you've recited it, the words will dissolve in your mind and need to be read again. What will you do if you need another fireball in battle?"

Rangvald began to reach for his satchel, then hesitated. Val watched him with a pleasant smile as Rangvald imagined taking out his spellbook, looking for the right page, and trying to read it in the dark, all while an army of warriors was trying to murder him. His eyes came back to rest on the vambrace with understanding. “Wait!” he said. “You can't give this to me. You will need it yourself! I can't take this. I will give it back. You must use it,” he said, reaching for the laces.

Val shook his head. “I want you to have it. I think it will do more good on your arm than on mine. Besides, there is no time now.”

Rangvald’s eyes followed Val’s finger as it pointed, and he nearly shouted with fear. As he had been distracted with the wizard’s gift, the enemy had drawn very near. His breath began to come in panicked sobs.

“Calm yourself, son. Remember, have conviction. Know why it must be done and believe in its doing.”

Rangvald fought to control his breathing as the ocean of torch-bearing men moved to within shouting distance. They came to a halt in unison, as if heeding an inaudible command. The enemy was just as Amazigh had described them, blood-soaked and grim-faced.

All along the defenders’ line, his comrades shouted taunts, clashing their swords into their shields or shaking their spears or farm tools. But the enemy stood still, making no reply. Then, from somewhere Rangvald could not pinpoint, a lone horn sounded. Again moving as one, the eerily silent torchbearers parted up the middle. Something could be seen moving up the road in the flickering firelight.

Rangvald looked to Amazigh, the giant man who stood towering over them all. He knew that his keen eyes would be able to see what was coming toward them. He watched as the man’s face scrunched up with disgust at what he was seeing. Rangvald stood on his tiptoes, trying to make it out for himself. It appeared to be a cluster of men carrying something. Perhaps a weapon of some sort? No, it was a litter of the type nobles sometimes used, made of dark, twisted iron. Atop it, a pale figure rode.

The sight filled Rangvald with more dread than if it had indeed been some terrible weapon. He instinctively knew who the figure riding atop the strange man-powered vehicle would be. He knew it would be the horrid and evil-looking woman from his dream. This foreknowledge braced him for the reality, and when at last she hove into full view, he was the only one among his companions not greatly affected by her pallid, emaciated, corpse-like appearance, with her lank, dark hair, her black, seemingly pupilless eyes, and her crooked, hideous mouth.

The iron platform upon which she rode bore no chair or couch. She rode on her bony knees. Around its perimeter was affixed a grotesque collection of severed heads. The skin on the faces, which were frozen in what looked like some eternal anguish, was shriveled and dried in a most peculiar way. Rangvald was surprised to find that, now that he was face-to-face with the terrible demon from his nightmare, he was more able to control his panic than when he was simply dreading its coming. He was here, and he knew now that he would not run.

Once again without any command that could be heard, the enemy moved in perfect unison, the ranks closing in behind the wretched woman. The cluster of men carrying her stopped at the front of their army. She stood. Turning her head this way and that, she seemed to take in the measure of her enemy. Then it appeared as if she were casting her senses beyond them. Closing her eyes and lifting her chin, she turned first one way then the other, searching with some unknown sight. She stopped and pointed a diagonal course to the north. Without a word, a hundred of her men on the left flank detached and began to run off in that direction.

"The princess and our people," Val of Kattegat groaned.

Eirik stepped forward and boomed, "Stay your men! I have not given them leave to depart!"

The woman turned, took in the boy at a glance, then threw her head back and laughed. The sound of her laughter was a pestilence to the ear. It was impossible to locate any signs of true mirth in it. It was more like the demented call of a crow with a broken wing. In spite of himself, Eirik blanched. Seeing that, his warriors shuffled nervously around him. The young king collected himself and stood up straight again. "Hear the words of the King of Vestmor. I command you to leave this land at once and to never return!"

The woman ceased her laughing at once and locked eyes with the youth. "I am the Witch Queen of Pretania, and yes, it is proper that I parlay with the monarch of this land. I claim this place by right of conquest, and I ask the King of Vestmor to recognize my claim and acknowledge that I am now the true Queen of this land and all of its subjects."

"I do not acknowledge it, and I order you to—"

"Shut your drooling maw, you child! I was speaking to the King of Vestmor. Let him step forward and answer for himself."

The litter she stood upon dipped slightly as one of its bearers stepped away from it, and reaching up, slowly removed his helmet.

"Father!" Eirik exclaimed. But King Gorm made no reply. Instead, he pointed up at the strange and hideous woman, and in a slow and emotionless voice, said, "I serve the Witch of Pretania. She alone is ruler of Vestmor."

"Father, no! You betray your people!" Eirik cried.

The army fell to murmuring and confusion. Doubt ran through them like a wildfire. The warrior behind Rangvald shouted, "The King lives. King Gorm is alive!"

"No! No! Listen to me!" Val of Kattegat called out, raising his arms to restore order. "The king does not live! None of these men live. Look, their faces are not simply grim—they are lifeless! They do not wear the blood of foul deeds. Look more closely; they bear the wounds of their own demise!"

Val's words did nothing to calm the warriors. If anything, they simply compounded their fear and confusion. "Steady, men. Steady," Eirik called out. "Is this true, wizard?"

"Yes, My King. Your father's spirit is sitting at the side of Odin and Freya right now! That is just his body you see."

"The wizard is right, King Eirik. See how our breath mingles hotly with the air of midnight and makes clouds? See how our chests rise and fall? Look to the enemy," Amazigh said, pointing.

"Yes, I see it. They are not alive." Eirik agreed.

"This foul witch desecrates your father's body and the bodies of your loyal friends and neighbors. There is no treachery here but hers," Val proclaimed.

"Very clever, wizard. But your cleverness will not save you. When this world is but one hour older, all of your companions' carcasses will be ridden like nags by the unclean things that dwell in shadow. And as for *you* —I will drink your power like nectar from the ivy flower and grow even stronger, just like I did with this one." The Witch Queen's bony finger pointed down to the front of the iron litter at one of the heads hanging there. Val of Kattegat saw the wisps of blonde hair stirring in the breeze.

"Ulfhild!" he cried. His lips moved in a blur and he thrust out his hands. A torrent of snow and ice poured forth. The witch's right hand raised up bearing the twisted black club topped by a giant glowing sapphire that Rangvald had seen in his dream. The blast of freezing ice split in two as it met the queen's unholy wand and rushed past her, causing warriors on either side behind her to turn into human icicles, which fell and shattered into thousands of pieces.

As soon as the blast of Val's frozen fury ceased, she pointed the gemstone at him. A pale light, flickering with indistinct shapes like the fluttering wings of shadowy moths, washed over him. Calmly, he turned and looked at Rangvald. "It's up to you now, son," he said, then he shriveled to an empty husk and fell to the ground dead.

"No!" Rangvald cried, falling to his knees, trying to gather the dry, frail body into his arms.

"I grow tired of this. Kill them. Kill them all," the Witch Queen of Pretania commanded, and her army came shambling forward.

Rangvald sprang to his feet in a rage. Screaming a spell in the tongue of the ancient ones, he waved his right hand. Sixty men fell to pieces in a wave of blue flames. More ancient words poured from his mouth. His left hand sent lightning leaping across the enemy ranks, turning fifty more bodies to cinder. All across the carnage, tiny fireflies of slightly differing hues flitted here and there above the falling warriors.

"Stop!" the witch commanded. Her charging warriors halted in their tracks.

Rangvald's pulse pounded in his ears. He felt the power humming in his heart, stronger than it ever had before.

"Another wizard! The most powerful wizard I've ever seen! Oh, this is a treat! And to think, I almost bypassed this little kingdom," the evil woman rejoiced.

"I command you to leave at once. You have seen the power of the wizard that defends this land!" King Eirik declared.

"Stupid boy!" the Queen said with a laugh. "You still do not understand, do you? I eat magic! You continue to send wizards against me, and I continue to use them to grow stronger. This one will make me more powerful than I've ever dreamed possible!"

Rangvald looked back at the desiccated corpse wrapped in gray robes that had been Val of Kattegat, and the truth of her words came crashing down on him. In desperation, he pointed at her and began to cast the Unseen Hand. In response, her ugly face split into a huge smile, and she held up her glowing cudgel to ward the attack. He knew that it would part just as Val's ice spell had and leave her untouched. As the last word was leaving his mouth, a thought occurred to him and he moved his arm.

The Witch Queen howled with rage and surprise as the iron litter and the men supporting it were swept away from beneath her feet, causing her to tumble to the ground. Rangvald brought the vambrace that Val had given him up before his eyes and read aloud, sending a fireball raking along the ground toward where the queen was getting to her hands and knees. Just as it was about to strike, he saw the sapphire staff raise. The storm of flame buffeted harmlessly by her, destroying warriors to her right and left.

He knew what was coming next, so he stood tall with his shoulders back and chin held high as the glowing purplish stone pointed and the fluttering light washed over him just as it had Val. The Queen smiled devilishly and rose to her feet. She took an eager step forward and thrust the weapon out at him. As another moment passed, her face began to cloud. She looked down at the wand in disbelief. The beam ceased. Rangvald stood still, his noble bearing unchanged and his body completely unharmed.

"This isn't possible!" the wicked woman screeched. "No mortal man can resist this magic. Tell me who you are!"

"You will have to work harder than that to learn my true name, you filthy conjurer. Until you hear it, you can know me by this mark," he said, ripping open his tunic and exposing his heart. A flash of silver from the goddess shone forth, and the witch screamed in terror.

Throwing her hands before her eyes, she shouted, "Attack! Attack! Kill them all!"

The army of the dead surged like a wave and the defenders' line broke immediately. Rangvald fell back with the men around him, who were lashing out desperately at the oncoming hordes. Everything was chaos and blood. He tried to raise his hand to cast a spell, but it was all happening too quickly.

He saw a glint of sapphire charging forward through the warriors, followed by the screaming face of the Queen, and he froze. This was it, this was the vision he had dreamed before. He was in the middle of a battle, surrounded by the dead and dying, and the demon's club was crashing down on him. Rangvald's arm moved on its own, some instinct or divine guidance taking over. A second later, a white shower of sparks brightened the night, followed by another and another.

The witch screamed with fury as Rangvald blocked her deadly blows with the sword the goddess Hefring had gifted him in the depths of the mere. Now it was his turn to strike and hers to block. He raised the blade on high and brought it crashing down. In anticipation of the blow, the Queen grabbed the thick haft of her weapon in both hands and held it aloft. A moment later, she looked up at him from the ground in shock. Her cudgel was cleft in two, as was her bloodied shoulder.

"You want to know who I am? Now I will tell you. I am Rangvald Gunderson, Wizard of the Oaken Stump. Blessed one of the Lifting Wave. Slayer of the Witch Queen of Pretania!" Rangvald lifted his sword to strike. Before he could, he was suddenly washed away by a sea of bodies. He struck out, again and again, stabbing and slashing with his blade, but the warriors carried him away from their Queen, heeding her unheard orders just as he had seen them doing before the battle.

The dead men dropped him in a heap, then turned as one and fled back the way they had come. Springing up, Rangvald looked around the battlefield and found the enemy in full retreat. He searched frantically and could just make out a cluster of them in the distance, carrying their stricken Queen. He ran a handful of steps in that direction, but it was clear that he would never catch up with them. "Stupid! Stupid! Stupid! I spoke when I should have struck, and now more mothers will weep because of it," he screamed at himself bitterly.

"Be kind to yourself, wizard. Some mothers yet will

be able to rejoice this day, and it is you they will thank for it."

Rangvald turned to see Captain Halfdan and a handful of men standing with him. "By Freya! So few!" he lamented.

Halfdan nodded grimly, then looking around himself, shouted to the men, "Did anyone see where the king fell?" When no one answered, they all set off to search. Here and there they found a wounded comrade and helped him to his feet, but of the king, they found no sign.

After a few minutes, one of the men called, "Here is brave Amazigh. The king will not be far away from him." All of the survivors converged and beheld the giant, fallen dead on his face with a hundred wounds in his back.

"He lives!" one of the warriors gasped, breaking the silence. "I saw him move!"

"Yes, and I hear him speaking," another said excitedly, bending over and listening for the faint noise to repeat itself.

"Quickly, help me roll him over. It is not he who lives," Halfdan cried, dragging at the big man's shoulder. Three more soldiers lent a hand, and Eirik gasped for air as Amazigh was lifted off of him.

"My King, are you all right?" Halfdan asked as he sat up.

The youth nodded sadly. "I fell, wounded to the thigh, and Amazigh shielded me with his very life."

Rangvald hurried forward, retrieving his book of magic. "Quickly, bring one of those torches closer," he ordered, trying to find the page for his healing spell.

"What has happened? Where is the enemy?" the king asked, bewildered.

"The wizard wounded their Queen and they carried

her from the field," Halfdan explained.

"We have much to thank you for today, Rangvald," Eirik said.

"No, I've made a mess of everything. I should have —"

"No," the king said, cutting him off. "This day still has hope, and that is your doing entirely. Without you, we would have fallen to the last man."

"Lay back, please, while I heal you," Rangvald said quietly.

A couple of minutes later, Eirik stood tall on his newly-mended leg. "Come, men, let's ride!"

"What about Amazigh and Val, and all of our dead?" Rangvald protested.

"It is of them I am thinking when I say leave them where they lay and ride. The Queen's warriors are heading for my sister and our people. If we don't save them, then all of these men's sacrifices will have been in vain. If we don't save them, then who will be left to mourn these who have died here?"

Rangvald stood, clutching his spellbook. "We are with you, King Eirik."

The youth took one last look at Amazigh. He bent down and placed the dead man's sword across his big chest, then, standing shouted, "To the horses! Let's ride!"

CHAPTER EIGHT

Revna reigned up beside the path. As the long column of refugees passed, she consulted her map.

"Are we on course, Princess?" Trygve the huntsman asked, riding up beside her.

"Oh, we are going in the right direction, but at our current pace, I fear we will never reach the caves alive."

"I don't see what can be done. There are too many children and elderly on foot to go any faster," Trygve said with a shrug.

"Look here," she said pointing at her map. "We will pause the wagons just up ahead. Have them emptied of their provisions. I want all of the people to abandon their possessions and mount the wagons. The small children and the elderly first. It must be done quickly."

"I don't understand, Princess. We can't trap ourselves in the caves without provisions. We'll starve."

"If we don't move quickly, we may never reach the

caves. There is a spring in the caverns. With water, the people can last for days while we try to gather food. But if they are caught out in the open by the enemy..."

"But what about your brother and every man who could bear arms? They went to fight them."

"They went to slow them down. They went to buy us time with their very lives. We must use that time to reach the caves. The enemy is not here to conquer us, Trygve. They are here to kill us. To kill us all and erase our kingdom from the world. Do you understand?"

The huntsman could only nod his reply.

"Good. Then carry out your orders. Let no one argue them."

"Yes, My Princess," he answered gravely before galloping ahead.

Revna folded her map and withdrew her spellbook, if it could even be called a "book." Eleven pages were all it contained thus far. Just eleven pages of magic she had learned since her training began. She selected the second to last page and committed the spell for fire to her memory. She could only summon a ball of yellow fire the size of a man's fist and cast it a dozen or so paces, so she wasn't certain how effective it would be in battle, but as the western sky was already carrying a tinge of orange in it, she knew that they would need light. This would save them from the necessity of stopping to create a flame. When Revna caught up to the column, the provisions were being heaped onto the ground, and children and grandparents were being lifted into the wagons.

"Hurry! We have to move faster!" she shouted, glancing again at the horizon where the sun was sinking ever lower.

"Most of the people will be able to ride now, Princess," Leif called up to her as he helped an elderly woman up into a wagon.

"Most. But not all," Revna said to herself disappointedly, scanning the column. "Wait! There are two more large wagons in the rear!"

"That family joined us at the last of the homesteads we passed. They refuse to unload their wagons and take on riders," Leif explained.

"We shall see about that," Revna growled, wheeling her horse and galloping to the back of the line.

"Unload these wagons and take on riders," she commanded the man who was driving the first of the two rigs.

"If anyone touches my belongings, I will kill them!" the man shouted, grabbing his axe and leaping down to stand between Revna and his wagons.

"But you're carrying beds and a table and chairs. Surely you can unload them so that the children and the elderly can ride."

"Why should I? These are my possessions. I worked hard to get them. Why should my family and I go without our beds so that a bunch of lazy beggars can ride? They should have worked harder and bought their own wagons."

Revna was flabbergasted by the angry man's words, but she remained calm. "They lost all of their possessions when the invaders burned their villages. They were fortunate just to escape with their lives. Most didn't."

"That has nothing to do with me! I'm not going to throw my provisions away; we will need them when we get to the caves, and I may as well tell you now that when we get there we will not share our food with any of you fools who dumped yours in the wilderness. I've worked too hard for what I have with no help from anyone. I refuse to be robbed by you!"

"Oh, you were never helped by anyone?" Revna spat, her temper rising. "You don't live in a kingdom with just laws and fair taxes? You don't live in a kingdom whose army fights to protect you and what you have? Seven years ago, my mother fought and died for you. Even as we speak, my brother and every man who isn't a coward are laying down their lives so you may escape to safety. A safety that you are being led to by myself and the huntsmen. We went out of our way to pass your farm and bring you with us. You live in a society. You have been helped, you are being helped now, and you will be helped in the future. Now it's your turn to help your neighbors and take them into your wagons."

"I will only tell you this one more time. If anyone touches my possessions I will kill them!" came his shouted reply.

"I am Revna, Princess of Vestmor, and I command you to unload your wagons at once!" she shouted back.

"You don't have your father's army here to back you up. You are just a spoiled child playing pretend. I'm in charge now, and my first act as leader is to give you the beating that you deserve for talking to me with such disrespect." The farmer dropped his axe, and rushing forward, grabbed her by the robe to drag her from the saddle. In response, Revna opened her hand and blew the pale pink powder clutched within into his face. Instantly, he stiffened and toppled back like a falling tree.

"Quickly, now. Unload these wagons. We have already wasted too much time," she directed. "Trygve, bind this man's hands. He will awaken soon, and I will not tolerate any more interference."

"Oh, I thought you'd killed him," the huntsman said, rolling the sleeping man over.

"He'll have a long time to think about his foolishness as he walks to the caves by himself," Leif said with a chuckle.

"No. See to it that he is loaded onto a wagon," Revna said.

"I don't understand. Why don't we make him walk?" the youth asked.

"Because we aren't like him," she replied. "Now, hurry. We must keep moving,"

◆ ◆ ◆

As the night wore on, Revna began to feel more optimistic. Even though the carts and wagons, heavily laden with people, did not move very quickly, they were still making good progress. She expected to reach the Nordhule by late morning. She rode in advance of the party, holding up Deathwhisper, whose charmed blade was glowing brightly to light their way. She was thankful for its enchantment, because at this point, she had been holding it for hours, and her arms were fatigued. She couldn't imagine what it would be like if the sword held any true weight. Now that the topic of fatigue had entered her mind, she realized just how weary of the saddle she had become. She knew that everyone must be just as sore and tired, especially since they were crammed into the wagons together, unable even to shift around to find comfort. Above all else, she knew that the horses and oxen were tired. Early in the trip, many had asked about breaks, but she had quickly quelled that notion. They could not afford to stop and rest. They had to make it to safety.

"How are we doing, Princess?" Trygve asked, riding

up beside her.

"I'm feeling hopeful. It will be dawn in another two hours, and we should arrive some time in the morning."

"So, still some hours yet to go?" he asked, sounding dejected.

"Yes, I'm afraid so."

"Is there no way we can stop for a rest? The drivers are falling asleep with the reins in their hands, and Snorri, that loudmouth farmer, is complaining nonstop."

Revna considered the idea. She was desperate to be out of the saddle, even if only for a few minutes. "No, I don't think we should," she said at last. "There is just too much we don't know. Halfdan told the messenger that he thought attack was imminent. Has the battle taken place already? And if so, did my brother and the other men make it there in time to help? There is no way to know for certain, but I believe our men did meet the enemy this night. My teacher, Val of Kattegat, said that he foresaw fires at night and that they would bring his death with them."

"Perhaps he was mistaken," Trygve suggested.

"Perhaps, but I don't think so. I fear that a battle has taken place and our army has fallen. If it has, then the enemy will push through to the fortress and, finding it empty, easily locate the signs of our trail leading north."

"If all of these things are happening, we have still been given quite a head start, haven't we?"

"Not so great a head start that horses at the gallop could not catch up to us."

"So, no stopping to rest until we reach the caves. Understood."

"Please keep the drivers awake, and if you need to gag that farmer to shut him up, so be it."

“With pleasure, Prin—” the huntsman stopped speaking abruptly as the sounds of panic broke out among the wagons.

“They're coming!” someone shouted.

“Keep going! Drive as fast as you can!” Revna shouted to the wagons as she and Trygve turned their horses and trotted back along the line.

“Do you see them yet? I don't see anyone behind us at all!” she called to Leif as he rode up to meet them.

“Not behind us—off across the field there, down in the valley beyond,” he said, pointing to the southwest, where a mass of torches was approaching.

“It could be your brother and the army, Princess,” Trygve said with excitement. “The enemy would surely be following us from the fortress, but if the king wished to catch up with us, he would come over land from that direction.”

Revna shook her head doubtfully.

“Come, Princess, the enemy couldn’t know we were coming here. Only our men would know. Maybe they come to bring us good news. Maybe it's all over and we can return home,” he reasoned, hope coloring his voice.

“I'm sorry, Trygve, but I don't think so. When have our men ever traveled with so many torches? It is strange. I am afraid that it is the fire at night that Master Val envisioned.” Revna saw the huntsman deflate as she spoke, and she added, “Listen, we don't know who it is yet. We will go and see. If it is our men, then we will welcome them.”

“Thank you, Princess, but you are right. No men of Vestmor would waste their torches when less than half that number would suffice to light their way. It is the enemy. They want to be seen; they want us to fear. I was only grasping at hope before. My son and I will go and fight at your side. We will do it with open eyes and hearts —no illusions. Won't we, son?"

Leif swallowed loudly and nodded.

"No one ever went to battle in finer company," she said, then turned to the passing wagons. "Make for the caves as fast as you can," she shouted. "We will hold them back if we are able."

"Stop! Stop the cart!" someone called out. One of the carts rolled to the side and halted. A stout old woman climbed out of the back. "You can drive on now. I'm staying with the princess."

"Wait I'm staying as well," declared a second voice, then another old woman got out, followed by three more.

"Get back into the cart at once," Revna commanded.

"I am sorry, Princess, but we must disobey. Driver, roll on, quickly," the first woman said.

"Driver, stay," Revna ordered.

"Listen, Princess, there is no time to argue. I am sorry to disobey you, but we are grandmothers. We are done raising our children, but our children and our children's children are on these wagons."

"You are right," Revna said, mollified. "You have the right to stay and fight."

"Thank you, Princess," the woman replied.

"Leif, didn't we leave some tools on the last wagon?"

"Yes; we left some food and supplies because the people all could fit already. Here it is coming up now."

"You there, stop," she ordered as it rolled by. "You women, arm yourselves. We must hurry; the torches are getting closer now."

The grandmothers hurried to the wagon and seized pitchforks, hammers, and anything they could find that looked strong enough to fight with.

"Back to rob me of the last of my possessions, I see," Snorri the farmer said in a self-righteous tone.

"You made a lot of promises to kill and beat people before. If you are eager for violence, will you come and fight the invaders with us?" Revna asked him.

"Fight your own battles, Princess," he replied dismissively.

"What?" Leif demanded. "It's everyone's battle! I can't believe we're going to fight, and probably die, for this wretched man!"

"Easy, son. We do not do the right thing for the gratitude of others. We do it because it is the right thing."

"Well spoken, master huntsman. Now let's ride," Revna said, lifting Deathwhisper to light their way and galloping off.

As they crossed the field, Trygve shouted to make himself heard above the wind, "Make for the hillock toward the center of the field!" He took over the lead, and Revna and Leif followed the huntsman to the indicated spot.

"Why do we stop here?" the Princess asked as soon they arrived. "Shouldn't we go out to meet them and try to hold them as far from the wagons as we can?"

"No, My Princess. This mound will offer us our only strategic advantage. From up there, my son and I can strike them with arrows as they enter the edge of the field, making them seek cover. We've slung extra quivers to our saddles, so if our arms and aim do not fail us, we may hold them for some time."

"Brilliant! I chose my companions well for this

journey, that is certain!" Revna cheered.

"Thank you, Princess. I see the old women making their way toward us. While we are on the top, the six of you stay hidden behind the hill. If they get past us and come to attack, I will let you know, and you can spring out. You will at least begin with an element of surprise."

"I understand. Luck in battle, Trygve. Luck in battle, Leif," she said solemnly.

"Luck in battle, Princess. Luck in battle, father."

"And luck to both of you as well. I'm so proud of you both. May Odin smile on our deeds this morn."

As the two archers scrambled up the rise, Revna took out her spellbook and again prepared the fire spell she had used to give life to the lanterns and torches of the wagon train. It was her only battle spell, and she knew it likely would not fell a grown man, but at least it might distract one long enough for her to strike with her sword.

The elderly women began to arrive as Revna put her book away. She waited until they had all drawn near before extinguishing the glow charm on her blade. Huddling in the dark, Revna explained their strategy.

The voice of the stout old woman who had been first to step off the cart said, "It is a good plan. Maybe our fine huntsman can stop our enemy themselves. Especially if the fools continue to light their targets for them with all those torches."

"What if they abandon their torches?" Revna asked.

"The moon is very low, all but gone, and the sun is still a long way away. If they have the sense to smother their torches, our archers will not be able to hold them."

"I thought it all seemed too good to be true," Revna said dejectedly.

"Don't give up hope, Princess. This is a good plan,

and our brave bowmen may inflict so much harm on them while the light allows that the enemy scatters and hides. But I want us to be ready for them if they break through."

"You speak with wisdom. Who are you?" Revna asked.

"As I said before, I am a grandmother now, and nothing more," the woman replied.

"My sister is called Signe. She was a shield maiden of the king, Princess," a second voice explained from the darkness.

"Signe, who taught my mother to fight when she was a girl?"

"That was I, Princess. But it was another lifetime. I am very old now and have no illusions. Neither does my sister Brita or the other grandmothers. If we are called upon to fight this day, then all we will do is try to slow them down before we die. We choose this end. It is honorable to die defending who we love. You must promise not to try and save us." This was met by a murmur of approval from the other old women.

"I understand, but you must promise the same. I am still but a child, though I know I do not act like one, and my magic is still very weak. I do not expect to be very effective in battle. I am also here to sacrifice myself if need be so that others might live."

No one spoke for a few moments, then, very quietly, Signe said, "You are just like her. Your mother would be very proud of the woman you have become."

"You honor me by saying so," Revna answered, thankful for the dark which hid the emotion in her face.

Above them sounded a whooshing noise, the unmistakable sound of an arrow being loosed. It was followed by another, then another, then dozens more at a remarkable rate.

"Hold fire, son. Their armor is too thick. Wait until they are a little closer and aim for their faces," came Trygves' command from the hilltop above them. Revna and the women waited for what felt like an eternity of minutes.

At last, the whooshing arrows started once more. The shots were a little slower now as father and son aimed with special care. Another minute passed, then Leif's stricken voice lamented, "This isn't real—it can't be!"

"Calm yourself, son. Steady on," Trygve soothed.

"What's happening?" Signe called up to them.

" We cannot stop them. They are advancing still," Trygve called down in reply.

Revna stood with her back against the hill and could see the flickering light cast against the ground on either side of their hiding place, and knew that the large host of warriors, still carrying torches, was drawing near. "Surprise will gain us nothing. Maybe words can stall them."

She stomped out and stood in front of the hill. A hundred grim warriors carrying a hundred torches that grew short in their hands were approaching with blank, expressionless faces. Revna stepped forward, and bringing forth the glow on her sword, she cast a fireball along its blade as she thrust it into the sky.

"I command you to stop!" she howled, standing in the light of the flame and blazing steel. To her relief, they did. "I am the wizard Revna. Raven of the Morn! Daughter of the Flame! I order you to leave this place!"

For a long moment, no one moved. At last, one of

the grim warriors stepped forward and jeered, "Look, it's a baby wizard. Oh, and there are her nursemaids hiding by the hill."

The warriors looked and sounded as if they were trying to laugh at his jests, but were somehow forbidden the practice of joy. Their smiles instead were ugly sneers, and the sounds they made were more like hisses. "Forward, my brothers, and we will eat their souls."

The grandmothers joined Revna as the men began moving forward again. "You stopped them for a minute. Even that was a victory that helped our wagons," The old woman named Brita said.

Revna looked around at the women who stood grimly in the approaching flicker. "Do not try to save me," she said. "I will grow old before your very eyes and fall dead at your feet. But remember, just like you, I choose this end. Now I will kill as many of these men as I can before I go."

Revna withdrew the Hand of Fate and the small parchment from her purse. She pointed the shriveled black hand at the jeering leader, reading the words aloud. The advancing warriors halted again as the man crumpled to the ground. She felt no pain, no sensation whatsoever to indicate her soul losing a piece of itself. She let the parchment fall to the ground. She knew that the words were etched into her brain and would be forevermore. A hush fell as from the yawning maw of the corpse on the ground, a strange reddish mote, a sort of eerily glowing ember, floated upwards. With a faint, oddly distant scream, the mote went shooting away to the north.

"What have you done to Baal of Philistia?" one of the warriors cried.

"I have banished him to the realm of Hel. He

belongs to the queen of eternity now."

A chorus of anguished wailing greeted this news. "She will cast him into the pit of Niflheim, the black, endless torture far beneath the bridge of rainbows!"

"Yes. Yes, she will! Did I not command you to leave this place?"

"Quick, kill the child!" one of the warriors, who Revna now knew was simply the dead body of a man being possessed by some vile demon, cried while rushing at her.

The words sprang from her lips. He, too, crumpled in a heap. This time, a blue ember went screaming to the north, but Revna did not stop to watch it go. Instead, she pointed the Hand of Fate again and expelled another loathsome soul, then another and another, repeating the spell as quickly as her lips could form the words.

In a terror, bodies began falling to the ground on their own to escape her wrath. A swarm of fireflies whizzed away, fleeing the land of Vestmor forever. A cheer broke out among Revna's tiny band. But she could not share in their joy. She looked wearily out as the torches began to burn the bodies of her dead and desecrated countrymen. The Hand of Fate had not made her body grow old after all, because it had done what it was intended for, but she still felt as though she had aged a hundred years by its use. *I can't remember when last I felt like a child,* she thought to herself.

"You did it, Princess. You were amazing!" Leif said, rushing up and embracing her. Instantly the feeling of being old and weary disappeared, and she blushed, feeling like a nervous girl again.

"Oh, I'm sorry, Princess," he said, releasing her. "I forgot myself. I was just so certain we were about to die."

"It's all right, but we don't have time. Trygve, you and Leif put the grandmothers on your mounts, two on each of your horses and one on my pony. We three will walk much faster than they. Now let's rejoin our people," she said. Her orders were swiftly obeyed. She saw a sort of respect, even reverence in their looks that had not been there before.

"I will lead you on the pony, friends. Let me get one of the enemy's torches to light our way," Signe said, hurrying to the bodies. Revna noted that she quickly belted on one of the dead men's swords as well. She knew that if battle came again, the old warrior woman was determined she would not meet it with a farm tool.

Revna nodded approvingly and called out again, "Come, let us rejoin our people."

CHAPTER NINE

Eirik and Rangvald went back up the road, stepping around the fallen bodies of their comrades, with Halfdan and the rest of the survivors trailing behind.

The large tent in which they had made their plans was now in tatters on the ground. The wave of undead warriors who had washed over them had destroyed the camp before turning back and bearing their wounded queen from the field. Even the new apple trees that Rangvald's magic had grown were broken and tilted to the side.

"The horses! Where are the horses?" Eirik cried out.

"Some lay dead. Still others have run off, My King," Halfdan reported.

"No!" Eirik shouted in despair. "See if you can gather some. We need horses!"

"Come, men, there are yet some apples on the trees. Let us take them and see if we can coax some horses back into our company," Halfdan said, rushing over to the splintered trees.

Rangvald called out with his voice and his thoughts, "Plowbreaker, where are you?" He listened for a response and thought maybe a scrap of a far-distant answer floated back to him, but he could not be sure. It occurred to him that his friend could be lying somewhere nearby, dead like so many others, but his mind rejected the thought and he turned away. His eyes settled on some of the warriors who were still being helped up the road. "Bring the injured to me," he called, rushing ahead and withdrawing his book once more.

Rangvald went from man to man, taking on their wounds and banishing them away. His newfound power made the process quicker than ever before, but each fresh hurt he felt, every gut-wrenching pain, drained him and assaulted his will to carry on. He pushed himself to continue. After the last of the wounded men were healed, he lowered himself to the ground and lay still.

"The wizard! Look to the wizard!" Eirik yelled, rushing to his side. Rangvald opened his eyes and found the king and the warriors he had healed huddled around him, wearing worried expressions. "Are you well, Master Rangvald?" Eirik asked him.

"I am not harmed. I am just wearied beyond what I can bear. Will this nightmare never cease?"

"Rest, my friend. I fear we may be done whether we care to be or not," the youth said miserably. "Halfdan can find no horses, and every moment that passes, the Witch Queen's ghouls slip farther from our grasp."

"I am sorry—" Rangvald began, but stopped speaking mid-sentence and tilted his head to listen. "Did you hear someone call my name?" he asked. The king replied with a look of confusion. "Of course you didn't hear it. It was in my head!" Rangvald said, sitting up. "Plowbreaker, is that you?" he shouted.

"Look! Horses!" one of the warriors shouted, pointing up the road where Plowbreaker came into view. He was leading a pack of horses behind him.

"Plowbreaker!" Rangvald cried. All of his weariness forgotten, he leaped to his feet.

◆ ◆ ◆

Hours passed as they rode through the dark, searching, craning their necks to catch a glimpse of distant torchlight.

When they had first set out, a trail had sometimes been visible, but having passed through some leagues of dense forest and fording a good-sized river in the dark, it had been a long time since any sign of the enemy's passing had been seen.

It wasn't until a little before dawn that one of their number spied something strange and pointed off to the south. Following the line of his finger, everyone saw the chaotic swirl of tiny lights that rose into the sky and scattered to the four winds. Rangvald remembered having seen similar lights scatter when his fireball and lightning had devoured the bodies of the warriors at the battle on the western road.

"It's the Witch Queen's minions! Someone is slaying them!" he yelled triumphantly, turning Plowbreaker and riding south.

The pale fingers of dawn were pulling back the curtain of night as they crossed a small valley. They could now see wisps of smoke trailing steadily to the sky in the field above them, marking their destination. A short time later, they stood gaping at the remains of the quarry they had been longing so to catch. Some were smoldering where torches had set them alight, some were staring vacantly toward the sky while flies circled their faces, but all were dead. Or, rather, dead and finally at peace.

"Who could have done this?" one of the soldiers asked in disbelief.

"Many of them have arrows in them," another soldier commented helpfully.

"This is not the work of archers. This is a wizard's work," Rangvald told him, then looked to the king. "Val of Kattegat told me that your sister is a wizard. This must be her doing."

"My sister is not yet fourteen winters old. The last magic I saw her perform was the levitation of a hen's egg. If this was her doing, it will be a tale for the ages."

"My King, over here," Halfdan shouted from the nearby hillock. "Three horses came from the path, followed by five on foot. They rejoin the path here, but with only three on foot, and one is a very small foot indeed."

"Revna!" Eirik exclaimed.

◆ ◆ ◆

The refugees had not been at the caves for long when the king rode into view. No one cheered at his arrival. On the contrary, many fell to their knees and wept when they counted the number of those who rode at his side. The men of Vestmor were all but gone. Their women and children, along with the elderly, had only barely escaped the same fate. They had come here to hide like shadows in the dark in caves abandoned long ago by the dwarfs of old.

The king and his men were greeted by a woman

who was strongly built but very old. She wore a sword at her side and was directing wagons up the long stone ramp that led to the entrance of the caves.

"I am Signe. Do you remember me, King Eirik?"

"Yes, you were a mighty warrior. You served my parents in days gone past."

"As I serve you now," she said solemnly.

"We saw the bodies of a hundred men the enemy sent to kill you."

"Yes. Vanquished by Princess Revna. She saved us all, My King,"

Eirik and Rangvald shared a look of elation.

"Where is she? Take me to her," the king pleaded.

"She is in the main cavern. Follow me," Signe replied, leaning them up the broad ramp.

Rangvald marveled at the place that had been called a cave by everyone who had spoken of it. That description had not adequately prepared him for the reality of what he beheld. It was a cave some thirty feet or so above the ground, set into the sheer face of a granite cliff, but that was where any natural appearance ended. Everything from the ramp they were now traversing to the giant statues of mighty dwarfish figures standing above it in huge alcoves was unmistakably the work of masons and sculptors whom no human craftsman could ever equal.

"This is an unforeseen problem," Eirik exclaimed, stopping at the opening to the cave where its two massive doors had failed. One hung tenuously by one fragile hinge and the other had fallen completely, its thick wooden planks and iron bands crumbling to pieces.

"Eirik!" Revna called out, running into his arms. "I'm so glad you made it! I was so worried!"

"I made it, but most did not. I'm sorry, sister, but Val of Kattegat fell."

"I know. He told me he had seen his death before we parted."

"He knew he would die, and yet he came," Eirik said solemnly.

"He was not one to run from his destiny. He hoped that he could be of some help, so he went."

"He was of help. He taught me to harness my new power, and he taught me courage," Rangvald said.

"Who are you, friend?" Revna asked him. "You do not look like one of our farmers."

"This is Rangvald the wizard, he has come from far away to aid us. Val said that he saw him in a vision," Eirik said.

"The man on the straw-colored horse?" she asked remembering her last conversation with her master.

"That's right, he does ride a horse the color of straw," Eirik confirmed.

"You are most welcome, wizard, and we are grateful for your aid in times such as these."

Rangvald bowed to her, but could not speak a reply. He found that the princess made him feel somehow sad. It was like the way he had felt when he saw the young king's face, struggling to hide his fear and indecision, but it was even more pronounced. She was small and slight, wearing oversized apprentice robes and carrying a gleaming sword that only made her seem somehow even more helpless. He knew that she was not a child. Not in the way she spoke or thought, nor in the way she accepted death with no time for mourning, and certainly not in the way she had single-handedly vanquished an army of the dead to save her people. He tried to imagine her at play or singing songs in a feast hall, but he could not.

"Rangvald, did you hear me?" Eirik asked, bringing him out of his somber thoughts.

"No, I'm sorry," he replied.

"I said you must be exhausted and needing food. I know that I am."

"Oh, yes. Very much so," Rangvald replied gratefully.

"I have some rather unwelcome news in regards to that," Revna chimed in. "Rest is available wherever you would like to lie down, and water is still flowing fresh and clean from the spring into the carven font made by the dwarfs, but food is very scarce, I'm afraid."

"What happened to the provisions from the fortress?" Eirik asked with surprise.

"I can answer that," said a man who was sitting atop one of the wagons parked in the giant stone hall they had entered. Eirik looked at him, and he continued. "The provisions were thrown into a ditch by the princess so that her lazy and useless friends could ride here in wagons they had no right to ride in."

"What about the provisions in the wagon you are sitting in? My warriors are starving. Let us pass out these provisions and—"

"These are my provisions!" the man interrupted hotly, causing Halfdan to step forward, drawing his sword.

"Wait," Eirik said, stopping the captain in his tracks. "You have grievances, that is clear. I am your king. Tell me what they are so that I may redress them if I am able."

"Your sister attacked me and tied me up. She robbed me of my possessions, and now you mean to rob me of the rest of them. For twenty-two years I have paid my taxes—two bushels a year to feed the army. My father paid those taxes before me. I am a free man. I have rights. You and your tyrant fathers are all the same. You Kings and Princesses do nothing while we toil and you grow fat off our labors."

"I have heard your words. Now I, Eirik Gormson, king of Vestmor will give you what you seek," Eirik dipped into his belt purse and pulled out a handful of silver. "Captain Halfdan, how much does a bushel of grain cost?"

"No the food in my wagon is not for sale! I need it. You can't—"

"Hold your tongue. You have spoken, and now I speak," Eirik interrupted him, but with no anger in his voice. "I do not seek to buy your food. Everyone assembled, hear the word of your king. The provisions in that wagon are that man's alone and are not to be touched. Now, Captain, how many bushels would the silver in my hand buy?"

"It would buy a large farm's entire harvest," the soldier answered.

"So more than forty-four bushels?" the king asked.

"Yes, My King. Many more."

Eirik walked over and thrust the silver at the scowling man. "Take it," he ordered when the man was slow to move. "Now you are the richest farmer in the land. This is most certainly true since almost all the others are dead."

"I said that you can't buy my food!" the man said.

"And I told you I'm not trying to buy it. I commanded that no one was to touch it."

"Then I don't understand."

"You have made it clear that you find the Kingdom

of Vestmor a land of tyranny and oppression. You find its rulers to be robbers unworthy of their people. These are your words, and I will not argue them. You find this country and its treatment intolerable, so I have refunded the taxes you have paid in your lifetime of torture. Twenty-two years, two bushels a year. You hold the value of that plus interest in your hand. Our dealings are done."

Eirik walked away, and Snorri the farmer's eyes darted here and there as if searching for the meaning of a riddle.

"Captain Halfdan."

"Yes, My King?"

"In ten minutes' time, I want you to secure this cave. We are at war with foreign invaders, so if you encounter anyone who is not a subject of my realm, put them to death. Is that understood?"

"Yes, My King," Halfdan said with a bow.

"Oh, and Captain, I want to be clear. Someone like the wizard Rangvald, who was not born here and yet has come and placed himself in harm's way to defend those who need protecting, will forever be a true son of Vestmor. Whereas that man," he said, pointing at Snorri, "has proven in word and deed that he cares nothing for the safety and welfare of his fellow people. He has renounced the Kingdom of Vestmor and been reimbursed for his contributions to it. He is not a subject of this realm. If he is here in ten minutes' time, carry out your orders."

"Please, My King," a frightened, mousy-looking woman with a bruised cheek spoke up in a trembling voice.

"If you think to plead for your husband, I implore you to save your breath."

"I seek to plead for the lives of my three sons.

Please, let them stay. My husband says that the princess lies and there are no invaders out there, but I know that is not true. Please, do not banish my children."

"Good woman, you and your sons are children of Vestmor. You are not banished. Stay and you will be members of my household. I will never eat unless you and yours have eaten first. I swear it by Odin."

"My wife and my children obey me. They are my property too, and they will not be stolen by..." Snorri stopped yelling as the woman and the three boys swiftly walked away and joined the king. "You come back! You come back right now or I'll—"

"Finish that sentence. You'll what?" Eirik said icily.

Snorri seemed to visibly shrink, and he stammered, "My wagons. Someone help me hitch my wagons. You, behind me, move your cart, or I can't move my wagons." Everyone assembled stared at the blubbering man without moving a muscle. "This isn't fair! You are all evil, just like your king. Why am I being persecuted? I don't deserve this, I was just standing up for my rights,"

Rangvald wandered out past the big open doors, not wishing to watch the whining farmer any longer. All of the refugees and wagons were now in the gargantuan main hall of the cave, and some of the soldiers were leading the horses and oxen out to graze with Plowbreaker and the other horses on which the warriors had arrived. Rangvald stepped out into the open field. Reaching into his satchel, he found what he needed, knelt down, and went to work. After a few minutes, he heard the sound of running footsteps and turned to see the crying farmer run down the stone walkway, then freeze in his tracks and gape at the field full of fruit and vegetables ready for harvest that Rangvald had just magically grown.

"It isn't fair!" the man sobbed, then ran off into the brightening morning alone. Rangvald shrugged and finished growing the last two seeds from his purse into full-grown trees. As the goddess' humming power went quiet in his chest, he gathered some pears and took them to Plowbreaker, who was merrily grazing with all the other animals. Then he gathered a little food for himself and trudged back up toward the cave with weary steps.

A commotion broke out on the landing above, and he saw excited people pointing down at the crops below. "Go, it's not going to eat itself," he called out to them with a tired smile, and they hurried down past him.

"Thank you, wizard. From the bottom of my heart, thank you," Eirik said as Rangvald passed him at the door.

"I've done what I can. Tell the people to save the seeds from what they eat. We may have to do this again," Rangvald said.

In a cheerful voice, Revna said, "My brother says you wounded the necromancer queen and she retreated. Perhaps we've seen the last of her."

Rangvald paused to consider the idea, then, shaking his head, said, "No, I don't think so. She seems to be made of pure hatred and arrogance. I think that when I dealt her that blow and failed to kill her, I only ensured that she would never leave us in peace again."

"I thank the gods that you struck it. That blow is the only reason any of us survived," Eirik replied. "Besides, she was never going to stop anyway. Not until all of Vestmor was a grave."

"Will we at least have some time to prepare for her next attack?" Revna asked tiredly.

"I fear even that will be too much to ask. She will know that our fighting men will have been reduced to but a handful, and she seems to know where we are. It was as if she could sense where you and the people were when she sent her warriors in your direction," her brother replied.

"Perhaps her wound will delay her return?" she said, still grasping for hope.

This time, it was Rangvald who dashed that hope. "She appears to wield powerful magics. I'm afraid she will be able to heal from her injury. The one thing in our favor is that she only attacks at night."

"Is it possible that she will march on us during the day and take us by surprise?" the young king asked, looking worriedly at the ruined doors.

"I can't say. I do not know if she simply chooses to move by night or she must. It may be that she and her vile minions must shun the sun or pay some consequence. I like that notion, but I do not know for certain," Rangvald answered, stifling a yawn.

"Very well. We will have to take a chance and leave the door for now. Rest is what is most needed. It is my wager that attack will not come until nightfall. We will sleep back deeper in the caves where it is dark, then rise refreshed in the afternoon and see what can be done to secure us."

Rangvald gave this a welcome nod and shuffled toward the back of the giant stone hall, longing for the cool, dark chambers beyond.

◆ ◆ ◆

When Rangvald awoke, uncertain of the time, he found himself alone in the chamber where he had lain down to rest alongside many of the farmers and remaining warriors. Either everyone had used the utmost care in remaining quiet as they rose, or he had slept as soundly as a stone. Rangvald searched for the will to rise, but instead, he found images of the army he had joined only yesterday who were now making a feast for crows out on the western road. He saw Val of Kattegat, who had, in the course of one fateful afternoon, become a kind of father to him. He could see him now bathed in the ghostly light as he shriveled to a lifeless husk.

Rangvald pulled his blanket up over his head, just as he had done when last he had been in his own bed. Had that really only been three nights ago? It seemed almost as if it had been in a different lifetime that he had hidden beneath his blanket, trying to block out the world. The thought hung in his mind for a minute, then he sat up and said, "That was a different life, and it was a different me. People need me. It's time to stop hiding."

Stumbling from the dim chamber to the hall beyond, he made his way to the large marble font which was fed by the cold crystal spring running deep below the stone halls of the long-absent dwarfs. He stopped and splashed the last vestiges of sleep from his face, then unlaced his kuksa from his belt, dipped it, and drank deeply. He felt the cold elixir of the earth restoring him, and he strode back to the large outer chamber, where all was a hive of activity.

Through the ruined doors, he could see a sky tinged by deep orange hues that framed a team of warriors who were leading Plowbreaker along with some of the other animals outside. The sunset sky gave him his first sense of the time of day. Rangvald ran to catch up with his friend as he was starting down the ramp. *Where have you been?* he thought to Plowbreaker.

I pulled some timbers from the nearby wood to help

block the doors.

Now where are you going?

I don't know, Plowbreaker replied.

"You there. Where are the animals being taken?" Rangvald asked one of the warriors.

"We are releasing them now that the barrier is being built."

"Releasing?" Rangvald repeated.

"By the king's command. He said that if we have to remain for a long time, the horses will starve because we have no hay for them."

"Oh, yes, that's logical," Rangvald agreed.

"If you say so," the warrior replied in a strange tone.

"Am I missing something?" Rangvald asked.

"Well, far be it from me to disagree with the king, but I think we should keep them in case *we* are starving."

Rangvald was confused for a moment, then grasped the man's meaning. "You men can go. I'll release my horse myself," he said coldly.

Once alone, they walked out past the crops Rangvald had grown. *You need to go, Plowbreaker. They're going to block the entrance to the cave before the witch and her army get here. Go with the other animals and get away from this place.*

But I don't want to leave here without you, Plowbreaker said, confused.

I know. I would prefer to stay together also, but I have to stay in the cave and try to protect the people, and you have to lead the animals away from the evil warriors like you did last night.

Will we ever see each other again?

I don't know, but I hope so. Without you, I don't believe I would have ever answered my destiny, and for that, I'm eter-

nally grateful, Rangvald said, hugging Plowbreaker's neck. *Now go, and get far away from this place.*

Goodbye, Rangvald. I'll miss you, Plowbreaker said, then reluctantly walked off toward the setting sun.

Rangvald arrived back at the doorway just as a team of horses was beginning to pull wagons laden with timbers in place to block the opening. Approaching Captain Halfdan, who was supervising, he said, "If animals are needed, I can call my horse, Plowbreaker, to come back. He is quite strong."

"Strong is an understatement, wizard. Your horse pulled logs as strongly as the oxen and twice as fast. But his enthusiasm for his work is almost reckless. This is finesse work, building the barricade. We're using some of the calmer, less spirited animals. Then they will be released as well."

"I understand, Captain," Rangvald said, disappointed that he would not have an excuse to see Plowbreaker one last time. "The barricade is already beginning to look impressive. Do you believe it will hold?"

Halfdan answered him with a look. It did not linger; it was little more than a glance, but in it, he communicated what he really thought without speaking it aloud for the already-frightened farmers to hear.

Rangvald nodded his understanding, taking Halfdan's cue for discretion. "Well, then, perhaps it is time I prepare my spells," he said quietly, excusing himself.

He spied Eirik and Revna whittling points onto some wooden poles along with a group of elderly farmers. Rangvald hurried over and picked up one of the poles. He withdrew his belt knife and began to work without being asked. Having slept in as others were already hard at work made him feel awkward, and he was anxious to lend a hand with something. "Are these to be part of the barricade?" he asked as he worked.

It was the old woman who had introduced herself as Signe who answered him. "No, these are to be spears for the grandmothers and those grandfathers who did not march with the king to the western road."

This answer surprised him, and it showed on his face. Seeing this, Revna explained. "I, too, had to be reminded that courage has no age limit when a wagon-load of grandmothers marched into the night and stood shoulder-to-shoulder against the dead last night."

Rangvald conjured an image of this in his mind, and still, he did not marvel at the thought of the elderly women half as much as the thought of the thirteen-year-old girl who led them. "You are quite right, it would appear that courage has no age limit," he agreed.

"We will defend the barricade. You and my sister with your magic, and me and my remaining thirty-six able-bodied warriors. If they should get past us, then they will meet the grandmothers. Beyond them, the children and their mothers will hide in the deeper chambers of the caves. If they fall, then everything that was left of Vestmor will fall with them," the young king said.

"Well then, we won't let that happen. We will hold them!" Rangvald declared with conviction. But looking from face to face, he found that his words had not landed with the desired effect. "Come, now, is it really as dire as that?"

"You will find no quit in the people of Vestmor," Signe said. "But arriving here and finding that time and neglect had done what no army for a thousand years ever had—finding the impregnable doors thrown down—we may have to face the truth."

Her words landed hard, and Rangvald braced himself for the fear or despair they would bring with them, but then was shocked when a wave of anger washed over him instead. "Listen to me, all of you. This foul stench from the grave will not end the kingdom of Vestmor. We will not allow it! Let her come with her abominations. We will meet them and drive them back to whatever dark pit they belong in!" Everyone in the big chamber had stopped what they were doing and turned to listen to his impassioned words. "This is not a challenge of power. This is a test of heart, and in all my days, I have never known of people with more courage, more strength of will. This place is the rock upon which the Witch Queen of Pretania shall be broken. And ours are the hands that will do it!" Looking to the sky above the growing barricade, he said, "Look, the night has come. She will be marching toward us now. Everyone, look to your preparations. Tonight, we wipe our enemy from the face of the earth!" This was met by a great cheer.

King Eirik leapt up and shouted, "You heard the wizard. Prepare for battle! Let's make a welcome for our guests that they will never forget!"

The people redoubled their efforts with a new spring in their steps. Even after all of the horrors they had endured, all of the loved ones who hadn't even been properly mourned yet, the angry and defiant words Rangvald had used gave them the will to carry on. They were all focused on the singular purpose of defending the last children of their realm, the last descendants of their shattered families, and now they felt as if they could actually do it.

Their faith was tested again however when the

warriors finished removing the wheels from the wagons, stacked them up, and filled them with what timbers the afternoon had allowed them to cut and drag back for their use, and still the barrier hardly reached the halfway mark of the giant doorway. The barricade was lashed together and braced as best as could be, but a quick survey was all that was needed for the same question to form in everyone's mind.

Was the Nordhule a safe haven or a trap?

Eirik observed the determined look slipping from the faces. “Excellent work, men! Even better than I imagined,” he declared in a loud voice. All around him, the faces, which a moment before had been falling, seemed to reconsider, and he saw them begin to nod with a reserved approval.

“How long until we will see them?” Eirik asked Halfdan more quietly.

“If they started for here when night fell, we could see them within the next three or four hours. We learned last night that the dead can run without stopping and cover great distances in a night,” Halfdan answered.

“Where is the huntsman?”

“Here, My King,” Trygve replied, stepping forward.

“Trygve, no one in the kingdom can match your eyes. Will you take a position on the barricade and watch for their approach?”

In answer, Trygve bowed, then began to scale the patchwork of wagons and timbers.

“I will accompany him,” Rangvald announced.

“Do you have keen vision as well?” Eirik asked with interest.

“No. I, too, will rely on the huntsman to see the enemy, but it occurs to me that my battle spells will be useless behind the barricade. From up there, I may be able to attack while they are out in the open, and perhaps wipe them out before they even reach us."

"That would be most welcomed," Eirik agreed.

The wizard followed the huntsman to the top of the barricade, where they looked to the southwestern horizon for the enemy's approach.

One hour passed, followed by another. As the third hour approached, the defenders felt their tension begin to rise. Eyes were continually darting up toward the huntsman and the wizard atop the makeshift wall, expecting at any time to hear the herald of approaching fires, but it did not come. As the fourth hour approached, the huntsman's alarm seemed more impending than ever, and all around, hands gripped sword hilts anxiously. Then the fourth hour came and went as well.

When the fifth hour approached, no weapons were being gripped with anticipation. Hour six was greeted by gentle snoring and low murmuring conversations. When the seventh hour of their vigil approached, Rangvald turned to Trygve and said, "Perhaps there will be no attack tonight."

The huntsman's lips parted to speak, but then he stopped and focused into the darkness with all of his attention. "I think I see something," the sharp-eyed archer whispered.

Rangvald strained his eyes, peering into the darkness. "Torches?"

"No, something else."

"Where?"

"Coming up the path from the south," Trygve said with uncertainty.

"What is it?"

The huntsman hesitated. The silence felt heavy and tense. "There it is! Right there at the foot of the ramp. The moonlight is glinting off something the color of a... What's that gemstone called again?"

"Sapphire," Rangvald answered with horror, rising to his knees and unleashing a massive ball of fire that turned the night into day. The giant sapphire glowed brightly as the deadly flames deflected to either side of the grinning witch. Squinting in the sudden light, he saw the long single-file column of ghouls, each of them holding onto each other, connecting to the queen and remaining safe behind her.

Rangvald knelt, feeling stupefied, as a series of distant whispers sounded from the darkness below.

"Move!" Trygve shouted, throwing himself in front of the wizard, then falling back against him, causing them to topple from the barricade. Rangvald screamed as he felt himself falling toward the stone floor below. To his great surprise, he landed with a watery splash and floated down, down into the deep, until he was resting on the sail-draped prow of a sunken ship.

Lifting his head, he saw Hefring, glittering and silver goddess of the waves, gliding into his arms. *There is nothing but this,* he thought. *There never was and there never will be. Nothing has ever existed but this one perfect moment.* Leaning down, she kissed his chest above his heart.

He awoke and found himself staring blearily into Trygve's lifeless eyes. The huntsman was hanging upside-down from the top of the barricade, entangled by one boot. Scanning his body, Rangvald saw the arrows that sprouted from his chest, arrows that had been meant for Rangvald. They would have been his had the brave huntsman not pushed him back and covered his body with his own.

Revna pressed the cloth to his nose and mouth for a second time, and the stench of deers' horn affronted his senses, causing him to sit up. Rangvald tried blinking away his blurred vision to no avail.

"I have no healing magic, I'm afraid," the princess said apologetically. "Do you think you can stand?"

Rangvald struggled to his feet and swayed drunkenly. Revna supported him as best she could and led him away as voices shouted, "Brace the barricade, men! Push with all your might!"

After shuffling along for several steps, his knees buckled and he sat down hard. His head swam as he scooted on his seat and turned around. He could see Revna rushing back toward the trembling, bulging barrier where the warriors were pushing back against it with all their strength. He was thankful for the dwarfs' masterful design; he knew that it was the only reason they had not already been overrun. The ramp that ran up along the wall was less than two wagons wide and ended on a walled landing high above the ground where one had to turn right to enter the doors. It meant that attackers could never use a battering ram or bring more bodies than the landing would allow against the doors. It was the wisdom of the old dwarfish craftsman that was saving the makeshift barricade from simply being swept away.

It was almost as if the enemy could read his thoughts for at that precise moment, the trembling pressure against the barrier ceased. A long minute of peace passed as the defenders caught their breath. Then the peace was shattered just as quickly as it had begun when the wretched ghouls began raining down on them from above. Rangvald jumped with surprise, and his vision finally began to clear.

Those who were lucky enough not to have a descending monster land directly on them fought back, raining blows on the enemy. Nothing they did could slay them, but they found that if you hacked the fiends' heads off, it made it impossible for them to function effectively.

The princess backed away. Turning her attention to the top of the wall, she found more warriors struggling up and over. As fast as she could point the Hand of Fate and murmur the words, she turned them into lifeless husks. This gave Rangvald hope, but it was a fleeting hope, as it quickly became apparent that there were just too many of them. For every one she killed, three more appeared.

"Fall back! Protect the princess!" Eirik shouted.

"Do not get in front of me!" Revna cautioned as they rallied around her. Then she pointed the hand again and again, dispatching more spirits.

Rangvald made another attempt to stand, but he felt his vision begin to blur once more, and so he sat back down. The enemy was now pouring over the barricade and overrunning the defenders. "Run! Run as fast as you can!" he cried. Not waiting to see if they had heeded his words, he lifted the leather bracer that covered his forearm and read aloud as enemy swords came swinging down at him. In a heartbeat, the air was sucked from the room as a torrent of white flame poured from him, disintegrating everything in its path.

The throbbing power of the goddess's eternal kiss surged through his heart, and his body healed itself even as it was being injured. His collapsing lungs and searing retinas repaired themselves along with his smoldering skin. Even the cracked and concussed skull he had sustained falling to the ground was made whole again. Getting to his feet and walking through the maelstrom, he strode across the great hall and exited the doors as the flames dissipated. Turning to the descending walkway, he began to read the fire spell once again, but then he stopped as he beheld the warriors huddling behind their sneering Witch Queen. She was holding forth her wand, now shortened from Rangvald's sword stroke, and its fist-sized gem glowed brightly.

"What are you waiting for?" she asked with a mocking laugh. "What? Did you only just now realize that you can do nothing to stop me? Go ahead, try your magic on me all you want, but I will be coming into your lovely cave, and I am going to devour all of your souls!"

"No, you are not! I will not allow it!" he shouted defiantly.

"Then stop me," she said with an ugly smirk.

With a scream of rage, Rangvald conjured the Unseen Hand and raked its power across the line of massive dwarfen statues that stood in their alcoves above the walkway. As they came raining down, smashing and obliterating hundreds of warriors, the queen's smirk vanished. Desperately, she hurled herself over the side of the walkway and tumbled out of view.

"No!" he cried. "Not again!" Scrambling up onto the wall of the landing, he peered down, straining his eyes to find her. This time, when the whispers came from the dark, he did not hesitate. He threw himself backward off the ledge and fell as arrows sailed above him. "No!" he growled in frustration, sitting up and nursing a bruised elbow. "Again she escapes me!"

Rangvald sat feeling miserable for a long time, until at last a thought occurred to him, a thought that changed his perspective and banished his misery. The women and children of Vestmor were still safe huddling in the caves behind him.

For now, that was enough.

CHAPTER TEN

Black hatred radiated from the Witch Queen of Pretania as she skittered from shadow to shadow, dragging her wounded leg behind her. Twice she had faced the young wizard, and twice she had been driven from the field, sent fleeing for her life. Rage threatened to consume her at the very thought of it. It made no sense! She was the mightiest necromancer who had ever lived! Her wand bore the Tear of the Dragon. It made her invulnerable to wizards' magic, and her army had swollen to nearly two thousand of the dead. How was it, then, that he had humiliated her each time they met?

She trudged on for a few minutes more until her litter-bearers came trotting up to meet her. Gingerly, she climbed aboard and settled down on the twisted iron platform, making her battered leg as comfortable as she could. At a thought from her, they set off.

Her army, their numbers now cut in half by the

Wizard of the Oaken Stump, was regrouping in the pastures alongside the southern trail. "You missed. Twice," she spat at the captain of her personal guard as she was carried up before him. "The most deadly archers in all the world, and yet you missed."

The trembling man remained silent, eyes downcast, while the queen spent a long moment drinking in his fear. At last, she said, "Have my black pavilion set up and send me my healers. We must hide ourselves from the coming day." The captain released a little sigh of relief now that her attention had left him, and he signaled his men to follow. "Not you, Captain Evander. You and your archers will return to the cave."

"But, My Queen, we cannot leave you. The dead cannot protect you at your slumber," he replied in shock.

"You will be protecting me. The only danger to me is inside that cave."

"As you wish, My Queen, but I do not see why they would leave the caves. The walkway is buried beneath tons of rubble, making it almost impossible to get in or out. Besides, they will feel safe in their hideaway, where they no doubt have food and provisions to last a lengthy siege," he said confidently.

"Those are all reasonable points, but by now they will be certain that we are only a threat to them at night. They will be quite sure that they are safe to come out and greet the day."

"I see. We will take up a position in the field outside and teach them that the day belongs to you as well."

"No. You will remain hidden and wait. If you show yourselves, you will remove the element of surprise. Besides, if the wizard sees you, he will wipe you from the earth without a second thought. Remain hidden with your bows at the ready. It is my hope that he will emerge and fall within your sights. Do not reveal yourselves for anyone else. Only the wizard matters. Kill him, and they will be defenseless against me."

"I promise we will not miss him again, My Queen," the captain swore with a bow.

"I know you will not. You would not dare fail me again, for if you did, I would cast you into an eternity of burning torment."

The captain swallowed hard and again stared at the ground, remembering bitterly how he had one night, long ago, bargained for his life and the lives of his men. He could still recall the hoards of blue-painted Picts and their own Belgae conscripts who had been killed and turned into her minions. He could still see them marching against his milecastle night after night. He and his nine were all that was left defending the old emperor's wall. The legions had withdrawn, and most of the provincial cohorts had gone with the fever in the middle of the year.

He and his men had cut peat moss every day, soaked it with lamp oil, and made fire arrows, which they shot into the faces of the ghoulish attackers. The witch queen had screamed with rage as each night they had successfully turned back her attacks. But then came the night when there were no more arrows and no more casks of oil. He and his brothers had said their prayers and prepared to join their ancestors.

He now knew that that would have been a better outcome. But instead of an attack that night, they had heard her voice calling out to them from the moors with a proposal. He had accepted and sworn an oath to protect the Black Queen, and in exchange, she had spared their lives. That had been more than four hundred years ago, and he had regretted the bargain every day since.

As if reading his thoughts, she said, "Go now, Captain. If, when I arise, you can bring me news of the wizard's death, then perhaps I will consider giving you that which you long for most. Maybe I will release you and allow you to grow old and die at last."

The captain gasped and turned to his men. "Come, men, back to the cave. I want two-man groups spread out and hidden before the sun rises."

The queen watched her newly-motivated guardsmen disappearing into the dark with satisfaction. "Yes, wizard, come out, enjoy the sun and take some fresh air. What's the worst that could happen?" she murmured to herself with a cruel laugh.

◆ ◆ ◆

At daybreak, the last of the defenders came out and stood on the landing just outside the gaping mouth of the cave. No vestiges of wagon or timber remained from their barricade. Only a few scraps of leg bones and teeth could be found as a testament to the possessed corpses and fallen defenders who had been there. In patches here and there, the surface of the stones had been transformed into a strange, mottled glass.

The walkway leading down was choked off completely by the broken fragments of statuary that had rained down, causing the very earth to rumble and shake. Closest to them stood the carven head of some long-forgotten dwarfen lord, his broad features and ornate helmet towering above them taller than a barn.

"Well, we have no door, but I would say we have never been more secure," Eirik remarked.

"They will have to assault this landing with tall

ladders or try to build scaffolds to reach us. Even reduced now to little more than a dozen warriors, we can defend the cave for a long time," Captain Halfdan replied.

"Defensively, it is very positive," Signe agreed. "But it does create some new problems for us."

"Yes; namely the hundreds of people hiding behind us with no food," Eirik said, nodding.

"This is my fault for throwing our provisions away on the trail," Revna lamented.

"No, it is my fault. I should have waited until the food was harvested and then used my magic to produce more. Then we could have stocked up for the future," Rangvald said with a sigh.

"Quiet, you two," Signe scolded. "You've both saved us more times than I can count. Whatever you did before, you were doing your best with what you knew at the time. It does no good trying to find out who to blame. That won't put food in children's bellies. We need to make a plan and get busy."

"Signe's right. Let's devise a way to get down to the ground and bring some food up," Eirik ordered.

"We can climb down on ropes and food can be tied to them and hoisted up," Rangvald suggested.

Halfdan shook his head. "We used every bit of rope we could find building the barricade. And we don't have any wood to make thirty-foot ladders."

"What about twisting our clothes and tying them into ropes?" Rangvald asked.

"Possibly," the king replied.

"The leather straps from the animals' harnesses," a voice said from behind Revna. All eyes rested on Leif as he stepped forward. He had spent the hours since the queen's retreat mourning the loss of his father, and his dirty face showed the trails his tears had taken from his reddened eyes to his chin. His voice, however, sounded strong and certain now. "The animals are gone, but we still have the straps and buckles."

"That's right, we can make a harness and lower someone down," Halfdan agreed.

Rangvald peered over the top of the landing wall and could see that most of the trees and plants he had grown the day before were still in good health. "Lower me down," he said. "My magic can call forth fruit and vegetables from the field once more."

"Excellent. Fetch the leather straps and any baskets you can find," King Eirik ordered, and his soldiers hastened to obey.

"They will not have much success finding baskets, I'm afraid," Revna said. "Any baskets that were accompanying us were laden with supplies and got left by the side of the path."

The answer was again provided by Leif. "Signe and Revna, lend him your robes, and Captain Halfdan, give him your cloak. He can put them on and climb down, then use the garments to tie the food into bundles and we can pull them up."

"Of course," replied Signe, taking off her pale green robe and giving it to the wizard. Halfdan surrendered his long, dark cloak as well.

Rangvald looked at Revna skeptically. She was only a child, and her garment would surely be too small, he thought. But as she unbelted it, fabric that had been gathered and tucked came spilling out. Seeing his surprise, she explained, "This robe belonged to master Val's apprentice, Ulfhild, when she was a young woman. It is actually quite a bit too big for me."

Rangvald accepted it graciously, and to his delight, it fit with only a bit of tightness in the shoulders. Next, he donned Signe's garment, then topped it off with the captain's cape. Some of the soldiers rolled a piece of statue over to serve as a step to climb atop the wall, while others prepared a long length of leather straps tied together into a rope. Once they were done, Rangvald perused the finished product. A pang of sudden panic seized him. "Perhaps we had better try another way," he suggested shakily.

"I can go," Leif volunteered boldly.

"Thank you, Huntsman. But you have no magic to bring forth food when you get there," Eirik said.

"No, it's all right, I am ready," Rangvald said, ashamed. He felt a stab to his heart at the memory of the boy's father sacrificing his life for his own. Trygve had not hesitated to throw himself in the way of the deadly arrows fired by those night ghouls, but here was Rangvald, hesitating to climb down a wall in order to feed everyone.

"All right, just hold on, and we will do the rest," Halfdan said as they fitted the leather straps around him. "If anything should go wrong, do not stiffen; make yourself go limp. It is a bad height for a man to fall from, but one that may be survived with luck," Halfdan said cheerfully.

Rangvald could think of a hundred objections to everything the captain had just said, but he refused to give them voice. He simply visualized being safely lowered down the sheer rock face, performing his spells, and loading the robes with as much food as he could again and again until everyone had food to eat. The visualization grounded him and calmed his nerves as he mounted the fragment of statue and was hoisted over the top of the wall. The warriors worked in unison, paying out the leather rope and lowering him down out of sight.

Rangvald's scream split the morning air as the arrow ripped through his thigh. “Quickly, pull him up!” the king yelled, grabbing the leather and pulling with all of his might. Halfdan, standing on the statute fragment, reached down, grabbing the strap and hauling with all of his strength. Then his chest sprouted an arrow.

“Halfdan, come down from there,” Eirik shouted, but the captain paid him no heed. Bending down, he hauled Rangvald up nearly to the top of the wall. A second, third, and fourth arrow struck Halfdan then, and silently, he slipped over the side and passed Rangvald on his way down. Another soldier began to step up to take his place, but Eirik screamed, “No! Stay behind the wall! Do not show yourself!”

Rangvald continued to scream as arrows struck him. Nine, ten, eleven arrows found his back before the men inside dragged him all the way to the top of the wall. The young King disregarded his own warning and jumped up on the statue fragment to wrench the wizard back over. Both of them came tumbling down in a heap, covered in Rangvald's blood.

“Lie still, Wizard!” Eirik ordered, trying to hold onto him as he writhed in agony and terror. “Get these robes off and bind his wounds,” the king implored his men, who laid hold of Rangvald and, with a struggle, stripped the garments off.

“He only has one wound, My King. To his thigh,” Leif reported, holding Halfdan’s cloak to the leg where the arrow still protruded.

“How can that be? I heard at least a dozen arrows

fly at him. Could it be that they all missed?" Eirik asked in astonishment.

"No, they did not miss. He was wearing Ulfhild's battle robe," Revna answered.

Rangvald reached back and felt with his hand, trying to touch where the arrows had struck him. "A charmed battle robe?" he asked in surprise. She nodded excitedly. Rangvald shook his head in disbelief. "I didn't think charmed cloth would turn that many arrows."

"They are hiding in the trees to the right and left of the field, no doubt, and firing at an angle. It helped the robe do what it does best: it made them glance. Had they been in the field squarely behind you, you would have been dead for sure."

"Oh no, noble Halfdan sacrificed himself to save me, and in the end, it's only a leg wound, I will live," Rangvald sighed.

Revna opened her mouth to reply, but her brother rose, laid a blood-soaked hand on her shoulder, and gave her a grave look. Rangvald was confused by the look until he shifted his gaze to the cobbles around them and saw that he was lying in an ocean of blood. Looking at the back of his hand, he saw that it was white as snow and dusted with a pale blue web. Turning his eyes to Leif, who was still pressing the cloth against his thigh, he asked, "Am I dying?"

"Just lie still. Everything is going to be all right," the youth told him.

"You don't have to lie to me. I'm through panicking. Am I dying?"

"Yes, Wizard. There is a mighty river of blood that flows through the leg, and the arrow has severed it. You are only still with us because I have not withdrawn the arrow. Its head is slowing the flow."

"I see," Rangvald said, suddenly feeling strangely calm. He lay his head back on the stones, then stared at the sky for a minute. Quietly, he said, "Remove it now, please. I am ready. I have tasted them, the apples of the moon. The apples of the sun. Just as the maiden of the gods promised."

"Thank you for your help, Wizard Rangvald," Eirik said.

Revna nodded, but she did not speak.

Only Leif had tears in his eyes as he said, "Tell my father that I love him, Wizard. Tell him that I think I will be seeing him soon."

The arrow was ripped free with a tug, and Rangvald drifted into the welcoming darkness.

◆ ◆ ◆

Rangvald was not surprised this time when he found himself beneath the midnight sky staring at Hefring, standing knee-deep in a pool whose surface had become a mirror reflecting the heavens. He saw her standing among the moon and stars, their lights casting sparks across her silvery skin.

Rangvald smiled and felt a warmth in his breast, just as one does when coming home after being out in the cold. This was a good place to be, especially now that he was dead. This was his most treasured memory, after all.

"Why did you not return home when you had your book of magic back?" she asked again, just as she had the night this had actually happened.

Rangvald tried to remember the exact words he had spoken. So many things had taken place since then that it seemed like that night had been a lifetime ago.

"Why do you hesitate?" she asked, tilting her head quizzically.

"I'm sorry, I was just trying to remember what my answer was to that question. Is it really that important?"

"It is more important now than it ever was," she said urgently.

Rangvald explored his memory for a moment, then replied, "Idunn told me that people were in danger and I could help them. I realized that I have to face outward, not inward. I've been given gifts and I have to use them. It's my purpose, my calling."

"And do you still feel that way? You have certainly earned your right to take your book and go home now."

Rangvald listened to the sounds of the night and felt the gentle breeze washing over his face. "This isn't a memory, is it?" he asked.

"No, this is here, and it is now, and I'm asking you this question once again. Do you still feel that you must help these people? Do you still feel that you must use your gifts for good?"

Rangvald thought for a moment, then a smile spread across his face. "You know the answer to that."

"Yes, I do, my love, and now so do you."

◆ ◆ ◆

Rangvald opened his eyes and called out, "Revna, come here, please."

There was a collective gasp from everyone assembled as the man they had taken for dead spoke. "Yes, Rangvald, I'm here," Revna said, kneeling beside him in the blood.

"Take out my book. Open it to the seventh page."

Revna did as he asked, then looked back at him.

"I've never tried this before," she objected

"I will instruct you, and we will go very slowly. That is, if you are willing," he said, his voice very weak now.

Revna hesitated, but only for a moment. "Yes, I will try."

◆ ◆ ◆

Captain Evander was waiting anxiously outside of the black pavilion when the Witch Queen of Pretania finally emerged. Examining his face, she threw her head back and cackled with triumphant joy. "You are absolutely sure it was him you killed?"

"Yes, My Queen. We let him come over the wall and fully expose himself. There is still a streak of his blood adorning the stones."

"Excellent. Let the preparations begin," she commanded. A moment later, a horn blew and the ground all around them began to move as the dead sat up in the shallow graves they had dug for themselves before the rising of the sun.

Heeding their queen's thoughts, they began moving through the forest, felling trees and hauling them to the path, building there as best they could what she was imagining. Building what they would need to make the rest of the people of Vestmor into vessels for the dead.

◆ ◆ ◆

As the night wore on, Eirik allowed his optimism to grow. He knew that the enemy was still nearby. He had heard them chopping and hauling trees. But with each passing hour that they did not assault the Nordhule, he had begun to believe more and more that tonight would bring a temporary reprieve. It was not so hard to believe, after all. The witch had lost a huge number of her warriors the night before, and whatever they were building, which was no doubt to aid in their assault, it would surely take them all night.

Mainly, he had let himself begin to believe because if they did attack tonight, he did not see how his people could survive. His fighting men numbered only fourteen now. With Halfdan gone, Signe had become his captain, and she had brought the eighty or so elders with their makeshift spears out to bolster the front line. Whatever knives could be spared she had given to the women watching over the children in the deeper caverns. They would now be their own last line of defense.

As for their greatest assets, the wizard Rangvald and his sister, Revna, they both lay back in the caves, helpless and unable to be of any assistance. Eirik was no wizard, but he knew that healing magic was one of the most demanding magics, one that took a toll physically and mentally on any wizard who would seek to use it. Under Rangvald's direction, Revna had brought him back from the brink of death and closed the wound. But that was all she had been able to do before falling into a fitful torpor herself.

Eirik's thoughts were interrupted as the cool night breeze brought the sound of a single horn from somewhere out in the dark. He had heard that horn at the beginning of the night, just as he had heard it at the battle of the western road. Every time it sounded, it sent chills down his spine.

"Leif, go see if the princess or the wizard can be roused," Captain Signe ordered.

As Leif hurried to obey her, the king quickly and cautiously approached the wall and peered over it to the south. He saw exactly what he expected to see, but his heart sank all the same at the sight of the bobbing torches coming up the path. After a minute, he picked another point on the wall, just in case one of the queen's deadly archers was waiting for his head to reappear in the same spot, and glanced over again. This time, in the light of the flames, he saw that some of them were pushing a tall ramp-like structure on a series of logs that others were carrying in constant rotation, laying them down in front of its path, then going behind and picking up the logs in the rear to repeat the process.

"They are coming now," he said, addressing his frail army. "Remember, they will not fall from wounds like a mortal man. If you can separate them from their heads or their limbs, it renders them unable to attack you effectively. Also, if you recognize them as one of your own, do not let it fool you. Nothing is left of your kinsmen there. If you ever loved them, then you will strike and let their body find peace, just as their spirits have."

Signe turned to the determined elders and smiled. "I have something to say as well, and that is that I am proud to die in such company. All your lives, you have grown the food of Vestmor. You have grown its sons and daughters too, and now you fight behind its king as warriors. It is said that cattle die, kinsmen die, you yourself die. But the things that never can perish are honor and noble deeds. I know that the blazing eye of the war father is looking down at us even now." Drawing her sword, she raised it to the sky. "See us, Lord of the Aesir! Remember our names and hear us roar!" Then she howled a battle cry, and every voice in the cavern joined hers.

Eirik's heart thundered in his chest, and he smiled savagely as the aged farmers shook their wooden spears and his handful of warriors hammered their shields with their blades. *Good!* he thought. *If we die, it will not be with fear in our hearts.* Taking a quick peek over the wall, he saw that the siege engine had drawn very near, and it was being doused with buckets of water to ward off any attempts at setting it alight. “Hurry up, you lazy demons. Put your backs into it. We haven't got all night!” he shouted down to the enemy, rousing another cheer from his people. He turned, still smiling, and shook his sword above his head. “FOR VESTMOR!” he cried at the top of his lungs.

“FOR VESTMOR!” the cheer was repeated.

Yes, if we must die, then this is the way, he thought. *We will make them choke on our defiance.* Reluctantly, he turned from the cheering farmers with faces filled with fire, the gray-haired couples who embraced and kissed with passions long forgot, and instead watched the siege engine come slamming forward. Its top hung above the wall by five feet or so, and the first dead thing to jump down into their midst inhabited the body of the giant Amazigh. With one slash of its sword, three of Eirik's warriors died.

“That body does not belong to you!” Eirik screamed, rushing forward and stabbing it in the throat. Then, evading the counterattack, he danced to the right and hacked it in the side of the neck. The giant swung fiercely, but Eirik glanced the attack off his shield and slashed deeply into the other side of the thick neck, causing the head to loll at an unnatural angle. The ghoul tried to back away, but more of its comrades were pressing forward behind it.

"Amazigh taught me to fight like that. Now get out of his body!" Eirik struck once more and toppled the head from its shoulders. "All of you, get out!" he howled, striking another across the face and seeing it stagger off blindly. "The eyes! Attack the eyes!" he yelled to his companions, warding a blow with his shield and hacking another across the eyes. He employed this technique on three more, smashing in their faces and leaving them crawling blindly, groping along drunkenly, or even becoming turned around and attacking their own warriors.

As more and more ghouls poured from the ramp, Eirik lost the space he needed to fight evasively the way Amazigh had taught him. Now he found himself shoulder-to-shoulder with the elders, who were stabbing out with their spears as best they could. Step by step, they were pushed back, their numbers dwindling as they went. This was it. The end was very near. The strength of their will alone would not be enough to save the women and children behind them in the caves. By daybreak, the people of Vestmor would be no more.

◆ ◆ ◆

Leif could hear the death in the outer chamber as he fumbled through Revna's satchel. On the third bottle he unstoppered, a great stench attacked his senses, and he knew he had found the one he had seen her use on the wizard the night before. Pouring it onto a corner of her blanket, he held it to her face and was relieved when she instantly sat up, coughing.

"What's happening? What's that noise?" she asked in a frightened voice.

"The enemy is attacking us. You and the wizard have been in and out of consciousness ever since you tried to heal him."

"Take me to the wizard," she ordered. Leif supported her as she rose and guided her to where Rangvald was lying. "I am beginning to remember now. I closed his wound, but the feat was too much for me; it took all my energy. Why is it that he has not risen?"

"You stopped him from dying, but he has lost so much blood that he is still too weak. Now please, Princess, I fear we do not have long. Can you come and banish the spirits like you did before?"

"I cannot banish enough of them to turn back the tide. I can only stop one at a time," Revna replied, speaking more to herself than to Leif. Then, in a determined tone, she said, "Quickly, hand me the wizard's spellbook."

◆ ◆ ◆

Eirik's forearm felt numb behind his shield as sword after sword thudded into it. His own sword strokes had become weak and ineffective as a burning fatigue invaded his limbs.

"To me! Rally to me; we will make our final stand!" Signe called from behind an overturned stone table. Surprisingly, the enemy halted and watched the nine bleeding mortals drag themselves together around the old woman, whose bony fingers still clutched her gore-stained sword even though she could barely lift it. "Thank you. We are ready now." She nodded to the teeming dead men amassed before them.

"Why do you fight so hard when you cannot win?" one of the slack-faced warriors asked with confusion.

"It's not about winning," Eirik began, lifting his weary eyes to the creature who had spoken and then freezing as a final rage overtook him. Pointing his sword at it, he shouted, “I am Eirik Gormson, King of Vestmor, and I command you to leave my father's body! I command you all to leave the bodies of our kinsmen!”

The ghoul inside King Gorm’s body began to laugh, but then turned to vapor as a bolt of lightning struck with an instant and deafening clap of thunder. The bolt continued past, incinerating a hundred more warriors and causing the others to flee in a panic.

Rangvald came limping past the young king and his last defenders while casting the Wind of the Gods, turning the great hall into a raging hurricane that swirled and smashed the retreating warriors into pieces. Lastly, he sent a fireball smashing into the siege engine, scattering burning corpses into the night and destroying the structure. Filled with the goddess’s power, which healed his body fully, Rangvald turned and strode back toward the defenders as the sound of the Witch Queen’s screams of fury echoed from the darkness outside.

“What has happened? I awoke and heard the sounds of battle,” Rangvald asked them in bewilderment. Before anyone could speak, Leif appeared from the deeper caverns. He was crying and carrying the body of the Princess. “What happened?” Rangvald shouted again.

“You only woke because she healed you.”

“I don’t understand. She was supposed to heal me little by little through the day as her strength allowed.”

“She managed to close your wound and keep you from dying, but then she fell unconscious from exhaustion and we could not rouse either one of you. When we were attacked, I finally woke her, and she healed you all at once so you could save us.”

“What? All at once?” Rangvald gasped. “She's not strong enough to use that much healing magic!”

"She knew that," Eirik said quietly. "Can you use your magic to heal her now?"

"No, I can't. It isn't her hurt to be healed. Once another's hurt is taken, magic must be used to banish it. I cannot heal her this way. If only she were awake!"

"Can you wake her, huntsman?" Eirik asked.

"No, My King. I tried her waking potion, but it had no effect this time," Leif replied, laying her down gently and pressing his head to her chest. "She's gone," he wept.

Rangvald sank to his knees and stared helplessly at the girl. "I should have just died when the arrow struck my leg. I never intended for her to trade her life for mine."

"Move aside!" Signe ordered, kneeling down and pushing the wizard out of her way. "Princess, come back!" she commanded and hammered her fist into the girl's chest as if pounding on a door.

"Stop! What are you doing!" Leif protested.

"Quiet. I once saw someone do this, and it worked. And if it doesn't, what's the harm?"

No one argued the point, and she did it again, pounding the princess's chest, and this time, shaking her and yelling for her to return as well. Revna released a tiny gasp and her eyelids fluttered.

"Leif, do you still have the deers' horn? The waking potion?" the astonished wizard asked.

"Yes, it is here."

"Use it now!" Rangvald urged.

Leif dumped some on his sleeve, and upon applying it to her nose and mouth, her eyes sprang open and appeared to focus on him.

"Repeat the words after me," Rangvald said desperately, and he began to chant the magic words to dispel the hurt. Revna's eyes began to close again, and Signe pinched her arm hard.

"Repeat the words!" the old woman ordered, and Revna's lips began to move. Rangvald continued to chant, and she repeated after him, reciting the words over and over. Her voice started as a hoarse whisper, but it grew stronger and clearer as they continued. Color gradually returned to her cheeks, as they watched, her breathing became normal.

It took several minutes, but at last, she sat up and took in what was left of the defenders. Grasping her hand Leif closed his eyes and pressed it to his lips, looking as though he never intended to release it. Rangvald studied her face, wondering if, after all this, he might at last see some sign of the child in her. *Surely now,* he thought, *after everything she has gone through, she will break down.*

But finishing her survey of the situation, she instead said in a firm voice, "Leif, please fetch the wizard his spellbook. We have wounded that need tending."

CHAPTER ELEVEN

Twelve defenders held vigil at the mouth of the cave as night came again. Two warriors were all that was left of the army of Vestmor. There was an old woman who had once been a warrior, along with five elderly farmers who had never struck a blow in battle before the previous night. There was a king and a princess and a huntsman, all of whom were children, although only the huntsman ever showed any sign of that. Then there was the wizard, who had been dragged kicking and screaming into this war, and who, for all of his newfound power, had failed to defeat the monster and her army of the dead at every encounter.

"I know we are few," began Eirik, sounding almost cheerful, "but we have the princess and the wizard Rangvald restored to us. We know about the archers who threaten us both day and night now, and we will not fall prey to them again. When the witch queen brings what is left of her army against us, it is we who will prevail, not she!" Almost as if to add an eerie punctuation to his words, the lone horn sounded from the deepening twilight outside.

After a few moments had passed, one of the soldiers ventured a peek over the wall and called out, "Torches approaching."

"Get behind me," Rangvald called. "Sentry, let us know when they are attacking, and then you, too, get behind me. This ends tonight!"

The warrior nodded, and then, moving to another spot, peeked once more over the wall. This time, when he ducked down, he had a confused look on his face. Moving to another spot, he popped up again, and they saw his head turn as he scanned the horizon for a moment. Then something flew past him, and he fell back, clutching his bleeding head.

Rangvald rushed forward and, grabbing the man's wrist, tried to pull his hand away from the wound. "Let me see it!" Rangvald demanded. The man moaned but allowed his hand to be pulled away. "It's going to be all right. The arrow just carried away a piece of your ear. Just breathe," he said soothingly. With an effort, the man drew a deep breath and tried to calm himself. "Good. Now tell us, are they attacking?"

"No. They are passing us and heading away to the north," he replied, wincing at the pain.

"All right, let me heal you," Rangvald said.

"May I try?" Revna asked, pulling out her book and turning it to the new page she had added earlier in the day.

"Yes. That is an excellent idea. This is the type of injury you should have started on anyway, had circumstances allowed," Rangvald said, still holding the bleeding man's arm. "Now, on a wound such as this, do not try to replace what is gone. Just heal the severed flesh."

"Yes, I understand," Revna said, bracing herself for the massive effort to come.

"That's it, read the spell slowly. Let the magic fill you. You decide when you're ready," Rangvald instructed.

Revna's body began jittering as one who is shivering in the cold, then she placed her hand on the warrior's bleeding ear and moaned in pain as the side of her own head throbbed and felt as if it were swelling to twice its size. She froze, letting the pain take over her mind.

"Banish the hurt," Rangvald urged, bringing back her focus. Quickly, she recited the magic words, and the pain vanished into memory. Revna took a deep breath and smiled with satisfaction as the warrior reached up and felt the new shape of his healed ear.

Eirik ventured his own quick glance over the wall, prompting another arrow, which he dodged. "Please, My King, don't," Signe barked. "They are waiting for us now."

"You're quite right. They are. But I wanted to make sure."

"And?" Signe asked.

"It's true. The torches are disappearing to the north."

"Perhaps they're finally leaving?" the warrior suggested, still exploring the new notch in his ear.

"No, that isn't it. They have left their archers who keep us trapped here both night and day. They are up to something else," Eirik replied.

"The villages of the deer herders," Revna said in a grave voice.

"That's it," Signe agreed, just as gravely.

"What's it? I don't understand," Rangvald asked.

"There is a land just north of here, the land of the deer herders. It is a place that is harsh and unforgiving, but its people are gentle and they keep to themselves. The Witch Queen's army has been devastated. She seeks to rebuild it," Eirik explained.

"So, on the bright side, it appears that there will be no attack tonight. But, unfortunately, we are still trapped inside with no food and no supplies to build a new barricade, so all we can do is wait here for the queen to return with a new army," Revna said dourly.

Rangvald began to pace restlessly for a time, then, stopping, he looked at the wall and wondered aloud, "How far will my powers reach?"

"Why? What are you thinking?" Eirik asked.

"I wonder if I can attack the archers in the trees off to the sides of the field."

"It won't work. They will fill you with arrows as soon as you show yourself."

"What if I wear your helmet and hold a shield? I will borrow Revna's robe again."

"I like the thought of going on the offensive when they least expect it," Erik said thoughtfully. "But I also saw these archers take a piece of Frode's ear when only half of his head was exposed for just one second too long. Your face, your neck, your hands will all be exposed, and even if the arrows simply hit the charmed robe squarely this time, they will pierce you. Can Revna heal serious wounds now?"

Rangvald shook his head. "No. If she tries to heal a serious wound again, it is likely to kill her, just as it nearly did before."

"No, Wizard. I like the thought of taking the battle

to them. Believe me, I do. But this plan threatens the loss of both wizards again, and that is exactly what brought us within a hair's breadth of defeat last time."

"So we just wait for her to kill the poor deer herders and then come back and attack us?" Rangvald protested.

"I am sorry about the northern tribes, I truly am, but yes. We wait for her to attack, and this time, we will not have put you in any dangerous positions like we have before. We have witnessed your power. It does not matter if she comes back with thousands; you can wipe them out and end this once and for all."

"And what if she does not attack for many days? How long can we go without food?" Rangvald countered.

"Well, if that happens, then you may still get to wear my helmet and carry a shield up onto the wall. But until then—" Eirik stopped speaking and stared back toward the chambers where the people were hiding. Everyone turned and beheld what he saw, the crying woman hurrying towards them.

"What are you doing here, Gertrud? It isn't safe," Signe said, but the woman ignored her and rushed up to the king.

"My youngest son, Bard, has wandered away. Please, My King, you swore that you would provide for us and protect us like we were your own family."

"Calm yourself, Gertrud. I shall not forget my vow. We will find Bard. He cannot have gone far; it isn't possible. He has to be in one of the three chambers we have been sleeping in."

"No, My King, he went deeper into the caves, through the hidden doorway," she said through tears.

"What hidden doorway?" he demanded, sharing a shocked look with the others.

"Come, I will show you," Gertrud said, turning and hurrying away.

"Frode and Aver, you warriors stay here with the huntsman and keep watch," Signe ordered as the rest of the party followed behind the frantic woman into the next chamber, past the font of crystal spring water, and into the middle of the three rooms. When they entered, everyone was astir. "Make way, make way for the king," Signe shouted as they hurried through the long dim cavern.

"We called to him some more, but he still wouldn't answer us, mother," one of Gertrud's other two sons reported as they neared the far end.

"Where is this secret doorway?" Eirik asked impatiently.

"There," the other child replied, pointing at the back wall of the long room.

"Is there a hidden latch or some mechanism we cannot see?" Revna asked, leading the way to the richly-carved wall.

"No. You will see it only once you get there. The children found it while playing a game of hiding and finding," Gertrud called after her. Revna hurried ahead and, reaching the wall, gave out a yelp of surprise before disappearing from view.

"Revna!" Eirik called out, causing her to step back into view.

"Some sort of glamour?" Rangvald asked.

"No magic necessary. Just a simple trick of the eye," she replied, drawing Deathwhisper and summoning its glow.

"Clever dwarfs," Rangvald exclaimed, arriving at what he now saw was two walls that shared one continuous pattern of carving, but one was two feet in front of the other, creating a secret passage hidden in plain sight.

"Follow me," the princess said, disappearing again. Eirik and Signe drew their swords and followed. Rangvald, bringing up the rear, ran his hand across the vambrace on his arm and brought forth its faint glow.

"Bard? Bard, can you hear me?" Revna's voice echoed as they entered a truly cavernous space.

"What is this place?" Rangvald asked, trying to make out the hulking shapes that were being partially illuminated by Revna's sword.

"It is the workshop of the old dwarfen craftsmen," Signe said with reverence.

Now Rangvald's eyes began to make sense of the shadowy shapes around him. He saw giant looms and turning wheels, kilns and anvils, rows of workbenches with racks of tools.

"These are the tools that forged the weapons of the gods," Eirik said in a hushed tone.

"Bard, answer me!" Revna shouted, her voice sounding all the louder in contrast to her brother's near-whisper a moment before.

"I'm here," came a distant reply from off in the darkness.

"Quickly, this way," Revna said, rushing ahead as the others struggled to keep up. "The voice came from down here!" she declared, rushing for a hallway that connected to the massive workroom.

"Be cautious, Revna," her brother implored.

The princess checked her excitement with an effort and, heeding Eirik's warning, proceeded down the hall a little more slowly, eyeing the closed doors to the left and right warily as she passed them. At last, they emerged into a room that was just as large as the one that had held the tools and workbenches, but this one seemed to possess a diffused glow all its own, as if the light from Revna's blade were somehow being reflected back at them from every direction.

"All the gods in Asgard!" Signe swore as recognition struck her.

"What is—" The question froze in the wizard's mouth as he, too, entered the chamber. All around them, as far as the eye could see, there were mountains of treasure reaching toward the distant ceiling. Gold and silver wrought into the most marvelous of shapes, jewels cut magnificently with gleaming facets, swords and armor gleaming like moonlight.

"There you are, Bard," Revna said, treading down a pathway between the piles of treasure and looking down at the little boy, who was sitting at the side of a jeweled hill next to a large golden table filled with an unimaginable bounty of breads, pies, and pastries. He was chewing a pastry merrily and wearing half its filling on his cheeks.

"What are you doing here?" she asked crossly.

"I was hungry," he slurred around another mouthful.

"I know you were hungry. We are all hungry. What did you do, just wander around until you found this?"

"No. I followed the piggy," he replied with a giggle.

Eirik tightened his grip on his sword and turned warily in a circle, scanning the treasure room.

"I don't understand. Who put this food here?" Signe asked. "A treasure hoard I can understand. That could have been left by the dwarfs of old. But fresh cakes and bread... they cannot be more than a few days old at most."

Rangvald considered for a moment. "Revna, hold

your blade here above them so I can see." As she did, he searched the items in the bottom of his satchel until he found a stone with a hole piercing its center. He held it up before his eye and examined the bounty. "The food is charmed; it can never spoil," he declared.

"Magic food? Is it safe to eat?" Signe asked doubtfully.

"Yes, and it always would be, no matter how long it has been here."

"I can do a magic trick. Watch," Bard said excitedly. Then he ate the last of the pastry from his open palm. Even as he lowered his hand, they saw the pastry reappear whole once more.

With a giggle of delight, he lifted it to take another bite, but Signe snapped, "No more, child, you'll make yourself sick."

"Bard, what did the piggy look like?" Eirik asked in a worried voice.

"Like a piggy," the boy said with a shrug.

"Did you see anyone else?"

"No, just the piggy."

"You are worried, brother?" asked Revna.

"Yes, very. We were hungry, and now, here is food. Think about it. How does a hunter set a trap?"

At his words, they all looked around themselves fearfully, at last sharing in the young king's caution. It occurred to Rangvald that an army could be hiding behind the massive piles of treasure right now and they would never see them. "Quick, King Eirik, take one side of the table and I will take the other. We will carry its bounty right back to the secret door," Rangvald said, rushing to the table and grabbing an end.

"Very well, but at the first sign of danger, we abandon it and flee," Eirik said, lifting the opposite end.

Revna led them back down the hallway, Rangvald saw her pause again and again as if this time she was certain that each door was about to be flung open so that a thousand ghouls could fall upon them all at once. To everyone's great relief, they all remained closed. As they moved swiftly through the giant workroom, the light from Revna's blade caused shadows to jump from every piece of equipment they passed, making their hearts pound with fear. The princess almost wept for joy as she passed through the secret door into the light again, followed by Signe, who had picked Bard up and carried him when he had begun to fall behind. His appearance was greeted by a cheer from everyone in the room.

Eirik appeared next, out of breath. "The table is too wide to fit. Help me gather the food!" he gasped.

At the mention of food, there was a second cheer, and people rushed forward to help. Rangvald pushed the table all the way against the opening and slid the baked goods forward as needed so that they could be reached from inside the room. After two days with no food, several of those at the front grabbed a piece and took a hasty bite before gathering an armload. "Don't worry, there will be enough for everyone to eat. Now hurry," he urged.

With many hands making the load light, the table was emptied in no time. Rangvald heaved it back, pulling it out of the way so he, too, could exit through the doorway.

The huge workroom darkened as he rushed around the table and ran his hands back and forth across the smooth stone wall that only seconds before had held an opening. Rangvald turned slowly and caught the glint of two large eyes watching him from the darkness.

The piggy, I presume, he thought, feeling like a fool. He began to tilt the glowing bracer on his forearm toward his eyes as he raised the other hand.

Just then, a cheerful feminine voice filled his head. *Why, yes, I guess you could call me a piggy. My name is Trufflesbane.*

CHAPTER TWELVE

Rangvald reached down to his belt and lifted the short iron rod that hung there. He summoned its glow and gasped at what he saw. *No, I don't think piggy quite does it,* he thought to Trufflesbane. She was almost as tall as a cart-horse and twice as thick, with dagger-long tusks and bushy reddish fur. No, she was no pig. She was a boar, a battleswine, like the one of legend that had fought by the side of the goddess Freya. *Are you going to hurt me?*

Don't be silly, Rangvald. I'm here to help you, she thought back, and the words carried a hint of laughter.

Wait, how do you know my name?

Idunn told me. Now hurry up and follow me, she thought to him, turning and trotting off into the dark.

Where are you taking me?

To see my friend.

All right, but can you open the door in the wall again so I can tell my friends that I'm going? I know they will be worried.

They aren't there anymore, Trufflesbane said, turning back toward him.

Yes, they are. They're just on the other side of the wall here. Rangvald pointed.

No, it doesn't work that way.

How does it work then? Rangvald asked mystified.

I don't know. I'm a piggy, Trufflesbane giggled. *I only know that it doesn't work that way. Now follow me.*

Rangvald looked at the smooth and seamless wall, running his hands across it once more. Then, with a shrug, he jogged off to catch up with the boar.

At the back of the workshop, she turned right and led him into a long hall lined with doors, similar to the one he had traversed earlier. When they reached the far side, they entered a vast chamber containing mounds of gold and jewels that stretched up to the ceiling.

A second treasure room? he thought to her in surprise.

No, there is only one treasure room, she replied.

But that can't be. We took the hall to the left of the workroom to reach it before.

I know, but it's here now, she said happily, standing motionless as if she were waiting for something to happen.

Where to now? Rangvald asked, beginning to feel a little dizzy from the whole experience.

Trufflesbane continued to wait for a few moments more before declaring, *All right, now back the way we came.* She took six steps into the hall before stopping in front of the first door on the left.

Wait, this is it? But we just passed this door, Rangvald objected.

No, not this door. It was a different door then, Trufflesbane explained, lifting the latch peg with her snout and pushing her way in.

Rangvald watched from the hallway as she trotted into what appeared to be a modest cottage with a warm fire at the hearth. She circled once, then settled down on the floor next to a short man seated in a chair by the fire. With a yawn, she laid her head against his leg and closed her eyes.

"Come in! Close the door! You're letting in a chill!" the little man snapped. Rangvald obeyed immediately, hopping in and pulling the door closed behind him.

"Yes, yes, come in; you are most welcome here. Any friend of my sister is a friend to us," the short man said, adopting a friendlier tone now that the door was closed. "Isn't that right, Trufflesbane?" he added, reaching down and stroking her head, which elicited a happy grunt from the massive porcine.

Stepping forward, Rangvald studied the man's broad, bearded face. "I've seen you before somewhere."

"I rather doubt that. Very few know how to find this place without being invited, and I rarely leave it."

Rangvald turned with a start as a rapping came from the door behind him.

"Ah, now there's someone now who knows how to find this place," the man chuckled. "Come in," he called in a louder voice.

Rangvald gasped as the door opened to reveal a small farmyard covered in snow instead of the hallway he had left just a minute before. A bundled figure hurried through the door, shaking off the snow, and slammed the door shut behind them. Throwing back the hood, the goddess Idunn beamed at them. Her smile literally made the cottage brighter somehow. "You're loving this, aren't you?" she accused, pointing at the little man with a laugh.

"Just happy to see you reminded that it isn't eternal spring everywhere," he laughed back, getting up and taking her cloak.

Rangvald was shocked, now that the man was standing, to see how powerfully he was built, as if his muscles were knit from iron. "You're a dwarf!" Rangvald exclaimed.

"Oh, you've chosen a smart one, haven't you?" the dwarf laughed.

"Be gentle. He is very new to being a hero," Idunn chided.

"A hero! Is that what I am?" Rangvald asked, startled.

"What do you think?" she asked.

"Well, I'm doing what I can to help, but I'm no hero. The word hero is reserved for... For..." He trailed off.

"For what? Someone who is chosen by the gods and sent on a magical odyssey to fight against insurmountable odds in aid of those they don't even know, simply because it is the right thing to do?" she asked.

"Oh my. I am a hero," Rangvald said with a gulp. He suddenly felt dizzy. Idunn said something else, but Rangvald did not hear her.

"All right, come along, hero," the dwarf said, steering Rangvald to a chair and sitting him down. "Here, drink this," he told him, pressing a horn into his hand and guiding it to his lips.

Rangvald blinked in surprise as the magical elixir touched his tongue. His body filled with warmth as his senses were instantly restored. "This is the most delicious thing I've ever tasted!" Rangvald said in wonder.

"It is the mead of the gods," the dwarf told him. "It comes directly from the udders of Heidrun, the goat of Asgard. Odin does not eat food; he drinks this instead. It nourishes him and brings him wisdom."

"Is it proper for me to drink this?" Rangvald whispered, suddenly feeling fearful.

"Yes, it is," Idunn answered. "You have much yet to do, hero. You will need wisdom and strength. Also, the drinking of Heidrun's mead will sustain you for days without needing to eat or rest."

"Hero," Rangvald repeated, remembering the revelation that had caused his head to spin. "So if I am the hero, what part of my saga is this?"

"This is the part when the hero quests for a weapon powerful enough to slay his foe," she replied.

"Ah! A dwarfen craftsman," Rangvald said, looking at the dwarf, who was settling back into his own chair once again.

Idunn shook her head and said, "Oh no, not just a craftsman. *The* craftsman. Dvalinn, greatest of the sons of Ivaldi. Dvalinn, who is called child of iron and stone. Called Asger, he who forged Gungnir, the spear of the All-father."

"At your service," the craftsman said, sitting forward and giving a little bow. "Now, tell me about your foe, Rangvald, so I may decide what can be made to vanquish them."

"She calls herself the Witch Queen of Pretania."

"Do you know her true name?"

"I do not," Rangvald admitted. "She knows mine, however. I was foolish and declared it to her when I thought I was about to slay her. Fortunately, no sorcery has been done to me because of it. Not as far as I can tell, anyway," he said with a touch of hopefulness.

"Do you know her true name, sister?"

"I do not, but if I sought it, I could learn it, I am certain. As for her casting a hex with your name, she has already done it, but it will have no effect on you for now, so put it out of your mind."

"Wait what does that mean?" Rangvald asked, feeling a spike of panic.

"It means precisely what I told you. It will not harm you at this time. She commands power over just one realm of magic, so you needn't concern yourself with her hex yet."

Rangvald's eyes grew wide with realization. "My spirit! When I die, my spirit belongs to her!"

"Yes," Idunn said, then locked eyes with him. "Unless you kill her."

"Right. Unless I kill her. How do I kill her?" he asked desperately.

"That is what we are trying to find out. Now please, stay on course and tell me about this witch," the craftsman interrupted.

"Of course. I'm sorry. Let's see, she looks like an evil walking corpse, and she commands real corpses to rise and attack the living."

"Hmm," Dvalinn drawled, stroking his beard. "You bear the mark of a goddess; your sorcery must be quite powerful indeed. How is it that your magic failed to slay her?"

"She holds a wand topped with a large stone of sapphire. Against it, my magic can have no effect. The stone also has the ability to drink the life of wizards, a power she attempted to use on me, but the hand of Hefring came to my defense."

Dvalinn nodded. "The stone of which you speak is called a Dragon's Tear."

"Do you know how to defeat it?"

The craftsman was silent for a moment, then his face lit up. "Yes, I know what to make! It will be just the thing to defeat one who defies the dominion of death and is invulnerable to your magic. First, I will forge a chain and stake from a world stone. We must get one from deep below the ground at the center of the world, or find one that has fallen from the heavens. Then I will call upon Huginn and Muninn; they will know where to find a troll. If we can prevail against it, we will hew a hammer from the mingling of the chain and the troll stone. Sister, if you seek out the Witch Queen's name, I will grave it on the weapon's face with the only tool that could accomplish such a feat, the tooth of the dragon Nidug that was stolen by our father Ivaldi in another age long forgotten. Lastly, I will chase that graven name with the single object that most represents the power and glory of life, a single strand of lady Sif's hair, gifted to me long ago when I forged her golden crown and earned the eternal enmity of Loki!" As he spoke Dvalinn's voice began to rumble with joyful anticipation. Trufflesbane lifted her head from the floor and smiled up at him, sharing in his rising excitement.

Idunn shook her head at her brother.

"No?" he asked.

"No," she replied patiently. "The witch will return tomorrow night, and unless you can provide Rangvald with something that can turn the tide by then, I fear no one will be able to stand against her."

"So we have just one day?"

"Yes, one day," she confirmed.

"Oh. Well, that leaves just one option then. We will have to go and get a Dragon's Tear of our own."

"We can do that?" Rangvald asked excitedly.

"Of course. Then you can use the same power against her. You can watch her shrivel to nothing as you drain her essence away."

"That sounds perfect! Why didn't you suggest that in the first place?"

"Because you most likely will not survive the attempt," Idunn said matter-of-factly. "To claim a Dragon's Tear, you must go to the Niflheim, the mist realm beneath all of creation, fight your way past the three goblin armies, and make your way across the corpse fjord to the Nostrond, the shore of the dead, where Nidhug the corpse-sucker dwells, he who chews at the roots of Yggdrasil."

Dvalinn nodded enthusiastically. "I'll get my armor!"

"Is there no other way?" Rangvald asked as the dwarf opened a large oaken trunk at the foot of his bed and lifted out a coat of scales made of a dingy bronze-colored metal.

"Not that I can think of. One day is not sufficient even to bring my forge up to heat. It must be the tear," replied the dwarf.

"But can it even be done? What if we die there, far below the world?" Rangvald argued.

"It can be done," the craftsman said firmly. "Our father took the Serpent's tooth and returned to tell the tale, and the witch herself bears one of its tears, so that's twice that we know the deed was done. As to whether we die or not, Idunn says that tomorrow night, the women and children of Vestmor, along with their defenders, will die if a weapon to defend them cannot be found. I say I'd rather meet my end trying than simply let that happen. What do you say, hero?"

"Oh, yes, I'm with you. It's just..." He trailed off unhappily.

"Speak your mind, Rangvald. You are among friends," Idunn assured him.

"This business of being a hero... Is any of it real? Does what I'm doing matter, or is it just entertainment for the gods?"

"Listen to me, Rangvald," Idunn said, taking his hands and raising him from his chair. "It matters. The necromancer who is attacking Vestmor is doing so because of her own dark and hateful ambitions. When you were called, you were given free choice to refuse this destiny, but you decided to come. And that is because you are a true hero. It is real. Even if the gods look on and take a hand in things, it is real. As for me, it is not mere sport that has drawn me to you. Our destinies are intertwined. If you survive your test in the Niflheim and return, then I will ask a favor of you."

"What favor? You can ask me," Rangvald said, curious to learn what destinies they shared.

"Everything in its time, Rangvald. You must focus on the task at hand, and so I will ask you, and again, you must freely choose. Will you quest for the Dragon's Tear and try to save the people of Vestmor?"

"I will," he vowed solemnly.

"Then ready yourself. There is no time to lose," she declared, turning and going to the pantry.

Dvalinn returned wearing his scaled armor, banded with a wide waist belt from which two hammers hung. They were shaped like long-handled forging hammers, but they were just a bit too large for any man to wield. He finished plaiting his hair, then pulled on an old, battered helmet that bore bands of tarnished copper knotwork.

"That's it. I know where I've seen you!" Rangvald said with a laugh. "Your severed stone head lies at the top of the walkway at the cave. It's as big as a barn!"

"My statue is broken?" the craftsman demanded.

"Yes; they're all broken," Rangvald answered, strategically omitting the means by which they had become so.

"The statues of my fathers and my brothers thrown down! That makes it personal. Come, let us go claim what is needed and end this witch once and for all." The craftsman looked to Trufflesbane, who was holding her saddle in her mouth. "You don't have to go, my friend. We probably won't survive this," he said, eliciting an audible gulp from Rangvald and a derisive snort from Trufflesbane.

"You're right. I'm sorry. Time is short, and you are the fastest battleswine who ever lived. Not this saddle, though. The other one, so two may ride."

Trufflesbane went to get the other saddle as the craftsman dipped back into the chest and withdrew a scabbard. "Here; I see your fine sword tucked in your belt unprotected. Take this."

Rangvald accepted it and found that the sword fit it perfectly. "It's almost as if it was made for it," he remarked.

You will need to put this on as well," the craftsman said, handing him a heavy coat of furs.

Rangvald obeyed, even though the cottage was quite warm. Trufflesbane returned with the saddle. Dvalinn strapped it in place, adding saddlebags loaded with supplies. "We're ready," he called out once he finished.

"Good," Idunn replied, coming forward bearing two bright red apples. "The closest I can get you is the gates of Niflheim. My powers will not penetrate the veil of the mist world. Unfortunately, that also means that you must return to the gates to come back. Here is the first apple. You must each take a bite, lie down, and close your eyes. When you open them again, you will be in the underworld." The craftsman stepped forward to receive the apple. "Now, here is the second apple. When you return to the gates, you must repeat the process. Each of you must take a bite, then lie down and close your eyes. You will return to this room."

"Give it to Rangvald to keep," the dwarf said.

"Why me?" Rangvald asked.

"If for some reason only one of us can make it back, it must be you. You must take the Dragon's Tear to Vestmor and kill the Witch Queen."

"I will take it," Rangvald said, placing the apple carefully in his purse. "But we are all coming back together."

Idunn stepped forward and embraced Trufflesbane, tracing a symbol on her broad neck. Next, she embraced Rangvald, and he felt her finger repeating the symbol on his back. Last, she hugged her brother, and as she drew the symbol on him, she whispered, "Bring them back."

"I'll do my best," he said with a smile, then he held out the Apple to Trufflesbane. After she had bitten into it, he took his own bite before handing it to Rangvald, who followed suit. They lay down, closed their eyes, and disappeared.

CHAPTER THIRTEEN

"That's enough," Eirik said. His words brought looks of relief to the tired warriors who had been working in shifts, using the only hammer they had. "The hole you've made in the wall is deeper than the wall was thick. You should have broken through by now, but still, we see nothing but more stone."

"I suspect some manner of sorcery is at play," Revna said.

"Aver, Frode, go and take some rest. The sun is up, and we should be safe enough for the time being," the king commanded.

As soon as the warriors were gone and Eirik saw that the two hundred or so people that were in this room were all lying down for sleep, he turned to Revna, and in a low voice, said, "I've killed us all. This is my greatest failure. I had just finished telling Rangvald that his safety must not be risked for any reason, and then we blundered into an obvious trap. Now he's gone!"

"It's not your fault," she protested.

"Oh, but it is. I'm the king. It's my responsibility. Now everyone is dead, or soon will be. The worst part is that I had finally figured it all out. Keep Rangvald safe. No more sitting on barricades or climbing down walls. Just keep him safe, and he can defeat her. Then the wall opens up out of nowhere and we walk right in like fools. I am the worst king who has ever lived!" He began to weep as he spoke.

Revna wanted to comfort him, to tell him that he was wrong, but seeing him openly crying removed the last of her resolve, and she simply cried too. Had anyone seen them, they would have finally looked like two teenagers with broken hearts, not the fearless leaders they had appeared to become over the last few days. Several minutes passed as they stood in the shadows, crying silently so that no one would see or hear.

"We have to get a hold of ourselves," Revna said, drying her eyes on her sleeve.

Eirik nodded, rubbing his cheeks with his cloak. "I wasn't ready for this," he said miserably.

"No one could be ready for this, Eirik," Revna insisted. "Our father was a great king, and even he was not ready for this. You have to stop this right now. You are the warrior king of Vestmor. You have to lead our people."

"You're right. I just need some sleep. When I wake, I will lead again. Even if it is only to Valhalla, I will lead."

Revna nodded tiredly, then, wiping her face once more, said, "Yes, let's sleep. We will need our strength for what's to come."

◆ ◆ ◆

Captain Evander's face was twisted into an endless silent scream. He turned it this way and that as if his empty eye sockets could still search the midday sky.

The nine archers who still remained stood in a circle, looking up at him as he writhed on his stake.

“We are agreed, then?” spoke one of the men.

“No, Lucius, we are not! Do you want this to be our fate?” the man standing next to him replied, pointing at their former captain.

“This is already our fate Felix. I heard Evander plead for us one last time, but it was in vain. The Witch Queen told him she would strike a bargain with some of the deer folk to the north to replace us. Then she told him that we would be coming to keep him company. Trust me, this is the only way. We cannot run or attack her, because we are bound to her. But what we can do is win back her favor.”

“Their wizard will kill us if we try.”

Now it was Lucius's turn to point up at the suffering man. “Look at our brother and tell me that being instantly burned to ashes by the wizard is a bad way to die.” He let his words sink in for a minute, then, no longer seeking their agreement, he simply turned and walked toward the cave. One by one, they all fell in and followed behind him.

It took hours for them to crawl quietly over the rubble of the broken statues blocking the walkway. Even when one of their number fell between two slabs of granite, he did not cry out. The only noise came from his tumbling body and the sickening sound of his breaking neck. The remaining eight held their breaths and waited. When no alarm rose, they continued slowly along their way.

When at last they reached the landing, they were delighted to find no sentries placed. Peeking carefully around the huge door frame, they were again surprised to find no warriors in the massive chamber.

Can this work? Lucius thought to himself, feeling a twinge of hope starting to stir. He led them across the big room toward the deeper chambers where he imagined the people would be sleeping.

They had made it nearly halfway there when he froze and watched an elderly woman wearing a sword emerge from the room to the right. With a yawn and a stretch of her arms, she walked to the marble font to have a drink. At the sound of Lucius's bending bow, she looked up and saw them just as the arrow entered her chest. She fell behind the font without a sound, and he allowed himself to hope again. He had just taken another step when the old woman screamed, “Attack! We’re under attack!”

◆ ◆ ◆

Revna was first through the door, and she saw Signe’s dead eyes looking up at her from the floor. Looking at the arrow piercing her lungs, Revna knew she must have struggled to muster one last breath with which to warn them. A red veil of rage descended over her vision. Lifting the Hand of Fate, she ran around the cistern and pointed it at the first archer she saw. The words sprang from her lips, and the man lifted his face to the ceiling and yawned one long final exhale before dropping to the floor in a lifeless heap. Revna did not see it, however, as her frame was instantly racked with pain. A scream of anguish escaped her lips and she crumpled to the ground. Two arrows struck her on her way down, but they glanced off of her battle robes.

“Aim at her face,” Lucius shouted, but before anyone could obey, Leif leaped in front of her, loosing arrows from his bow in a flurry.

“Don't you hurt her!” he screamed.

Lucius put an arrow into the youth’s stomach, but to his surprise, the young man plucked it out, nocked it, and fired it back at him. Lucius grasped the shaft of the arrow that now protruded from his own stomach, hoping to pull it free and copy the feat himself. Instead, he moaned and toppled to the ground. Whatever passion, whatever strength lay in the boy, Lucius knew he did not have it in himself. He had seen war for more than four hundred years, and he had never seen such a deed. The archer looked up and saw yet another boy striding toward him. This one bore a sword from the desert such as Lucius had not seen since he and his brothers had marched in the legions of the Emperor. He nodded gratefully to the youth, then closed his eyes as the sword came down and sent him to Elysium.

Eirik dispatched the others, all of whom had fallen to arrows from the young huntsman’s bow. Leif waited until he saw that the danger had passed, then took a few staggering steps and lowered himself to the ground. “I'm coming, father,” he whispered.

Revna hurried to his side, and Leif reached up and grasped her hand. “Princess, I have to tell you something before I die. I love you. You are the bravest, most wonderful person I've ever met, and I love you with all of my heart. Isn't that just silly? Me, the son of your father’s huntsman, in love with you.”

“No, it isn't silly,” she replied gently.

“I would have never told you, I promise. But I'm going to die now, so what harm can it do?”

"None at all, Leif. But you are not going to die," she said, taking out her spellbook and opening it to the last page.

"What are you doing, Princess?" Leif protested fearfully.

"I'm going to heal you."

"You mustn't try it! This wound is even worse than the one the wizard had, and that nearly killed you!"

"Yes, but I didn't know what I was doing, and more importantly I was just too small and weak then."

"I don't understa—" Leif fell silent and his eyes focused on her with a look of shock.

Revna placed her hand on his stomach and began to read. Her voice sounded strange in her own ears. It was deeper, especially when she grunted in pain as she received his hurt and magicked it away.

"Your voice? Your face?" Eirik said in confusion as he slowly approached them. He gasped when she stood to meet him and they were almost eye-to-eye. "You look my age now!"

"Yes. I was enraged by Signe's murder, and in that moment, I did not care what happened. I used the Hand of Fate on a living man and paid with some of my own life."

Leif got to his feet and sheepishly said, "Uh, Princess, I am so sorry. I never would have told you…"

"It's all right, you don't have to apologize. I feel…" Revna paused and searched for her true feelings, but was quickly overwhelmed and retreated from them. "Come, Leif, help me lift Signe from the ground," she said instead.

"Poor Signe," he said, beginning to tear up.

"No. Do not say that. She lived and died the way she chose, defending those whom she loved. May we all hope for the same," Revna said solemnly.

The princess withdrew the arrow from Signe's breast and laid the warrior woman's sword in its place. Then she kissed her brow and rose so Leif and Eirik could bear her from the ground.

As she stood, Eirik tilted his head, and a queer look stole across his face. "What is it?" she asked, noticing the look.

"I just realized that your robe fits you now."

Revna looked down at herself, taking stock of her strange new body for the first time and noting that the robe was, in fact, the only garment that still fit her without straining at the seams. Quietly, she replied, "Yes, this wizard's robe, I seem to have grown into it, haven't I?"

CHAPTER FOURTEEN

A great shiver of cold enveloped Rangvald, and he pulled the coat of furs the craftsman had given him tight around himself. Opening his eyes, he sat up to see a realm gripped in the forever twilight of ice and snow.

"Get up, Wizard. The ground here has a hungry frost. It will suck the warmth from your bones and kill you if you give it the chance," Dvalinn cautioned.

Rangvald scrambled to his feet and looking at his companions through the plumes of his breath asked. "You do not need heavy furs?"

"Trufflesbane never takes hers off," Dvalinn said with a chuckle, giving her a pat. "And as for me, we dwarfs are made with very thick skin. Whether it's the heat of the forge or the frozen tunnels at the bottom of the Trollheimen, it bothers us but little."

At this answer, Rangvald began to turn slowly in a circle, searching for his bearings. Off to his right, he saw a river that was surprisingly not iced over, as one might expect, but instead was fast-moving, with floating chunks of ice whipping around a bend and disappearing into the distance.

"That is the river Ellvagar that flows through the underworld," the craftsman explained.

Turning further still, Rangvald stifled a cry and stood transfixed at what he saw had been looming behind him. To call it *fire* wasn't quite right. That might suggest that something had caught fire and was burning. This was something different. This was a realm made entirely of swirling storms of flame. It stretched up out of sight of the human eye. The same could be said of the span of it going to the right and left. Somehow, it obeyed an invisible border, preventing it from coming any nearer or retreating any farther away. Rangvald could feel no heat emanating, nor, in fact, any light that might be called intense. Where the land of ice met the land of fire, Rangvald could see a jagged fissure from which a curtain of steam rose with a steady hiss.

"We don't have to try and go there, do we?" he asked, preparing to forfeit his sanity depending on the dwarf's answer.

"No. That is the Muspelheim, realm of fire. You are standing where no man was meant to stand, Rangvald. At the cradle of all living things." At the craftsman's words, Rangvald's sanity remained poised to abandon him. "This is it," Dvalinn continued. "Here where the frost realm and flame realm meet. Where the steam mingled with a yeast and produced Ymir, whom the Rime-giants name as Aurgelmir. It was from Ymir that all life sprang."

Rangvald's mind began to slip and he started to laugh, softly at first, then louder and louder. He tried to stop his hysterics but found that he was powerless to do so. Not until he felt the dwarf's grip of iron on his shoulder turn him and begin to march him away.

"Look down. Focus on your feet. One in front of the other. Step after step."

Rangvald obeyed him and watched his own feet as they trod the hard-packed ice and snow alongside the river. He was not sure if they walked for minutes or hours, but when the party came to a halt and he looked up, he had possession of his senses once more.

"The gates of Niflheim," the dwarf announced.

"But they are left hanging open and with no one to guard them," Rangvald observed.

"I don't believe they receive many visitors. There are places where only the very brave or the very stupid wish to enter."

"And which are we?" Rangvald asked.

"Both!" the dwarf laughed as he strode through the gates. Rangvald and Trufflesbane exchanged a look then followed him in. After they had gone about a hundred paces, they reached a clearly marked path, trodden by many feet over many years, with a dense forest of leafless and stunted trees growing on both sides.

"Good, a road. We can mount and make up some ti —"

The dwarf fell silent without finishing his sentence. Rangvald was about to inquire what the matter was when a sound reached his own ears. It was a single scuttling noise across the icy snow under the trees. Then he heard two scuttles, followed by a third, and then a thousand.

"Quick, in the saddle," the craftsman shouted, leaping up and hauling Rangvald up behind him just as Trufflesbane lurched into a run.

Rangvald glanced into the trees for the few seconds he had before Trufflesbane's speed turned the world into a blur, and he thought he saw eyes—thousands of eyes—scuttling towards them. He squeezed his own eyes shut and held onto the dwarf for dear life.

With an earsplitting chorus of shrieks, they struck, instantly flooding the road with their black, furry bodies. Rangvald opened his eyes and now could see glimpses of the spiders, each as big as an elkhound. The craftsman lay forward, pulling Rangvald down with him. The mighty Trufflesbane did not lose an ounce of speed as she plowed through the arachnids, sending pieces of their exploding bodies tumbling past and rolling off Rangvald's back.

As they continued to thunder down the road, the battleswine smashing the spiders into furry kindling, Rangvald realized that they were going to make it. He chanced a glance around Trufflesbane's flank and what he saw confirmed it. The giant spiders were skittering out of the way ahead and giving them the road. He breathed a sigh of relief as she began to crest a small rise, but at its top, he once again closed his eyes and squeezed them shut with all of his might. Trufflesbane tried to stop, her hind legs digging deep ruts in the road as their momentum carried them forward. When she did come to a jarring halt, Dvalinn and Rangvald were thrown from the saddle, then they, too, stopped abruptly.

Rangvald reluctantly opened his eyes again. He could see Trufflesbane and the craftsman hanging helplessly. All three of them were caught in the massive spiderweb spanning across the roadway. Off to the sides, he saw that some of the strands of web had snapped where they led to the trees. Even a couple of the trees themselves had been uprooted by Trufflesbane's devastating impact. Unfortunately, many more strands were perfectly intact, and when he tried to wrench himself free, the grip of the webs felt as solid as stone.

Once again, scuttles drew his attention, and looking up at the rise, he saw the huge spiders looking down at them from the crest.

"Wizard, a little battle magic would not be unwelcome about now," the dwarf said with an edge of concern in his voice while trying to pull himself free of the webs.

"My hands are stuck fast. My battle spells must be directed," Rangvald replied with more than just an edge of concern.

"Well, this may be goodbye, then," Dvalinn pronounced gravely.

The spiders, satisfied with their tentative moment of surveillance, joined once more in a communal screech, this one holding an even more triumphant note than the first one. They started down the road toward them. Trufflesbane let out an earth-shattering squeal of fear and rage and began to writhe, twist, and hurl herself all around. As the spiders crawled nearer, their long, sharp fangs protruded, dripping with milky venom, and they hopped up and down, vibrating with murderous ecstasy. Rangvald and Dvalinn were tossed around wildly as Trufflesbane leaped and strained against her bonds with all of her prodigious strength. Rangvald was so dizzy that he was afraid he would lose consciousness, although he was not certain whether this would be a blessing or a curse under the present circumstances.

His focus became clear in an instant, however,

when he heard a sound his imagination likened to the string of a giant harp that had been drawn too tightly. After the first one, several more sounded, followed by another ear-numbing squeal. Then, with a final lurch, Trufflesbane was down among the beasts, snorting and stomping them into horrible, twitching piles of goo. Rangvald watched her path of carnage as she drove the spiders back over the rise. Relief had just begun to wash over him when the craftsman spoiled it with, "Off in the trees to my side. Look, some of them are coming for us as she chases the others away."

Rangvald saw four of the creatures skittering closer, and he tugged helplessly where his limbs were stuck. *If only my arm were free,* he thought. Then, with a gasp of realization, he said, "I have an idea! This might kill us, but..." Leaving the rest unsaid, he summoned a bolt of lightning and released it directly from his hand into the web that was ensnaring it. Tendrils of arcing energy leapt from the web into both him and the craftsman, but neither of them died.

The smoldering webs released them. Dvalinn's hammers were already swinging as he fell. When he hit the ground, two of the arriving spiders died. With another swing, he obliterated a third, but when he struck for the fourth and final spider, he found that it benefited by not being side-by-side with its brethren. As he struck, it dodged to the side faster than the eye could track and was nearly successful in plunging its fangs into him.

Rangvald observed this, but he knew he could not cast any magic without hitting the dwarf. Instead, he drew his sword and ran around behind it to attack. Seeing the wizard, the spider spun to face him, and in that moment of split focus, Dvalinn was able to smash one of its legs with his hammers. Seizing his opportunity, Rangvald lunged as fast as he could. The point of his sword punctured through a cluster of eyes and drove into the creature's brain. With one final shriek, it rolled over, its legs shriveling above it.

Together, they ran up the rise to join the battle, but upon arriving, they instead sheathed their weapons and watched as Trufflesbane trotted back towards them on a thick carpet of spider ruin.

Turning to Rangvald, the dwarf said, "I felt the lightning, but we were unhurt."

"Yes; I remembered my lessons on wizards' lightning. It is said that it has a deep and passionate love for the earth. You can cast it into a man, but all it will do is seek the ground. As it goes to it, the heat of its passion cooks his flesh, and so he dies."

The craftsman thought for a moment, then laughed. "We were floating in the webs, away from the ground."

"Precisely," Rangvald said, smiling.

"Come, let's be away. By Odin, with the two of you around, we just might make it after all," the craftsman said cheerfully. Then, mounting up, they ventured further into the realm of mists.

Trufflesbane bounded down the road until they reached the end of the forest of leafless trees. Before them stretched a vast plain bearing the tokens of some long-ago battle. Everywhere around them peered the gray, frozen faces of the dead from the icy snow. Swords and shields and spears lay mute now where they had fallen in some forgotten age, but in the trio's imaginations, they could almost hear the ring and thunder of their clashing still.

Trufflesbane picked her way carefully around the ghoulish relics of the past until at last, they reached the other side of the plain. A little further on, she entered a strange pathway bordered on both sides by long white timbers, or perhaps they were columns of stone, lying on their sides. These led to a platform, where she paused at a walkway of the same white stones in a line.

"This is the way," Dvalinn said reassuringly, and she went on, her hooves clacking against the odd surface.

Ahead loomed huge spires of the same white material arching above the walkway. When they passed beneath them, Rangvald gazed wonderingly at the strange rafters high above. "What is this place? Who built it, Craftsman?" he inquired.

Dvalinn chuckled. "I wouldn't say anyone built it. We are simply passing through the bones of a frost giant."

Rangvald looked down again, this time recognizing the giant backbones upon which they trod for what they were, then up at the curving rib bones above. Trying to imagine the size of the being when it had lived made his head begin to swim.

As Trufflesbane ventured into a huge dark chamber, Rangvald saw two towering lines of teeth ascending to their left with dim gray light spilling in here and there around them. Further on, he could see a little more hazy light filtering in from where the nose or an eye had been. At the sound of a rustling from somewhere close by, Trufflesbane quickened her pace. Rangvald peered into the darkness, but he could see nothing in the deep recesses of the cavernous skull. He knew something was there, however. He could hear it, smell it, feel it. Some alien presence uncoiling itself in the darkness.

"Hurry!" Dvalinn whispered urgently, and Trufflesbane ran for the patch of hazy light ahead. Rangvald hung on tightly to the craftsman as they sprinted for safety. As she reached the hole and leapt through, Rangvald heard an echoing laughter from behind that froze his blood inside his veins. He was certain that some oozing tentacle was about to reach out and drag him back in, but Trufflesbane swiftly rounded the big white dome and picked up the trail again, leaving the accursed place behind.

The path rose gently as they trotted along and a long stretch of the journey passed without event. Were it not for the frigid cold and the bleak landscape, Rangvald could almost imagine they were just out for a pleasant ride.

After a time, the road began to rise a bit more steeply, and they found themselves stopped at a point overlooking a valley, the floor of which was covered entirely in mist.

"Oh no," the craftsman breathed.

"I knew it had been too long since anything tried to kill us," Rangvald said, straining his eyes to see through the mist below. "Is something hiding in the fog down there, waiting for us?"

"No. I can assure you that nothing is waiting for us in that fog," Dvalinn replied.

"Then what's the matter?"

"It is the fog itself. To take one breath is to go to sleep forever. I had hoped this place would not be in our path."

"What can we do?" Rangvald asked, eyeing the fog despondently.

"Well, we could try holding our breath, and Trufflesbane could run across as fast as she could," Dvalinn suggested, sounding uncertain.

"Right, that could work, couldn't it? Trufflesbane is the fastest mount there is!" Rangvald said, his hope returning.

"Odin's horse, Sleipnir, is faster. But it takes him eight legs to claim that distinction," the craftsman said, gazing across the valley and measuring it with his eyes. "No, I don't like it."

"Why not?"

"Have you ever run as fast as you could?"

"Yes," the wizard replied.

"When you did, did you find that you had to breathe more or less?"

"Ah. I see your point," Rangvald said. "Then what are our options?"

"I could go on alone. We dwarfs can dig tunnels so deep that air is only a memory. I could hold my breath through that valley without any trouble. But the journey has already been so long, and I fear it will be longer still. Without Trufflesbane's speed, I do not believe I will ever be able to get the Dragon's Tear and make it back before the Black Queen returns to the cave."

"What do you think, Trufflesbane?" Rangvald thought to her, speaking the question aloud as well.

I can make it! she thought back confidently.

"All the way across, while holding your breath?" he pressed.

Trufflesbane surveyed the valley and replied, *Yes, the road slopes down steeply into the valley. I will go faster than I ever could on flat ground.*

"She says she can make it. The slope down into the valley will give her greater speed than ever," Rangvald relayed.

Dvalinn stroked his beard while looking over the

valley again. "Yes, I think we must try it," he said. Trufflesbane trotted back up the road to give herself a head start. "Hold onto me, Wizard. If the sleep takes you, you mustn't fall off!"

Rangvald wrapped his arms around the dwarf's waist. He felt a big hand seize hold of the sleeves of the heavy fur coat and hold him fast. Then Trufflesbane was off, starting at a jog, but then picking up pace. As she reached the downward slope, a burst of blinding speed took Rangvald by surprise, and he held on for all he was worth. They were now traveling at an unimagined speed, and all three held their breath as the fog approached.

Trufflesbane plunged into the mist. An instant later, her front legs smashed into the vast pile of bodies lying hidden by the fog frozen in eternal slumber. These were not like the soft bodies of the spiders she had encountered before, which had smashed to pieces. These were the hard bodies of armored adventurers, the bony bodies of goblins, and thick-hided trolls.

Rangvald felt them go somersaulting through the air and braced himself for an impact that never came. Or, rather, for an impact that, when it did come, he knew nothing about, for he had been swallowed up by the blackness of endless sleep.

◆ ◆ ◆

A great shiver of cold enveloped Rangvald, and he pulled the coat of furs that the craftsman had given him tight around himself.

He felt confused. Had he just arrived in the Niflheim after eating the apple? Then what about the spiders? What about the bones of the giant with foul things living in its skull? What about the...

Rangvald staggered to his feet and found himself alone up on the opposite side of the valley. How had he gotten here? And where were the craftsman and Trufflesbane? The last thing he remembered was Trufflesbane tripping while running at great speed, then all of them hurtling through the fog together. So how was he here, and where were his companions?

"Hello!" he shouted, cupping his hands to the sides of his mouth. "Where are you?" he called again. When there was no reply, he turned his back to the valley and looked up the road, searching for them further along the trail.

"We're here!" he heard the dwarf's voice shouting in reply.

Spinning back around, he saw the craftsman starting up the slope toward him, carrying the massive boar in his arms. All at once, everything became clear. Dvalinn had told him that he could hold his breath without trouble. He had managed to do so even as they had come crashing down. Then he had carried him up into the fresh air before going back to retrieve Trufflesbane.

Rangvald watched as the craftsman's pace began to slow coming up the steep slope. His strength seemed more than adequate to carry her without any strain, but she was so large that he couldn't see where he was going, and as his foot came down on a patch of loose gravel, he was so top-heavy that they tumbled back into the fog in the blink of an eye and were gone.

Rangvald nearly cried out with surprise and craned his neck trying to see through the mist. "Craftsman?" He called. "Craftsman, can you hear me?" A minute passed with no sign of them. It had happened too quickly, too unexpectedly, for the dwarf to have held his breath. *Now they are both slumbering in the mist down there,* Rangvald thought despondently. "I have to try something," he said out loud as he moved down the slope, cautiously avoiding any loose spots. Taking a deep breath, he entered the fog.

If he could drag the dwarf up into the fresh air and wake him, he could try to carry Trufflesbane to safety again. Feeling his way forward, he found them not far inside, lying together in a heap. To Rangvald's chagrin, he found that Dvalinn was pinned halfway beneath the big boar, and he could not budge him. Giving up, he hurried back out of the fog to breathe.

I can't lift them. I'm not strong enough, he thought, despairing. "Wait! What do I mean, 'I'm not strong enough?'" he cried, then took another deep breath and ventured back into the fog. He summoned the spell of the Unseen Hand. Before the blessing of the goddess, he had been able to use its magic to give things a little push, but now, it was so strong that he had brushed a hundred tons of marble down on the witch queen's army. Of course, he could push his companions out of here. Placing his hands close behind their bodies, he felt the power of Hefring stirring in his heart, and he cast the magic.

Rangvald made his way up the deep furrow that was now carved in the road and found his companions sprawled at the top. Neither seemed injured as best as he could tell. He shook them both, but they would not wake. So he sat down and re-read his spells while the fresh air did its work.

Dvalinn was first to wake, sitting up with a start. "What happened?" he asked, looking disoriented.

"You slipped carrying Trufflesbane up the slope and the mist took you."

"Ah, yes, I remember now," he said, standing.

A few minutes later, Trufflesbane sputtered to consciousness, looking just as disjointed. Seeing her looking around herself in confusion, Rangvald explained, "You tripped in the fog, but Dvalinn carried us out."

Yes. Yes, that's right, I remember now, she replied, calming down.

"Are you able to run?" the craftsman asked her. In answer, she stood up enthusiastically, ready to go. Rangvald had noticed that they seemed to communicate just fine without the aid of wizards' magic. As they mounted the saddle once more, the dwarf asked, "How long did I sleep?"

"From the time you fell back into the mist until you sat up again, I would say only twenty or twenty-five minutes had passed." The craftsman grunted an acknowledgment, and Trufflesbane galloped off down the road. "You're keeping track of the time, aren't you?" Rangvald asked, having to shout to be heard over the freezing wind rushing by.

"Yes," the craftsman shouted back.

"With no sky that I can understand and so many strange things happening, I have lost all sense of time myself. How are we doing?"

The dwarf remained stiff-lipped for a few moments, then said, "It is further than I'd hoped, and the going is harder, but do not lose hope yet."

After they had gone a little further, a river hove into view on their right. "Is that the same river we saw outside the gates when we arrived?" Rangvald shouted.

Dvalinn nodded. "The river Ellvagar. It has been with us the whole way, usually just out of sight."

Rangvald was watching the swiftly moving waters that were free of ice here when he felt Trufflesbane slowing and coming to a halt.

"This is encouraging!" the craftsman, said pointing up ahead.

Rangvald saw the trail closing in and becoming almost a tunnel, formed not of stone or dirt, but of the twisting, entwining roots of trees.

"In there, we will find the lair of Nidhug. At last, we are getting close."

"Idunn said that Nidhug chews on the roots of Yggdrasil?" Rangvald asked as Trufflesbane began moving forward once more.

"That's right. The tree of life has three roots, one in the realm of the Rime-giants, one in Midgard, and one here in Niflheim that we are now entering beneath. Everything that lives in these deepest chambers of Nifl chews and hacks and injures the roots of Yggdrasil."

"I find it insane that anyone would want to kill Yggdrasil," Rangvald said sadly.

"The world tree suffers more greatly than any man can ever know. The four mighty stags crop its crown, and serpents gnaw its roots. In between, its trunk is slowly rotting. It is the defining feature of higher-thinking beings that they dirty and desecrate and destroy the world around them."

"But why? I just don't understand that."

"You were chosen to be a hero, Rangvald, precisely because you do not understand this impulse to conquer and destroy. Because you would spend yourself in the service of others and wish peace on everyone."

Rangvald considered these words for some time as they traveled deeper into the bowels of the mist realm. Then, remembering Idunn's words, he asked, "What's a goblin?"

"Ah, yes. They are down here in the deeps as well. Most speak of them as serpents. That is, if they dare speak of them at all. I guess that is what they are. They look something like the melding of a lizard and a man. Idunn knows all the tongues that were ever spoken or ever will be, she calls them goblins."

As they traveled on, they came to a tunnel branching off to the right, and Dvalinn pointed to it. As Trufflesbane turned down it, the way became much darker. Rangvald pulled the small rod from his belt and commanded it to glow. He tied it securely around his neck, and since he sat taller in the saddle than the dwarf in front of him, the rod was able to light the surroundings for them all.

"Idunn said there were three armies of goblins?" he asked, picking up the conversation again.

"Yes. My father told us there are three warring tribes. But their domains are in the furthest corners of the deeps so as to keep separate from one another. Our path takes us straight down the center between their lands. So, at most, we should only see a patrol or two." Again, Dvalinn indicated a turn, and Trufflesbane followed it, taking them down yet another path.

"Is it true that a dwarf cannot lose his way?" Rangvald asked, remembering his lessons in lore from the wizard school.

"Yes, as long as they don't question it or second-guess themselves, a dwarf is never lost," the craftsman replied.

On the next turn, they traveled for a time next to the swiftly running river Ellvagar, the roar of its waters reverberating through the wooden tunnels.

They passed into a huge chamber being watched

by dozens of glowing red eyes. The craftsman placed a hand on one of his hammers, and Rangvald brought the glowing runes on his bracer to life. Rangvald struggled to make out any details of the creatures behind those eyes, but they haunted the shadows around the edges of the room and remained a mystery. Just as they were trotting out of the cavernous room, the light from the rod revealed a cluster of the creatures that were watching them from near the doorway. They were little men, or at least they stood on two feet as men do. Filthy and hairy and not at all frightened of the trio of newcomers, they watched with interest as they rode by.

"Were those goblins?" Rangvald asked in a hush.

"No. Those were... I don't know what they were," the craftsman admitted. "But not goblins. We are making excellent progress. I don't believe we will see any goblins." He leaned forward and pointed left so Trufflesbane could see.

They entered a spacious, well-lit tunnel. After a few steps, Trufflesbane lurched to the wall and crouched down beside it. Dvalinn and Rangvald lay forward, trying to make themselves small.

"What is it?" Rangvald asked in a barely-audible whisper, peering towards the open space ahead of them, which was filled with firelight and clambering voices.

"That would be the goblin armies... All three of them," Dvalinn whispered back, sounding exasperated.

A jangled chorus of horns sounded from the clearing, causing Rangvald to jump with fright.

"Creep a little closer. No one is looking this way," the craftsman told Trufflesbane, and much to Rangvald's disapproval, she did. Now he could see some of the goblins in detail, and he did not care at all for what he saw.

Their skin was a pale and mottled green. Their faces reminded him more of bloated toads than lizards. They wore a wide assortment of patched-together piecemeal armor of bone and hide and rust-bitten steel. Every type of weapon could be seen, ratty and rusty, but all honed to a razor's edge. At the sound of the horns, they all screamed out with murderous battle cries. At the sight of their cracked and cancerous lips screaming, slavering, and drooling for carnage, Rangvald clamped his eyes shut in terror. Over the last few days, he had faced armies of the dead on multiple occasions and had not thought that anything could strike such fear into his heart again. He had been woefully mistaken.

"We don't have time for this," he heard the craftsman lament.

"What do we do?" Rangvald whispered, still not daring to open his eyes.

"I don't know. There are at least thirty thousand of them. One army to the left, wearing blue paint on their arms, one to the right in red sashes, and an army with handprints of yellow on their chests and shields straight ahead on the path that we must take."

"Is there another path?" Rangvald asked, opening his eyes again and looking at the dwarf hopefully.

Dvalinn paused for a moment, considering the question carefully, then shook his head. "Not one that we can travel."

Up ahead, an especially greasy, unwholesome voice boomed out, "Hear us. We are Goinn and Moinn, the sons of the gnawing grave, commanders of the army of the blue claw. We alone are the true kings under the root!"

"Wrong!" a voice screeched from the opposite side of the clearing. "You are pretenders! Ofnir and Svafnir, sons of the grave wolf, brothers of the blood-red rag, are the only true kings!"

"Silence! Grabak and Grafvolluth are the true high kings under the root! We are the sons of the bewilder! The bringer of sleep! The unraveller of that which has been woven, and once and for all, the yellow hand of bile will wipe the blue claw and the blood-red rag from all memory!"

"They have finished declaring themselves. They will fight soon," Dvalinn said, not bothering to whisper now as the armies screamed and the horns blew again.

"Can Trufflesbane's speed carry us through them safely?" Rangvald asked, sweat breaking out across his brow in spite of the freezing air.

The dwarf shook his head. "No; they have archers. She cannot outrun their arrows."

"Very well, then. We will fight our way through them in the chaos," Rangvald said, finding his resolve again. "My battle magic has been strong ever since Hefring's kiss. If it must be battle I just wish they would start already. We are losing time."

"Soon, but not yet," the craftsman told him. "There will be a few more minutes of this. It is a tense moment. No one wants to..." Dvalinn trailed off without finishing his thought, then in an excited tone said, "Dismount—I have a plan. It will seem like madness, but at this point, madness may be just what is called for."

The clamor of the armies was dying down again, so he whispered into Trufflesbane's ear. Then, turning to Rangvald, he whispered, "Follow my lead."

A few moments later, Trufflesbane pranced into the opening between the three armies. More than thirty thousand goblins watched in stunned silence as she stopped in the center, snuffled at the ground for a moment, then pranced merrily on. The army of the yellow hand of bile parted down the middle, making space for her as she frolicked through their ranks and disappeared down the path.

A moment later the dwarf and the man hurried into the clearing. They, too, paused in the center, where Dvalinn asked innocently, "Has anyone seen a pig?"

Without hesitation, thirty thousand bulging goblin arms pointed, and Dvalinn and Rangvald hurried after her. Once they were out of sight, they broke into a run and caught up with Trufflesbane. As they met up with her, the sounds of battle finally erupted from behind. Mounting up once more, Rangvald sputtered, "What just happened?"

"The answer was staring me right in the face," Dvalinn laughed. "That time just before battle. The most uncertain time that can ever be!"

"What? I still don't understand!" Rangvald said, feeling lost.

"Say that you are the commander of an army facing not one, but two other armies. The fate of all your people will be decided by what happens. You will be rulers or you will be slaves. You are trying to anticipate any strategy your foes may employ, looking for anything you may not have thought of. You are leery of any trick, any deception. Then all of a sudden, a giant pig wearing a saddle comes dancing by, followed by a lost dwarf and a man. They are here on this day, here where no one from the outside ever comes. What do you do?"

Rangvald began to laugh as well. "Well, it's all too bizarre to be a coincidence. It has to be a trick by one of the other armies. I can't be the first to act, the first to commit myself to anything and expose a weakness."

"Exactly." The dwarf laughed.

Both of them were still laughing as they rode into a long, dark, cavernous chamber. "You are brilliant Dvalinn," Rangvald said, reaching forward to pat his shoulder, but the dwarf was gone. Trufflesbane stopped trotting and Rangvald called out, "Dvalinn? Where'd you go?"

When he received no answer, Rangvald quickly leaned forward to hold onto the saddle and dismount. At that moment, something brushed his back. With a scream, he leapt down. "There's something here, Trufflesbane! It tried to grab me!"

Just then, Dvalinn came plummeting from above and slammed into the ground with a groan. Rangvald held the illuminated rod up and peered into the blackness overhead. A second scream escaped him as he saw the bats, each one almost the size of Trufflesbane. They beat their wings, but for some reason, it produced no sound. One of them dove towards him. The beast was darker than darkness and utterly silent, but he could see its outline swooping through the air. Rangvald's hand came up just as the craftsman shouted, "No, not upward!"

A jagged torrent of ice shot from Rangvald's hand, capturing all of the bats and slamming them high up into the ceiling of the chamber with a crash. Then two tons of thick black earth and a large chunk of broken root buried them in a silent tomb.

Almost instantly, Rangvald felt a frenzied movement beside him, and he was pulled into a tiny pocket of air. The frantic movement shifted away from him as he spat dirt from his mouth and tried to breathe. He felt the scrambling movement come back, and now he knew it was the dwarf doing what only a dwarf could do: digging, even when they were pressed beneath a mountain of earth. A few moments later, his tiny pocket was opened up. As his glow rod became exposed, he saw that his space had been joined with a larger one, where Trufflesbane's muddy head had emerged. She blinked as the glow illuminated the larger pocket.

Where is Dvalinn? he thought to her.

I don't know, she replied, her thoughts sounding hazy and drunk.

Rangvald lay still, trying not to breathe too deeply. He felt his consciousness starting to leave him. He had to fight to stay awake with all his will. Looking at Trufflesbane again, he saw that her eyes were closed and she was not moving. *Trufflesbane,* he called out to her mind, but he received no answer. *Trufflesbane!* Still she did not answer.

I'm sorry, he thought to her. Almost as if in reply, her head slid backward out of view and she was gone. The dirt caved in where her body had been, but Rangvald squirmed over and began to dig with his hands, trying to follow her. His movements were labored and he made almost no headway. Just as unconsciousness was descending once and for all, a thick and powerful hand found his, and then he was being pulled to safety.

The three of them lay sputtering on the floor of the passage they had left before encountering the chamber of the bats. The ceiling of intertwining roots above reassured them that no danger was looming there. When at last he could speak, Rangvald asked, "How could you dig under all of that earth?"

"Well, it's not so much a matter of digging at first, it's more compressing, and then... Well... Let's just call it dwarf magic. I will tell you, however, that if we had been any further in there, we never would have made it out."

Rangvald stood wearily, wiping dirt from his face and regarding the mountain of soil. "I'm so sorry. It was all my fault."

"There is no good to come from blaming yourself. You couldn't have known," the craftsman said, getting to his feet as well.

"So how do we get through now?"

"We don't. Not without spending an amount of time that would render the whole errand useless," the craftsman said frankly.

"So that's it? We just go back?" Rangvald cried.

"Well, going back won't be a treat right now, either. Listen," Dvalinn said, cupping a hand to his ear. As if on cue, a distant death scream from the massive battle came faintly through the tunnels.

Rangvald sat back down heavily. "But we've come so far."

Dvalinn put a comforting hand on his shoulder. "I know. Even if we had some tools, we might get somewhere. But we have nothing."

Rangvald sat staring at the floor for a few moments as the craftsman's words hung in the air. "Wait, we do have something! We have my magic!" he said, standing up again. "My magic brought it down—maybe it can move it out of the way!"

"Yes. Anything is worth a try," the craftsman agreed.

"Stand back," Rangvald cautioned, summoning the magic of the Unseen Hand. He held it within himself, building its power until he was breathing hard with exertion. The power of Hefring thrummed in his chest, and as he pointed his hand, the power surged into the dirt, plowing a pathway straight through its center. As soon as the magic was spent, he pulled back his arm and watched the soil fill back in, leaving it completely unchanged.

"No!" he cried, leaning over with his hands on his knees, breathing hard from the effort.

Dvalinn waited until the wizard's breathing had slowed before saying, "Do not lose faith. Do you remember what I said about compressing the dirt? If you can give the force a round shape and pack the earth, it may work."

"I don't know if I can. I've never practiced finesse with this spell. I have seen other wizards stirring a cauldron or turning a key. They practiced hard to gain that control. But I was always satisfied just giving things a push."

"Have faith, Rangvald. If other wizards can do it, then so can you. You have the power of a goddess inside of you," Dvalinn said encouragingly.

Rangvald paced back and forth, rubbing the silver patch of skin above his heart. Coming to a stop, he said, "All right. I'll try it. What do we have to lose?"

He took out his book and studied the spell. Again, his body began to rock back and forth as the magic filled him. Abruptly, all his movements ceased, and he took a deep breath. "No, that's not right," he said to himself. Starting again, he let a great calm come over him as he summoned the power. Instead of his breath quickening, it slowed, and he focused on the beating of his own heart. "Hefring, daughter of Ran, guide my hand." He called and felt her power vibrating through his chest as he stretched his arms out, and the magic of the Unseen Hand began pressing a perfectly round tunnel through the dirt.

When he had finished, he waited half a minute without moving, not even daring to breathe. The tunnel stayed. "Thank you, Hefring," he said and turned around with a smile. "I did it!" He laughed with joy.

The dwarf stepped forward and placed his hand against the smooth-packed floor of the tunnel. When he turned back around, his face was grave.

"What? What is it?" Rangvald asked.

Dvalinn sighed deeply, but did not speak.

"Talk to me! What is that look for?" the wizard demanded.

"I'm sorry. I never should have suggested it and gotten your hopes up. It will not hold. This tunnel will be our grave if we climb into it."

"No!" Rangvald shouted, turning away.

"If we only had some wood, we could bolster it like a proper tunnel," the dwarf said.

"What do you call this?" Rangvald shouted touching the wall. "And what do you call this?" he repeated, pointing at the twining roots above them. "Here; my sword is sharp, you can have all the wood you want!" He grasped the hilt of his weapon.

"Oh, no, Rangvald. No. Those roots belong to Yggdrasil. We are not the ones that chop and kill the tree of life. If anything, we are the ones who would try to heal it and help it grow."

At these words, Rangvald hid his muddy face in his hands and wept. It took some time, but when he could finally speak, he removed his hands from his face. "I'm sorry I shouted at you. It was not you I was angry at. It was just the disappointment. And as for what you said about the tree..." Rangvald stopped speaking, and his eyes grew wide as he remembered the dwarf's words. "That's it!" he said, taking out his spellbook and rushing to the spot where the chambers met. "'If anything, we are the ones who would help it grow!'"

Rangvald crouched down. Placing his hand against the thick, twining roots of the world tree, he read his spell. All at once, he remembered being behind the tent before the battle of the western road, where Val of Kattegat had taught him to harness the power of Hefring. He felt her kiss burning in his heart and heard the groaning of live things growing and twisting at the speed of magic. "Make sure when you do a thing, you know why it must be done and believe in its doing," he murmured, remembering Val's lesson.

Looking up from the book, he watched the roots of the wall springing out and reaching into the tunnel, weaving and meshing into a wooden portal. A radiant heat began to enter his hand where it touched the roots. It was not an unbearable heat, not yet, but it was growing. Rangvald focused on his hand, and without warning, his mind went hurtling away.

Some time later, he knew not how much later, it returned. He found himself being dragged through the long wooden tunnel that had formed through the heart of the soil. "What's happening?" he asked, looking up and seeing that it was the dwarf that was doing the dragging.

"You fell senseless. I fear you have been using too much magic in too short a space of time."

"I do not doubt the truth of that, but I think this was something different. The tree… it called to me."

"What did it say?" the craftsman asked, still dragging him by his arms.

"I don't remember. I don't think it called to me in words, but it called me and I went," Rangvald answered, content to still be dragged.

"Do you remember anything about it?"

"I remember a man with one eye looking at me. He was hanging from the tree of life."

"Did he say anything?" the dwarf asked. His voice had become a whisper.

"No. He just looked at me and slowly nodded."

Dvalinn dropped his arms. "Hurry. Come along now."

"Dvalinn, it was Odin, wasn't it?" Rangvald asked, adopting a whisper as well.

"Yes, it was Odin. Now hurry."

CHAPTER FIFTEEN

Trufflesbane had only been running for a few minutes when they came to a fork in the path. One trail seemed to broaden out up ahead, and if Rangvald was not mistaken, the air that way seemed slightly warmer. The other trail, however, ran into a dank, narrow tunnel formed of wet, lichen-coated stone instead of the interweaving roots of the great tree. Issuing from that tunnel was an almost deafening noise that caused Rangvald to tremble with fear. It was an indistinct roaring, and he felt instantly certain that they had reached the lair of Nidhug the dragon. Rangvald braced himself for the imminent confirmation of his dread, but Dvalinn paid no heed to the noisome tunnel and instead urged Trufflesbane onward past it and down the other path.

After they had trotted along for a few minutes more, the craftsman declared, "At last!" As he pointed ahead. Rangvald's glow rod struggled to contend with the deep gloom surrounding them. He could not see what Dvalinn had been pointing at until Trufflesbane stopped at the foot of the lapping waters.

"Some kind of underground lake?" he asked.

"It is the corpse fjord," the craftsman said. "Across these waters, the dragon makes its lair."

"Is there a boat?"

"No. There will be no boats here."

"Then how do we get across? Must we swim?" Rangvald asked, staring into the black water.

"Dwarfs cannot swim. We sink like anvils. But Trufflesbane floats like a longship at sea. She has carried me across many a body of water in our adventures."

Before Rangvald could ask another question, Trufflesbane strode down the bank and into the water. The wizard was shocked at how swiftly she paddled them across the fjord. His glowing rod revealed icy cliffs bordering the waterway on either side of them. Ahead, he could see light coming from around a bend. Rangvald lifted his hand to point it out, but then Trufflesbane jolted to a halt. She gave a gasp and was jerked halfway underwater before bobbing back up. *Hands from below,* she thought to Rangvald in a panic.

"Something is grabbing her from underneath," he told the dwarf as she began sinking again.

"You two, get the Dragon's Tear. Save the people of Vestmor," the craftsman said. Then he took a breath and slid sideways off the saddle. As promised, he sank like an iron anvil and was instantly gone. Trufflesbane suffered one more giant tug from below, but then was free again and began paddling away. After a short distance, she turned and swam in a circle. Rangvald searched the water all around them for any sign of the dwarf, but all was dark and still. There weren't even bubbles to mark the spot. It had happened so quickly. So easily had he sacrificed himself for them. He had slid off the saddle and went down to fight whatever horrors were waiting below in the pitch black. It was true he could hold his breath a long time, but in the middle of a body of water like this? Rangvald knew that it was too much to hope for. "I mustn't fail. Not after all of this," he whispered to himself.

Trufflesbane reluctantly gave up the search and swam up around the bend. A little further on, they entered a lagoon bathed in a ghostly light. The shore was carpeted completely with rotting, stinking corpses. This was the place Idunn had called the Nostrond, and right there on this gut-wrenchingly putrid beach was the dragon Nidhug itself, reaching up and gnawing on the roots above it.

Rangvald had been longing to find the serpent with every fiber of his being, but now that it was in front of him, he was filled with inescapable dread. What was his plan? He didn't have one! He had been relying on the craftsman to know what to do, and now he was at the bottom of the corpse fjord, being torn to bits by he couldn't guess what. Rangvald did not know what to do.

The dragon had not seemed to notice them yet. Trufflesbane climbed quietly over the bodies onto the shore, and Rangvald dismounted. Perhaps they could continue to go unnoticed while they found a tear and stole away. In the absence of any real plan, this seemed as good a course as any, so he began to creep forward. On his third step, his left foot clattered against some bones. The dragon at once abandoned the roots and stared directly at him while drawing in an enormous breath. The words flew from Rangvald's lips. As a surge of blue dragon's fire raced towards him, he cast his own fire to meet it. The power of the goddess sang in his breast, and the dragon's fire was easily defeated. Nidhug staggered back a step as the inferno washed across its face, but it was otherwise unhurt.

"More light," the dragon's ancient voice commanded, and at its words, the Nostrond grew brighter, though Rangvald could not detect from whence the light was emanating. Now the two of them were able to see the other more clearly. The scales of Nidhug were a dull black, traced in a faded lavender hue. Its face was jagged with fang and horn, but the scene was dominated by the glittering yellow eyes, which were calm and intelligent. Its demeanor was nothing like the roaring, savage beast Rangvald had been imagining. He felt compelled to try reasoning with it.

"I did not come to fight with you."

"That suits me. Only a fool would seek to do battle with a wizard as powerful as you are. What is it you do want of me then?" the dragon said quite pleasantly.

"One of your tears. I would not ask if it wasn't of the greatest importance."

"For you to come all the way here, riding on a descendant of Hildisvini," it said, nodding to Trufflesbane, "I could not possibly doubt the greatness of your need."

"Then may I have one?" Rangvald asked, beginning to feel almost optimistic.

The yellow eyes of the great serpent bored into Rangvald for a long moment, but then it replied, "Yes, of course you may." Reaching down, it scraped its claw through the scattered bodies and bones at its feet and lifted a handful of the bluish-purple stones. "Here, take one," it said, holding out its hand. Rangvald began to reach out, but halted as the dragon added, "And in return, I will ask but one small token."

"And what would that be?" Rangvald asked hesitantly.

"But one kiss. That is all I desire."

"A kiss?" Rangvald repeated, taken aback.

"Yes, a kiss. What? Do you find it so strange that I could want a kiss? You believe me devoid of all tenderness, don't you? You know nothing of my existence. I have been left here all alone, playing a role I never asked for. I would treasure one pure kiss from a hero, but if it is too much to ask..." The dragon trailed off bitterly.

Rangvald thought about the dragon's words for a moment and narrowed his eyes suspiciously.

"Ah, yes. I can see that you fear deception. That instead of a kiss, I will wait until your guard is down and strike."

"I will confess that that is precisely what I fear," Rangvald said.

Nidhug nodded its scaly head. "I see. Well, it was a nice thought anyway. You know, these tears mean nothing to me. They litter the floor of my prison by the thousands. They are not even a token of my true sorrow. They are just the way the sap of Yggdrasil passes through my body. Parting with one is of no great concern. But now I will never give you one."

"Please, it is very important! Is there no other way?" Rangvald pleaded.

"I need nothing from you. That is why I asked for something intangible. But you have refused me and made me a fool. And so I shall never give you one of my tears. And now I will say one last thing. Then you must either leave here or we must do battle."

"Yes, I'm listening," Rangvald said when Nidhug paused.

"Good. Listen, not just with your ears, but with your hero's heart as well. Once Nidhug makes a bargain, it is honored. I would truly have given you one of my tears in exchange for a kiss. This is my word, and it cannot be broken."

Rangvald instantly knew in his hero's heart that this was the truth. His rational mind told him that it would be madness to trust the dragon, but he could not stop himself.

Again, Nidhug read his thoughts on his face. "You know the truth when you hear it."

"I believe I do," Rangvald agreed.

"Then we have our bargain?" the serpent asked. Rangvald nodded and began to step forward. "I need to hear you say it. It can only be given freely."

The young wizard stopped and cleared his throat then declared, "I, Rangvald, do freely give you my kiss, Nidhug." He made to take another step forward, but then his knees gave out and he sank to the ground.

"Are you all right, Wizard?" Nidhug asked.

Rangvald was confused by his sudden affliction. He struggled back to his feet but did not answer. He could not trust himself to speak. He was suddenly choked up, as if fighting back tears. As soon as he had made his pledge, a profound sense of loss and despair had descended upon him. It was just like the day that he had learned of his parents' deaths—the feeling of being completely alone in the world. The feeling that he had felt again when Astrid had forsaken him, leaving him broken inside once more.

"Here, Rangvald, take your prize," Nidhug said, stepping closer and reaching out its big clawed hand.

Rangvald plucked one of the gemstones from the pile, and the dragon tipped its palm, letting the others fall to the ground.

"What about the kiss?" Rangvald asked weakly.

"Oh, you've already given me that," Nidhug replied, running a claw gently over Rangvald's chest.

Understanding washed over him, and he pulled open his tunic, searching his chest for the silver shimmer. Looking up, he saw it now upon the breast of the dragon. His despair grew even deeper, and the absent kiss of the goddess burned like a wound in his heart. He opened his mouth to protest, but could not find the spirit.

"Whatever is the matter?" Nidhug mocked.

Rangvald sighed and shook his head. He had been duped, and the great serpent wanted to gloat about it. But Rangvald had no intention of staying and enduring its taunts. He had still gotten what he had come for, and time was running short to return and save the people of Vestmor. "Come along, Trufflesbane. We are finished here. Let's go," he said.

"Go?" the dragon asked, feigning surprise. "There is no 'go.'"

"But you promised," Rangvald protested.

"I know precisely what I promised. And as I told you before, my promises can never be broken. You have been very careless in your bargaining, boy. You have willingly given me a kiss. A very sweet kiss, filled with power, I might add. And I have given you what you have asked for. A single tear. Now our business is concluded. I said nothing about letting you leave with it. Now that you are weak, I will kill you and your battleswine and suck your bones clean."

As the dragon reared up, Rangvald's despair turned

into a reckless rage, the type of fury only known to those who no longer care whether they live or die. He read the runes glowing on his vambrace and cast a fireball with every angry fiber of his being. As it struck, its effect on the dragon was instantly evident. Unfortunately, its effect was a bout of raucous laughter as the paltry burst of yellow flame fizzled and sputtered around the beast.

Once its laughter had subsided, Nidhug's voice took on a new level of menace. "You die now."

"Are you sure about that?" Rangvald shouted, meeting the dragon's eyes defiantly. "It seems to me that all you ever do is talk. Blathering on with your little deceptions and your little threats. If you are going to kill me, then just kill me already!"

Nidhug was struck dumb for a moment, astounded by the angry words and fearless demeanor, but then his own anger flared, and he screamed, "As you wish!"

The mighty jaws parted, exposing rows of razor-sharp fangs as the dragon began its strike. Rangvald did not flinch as the monster came for him. Nor did he flinch as something burst from the water and landed on the beach of corpses beside him. The flying hammer collided with the dragon's lower jaw, slamming its mouth shut and sending the beast careening back with a crash.

Nidhug shook its head to clear its vision, then, focusing on the newcomer, screamed in rage. "Ivaldi! How dare you show your face here again?"

"You honor me by mistaking me for my noble father," Dvalinn said calmly.

"Oh, son of Ivaldi, is it? Well, your father came here once long ago and took my tooth," Nidhug raged, peeling back its lips with a long claw and revealing a conspicuously absent fang among the rows.

"That was just like father. Picking up useless trifles wherever he went."

The Nostrond echoed with the roaring anger of the offended dragon. "I was just about to rend these two to bloody pieces. Now you can suffer the same fate, son of Ivaldi."

"That is going to be a problem," the craftsman said, still using a pleasant tone. "You see, these two are under my protection, and if you attempt to harm them, I will punish you."

The enormous eyes of the beast appeared to almost double in size. "I do not believe this! First, this one does not show an ounce of fear as I come to kill him; in fact, he has the audacity to tell me I talk too much. And now you say what? That you will punish me? This is insanity! I am Nidhug, the Malice Striker! I chew the corpses of the defilers, the oath breakers. I am eternal. None can slay me until the hour of Ragnarok!"

"He is right. You do talk too much. Now step aside, or you will be sorry," the dwarf said.

With a roar, the dragon charged. Dvalinn ran down the beach, leading it away from Rangvald and Trufflesbane, who both followed after, joining into the melee. Trufflesbane charged one of the thick hind legs, but she went careening off on impact, doing no damage to the monster. Drawing his sword, Rangvald ran alongside, slashing at its tail. He struck with all of his strength, but he may as well have been smashing his blade into solid stone.

The wizard dove to the ground just in time to narrowly avoid a swish of the spiked tail that threatened to smash him into oblivion. Scrambling back to his feet, he witnessed the dragon tumble to the ground, screaming in pain and terror. Dvalinn advanced menacingly, causing the dragon to skitter back, clutching at a long, jagged wound in the side of its neck.

"No fair!" Nidhug screeched. "What kind of weapon did you find that could pierce my perfect scales?"

"Oh, so that's where my father's trifle got to," the craftsman said, holding up the dragon's own long, sharp tooth. Dvalinn pretended to lunge once again for the dragon, causing it to turn and run headlong from the battle, disappearing into the tunnels leading down to the blackness below the Nostrond.

◆ ◆ ◆

Trufflesbane swam them across the corpse fjord as fast as she could, afraid that at any time the dragon might return and launch a fresh assault. But to everyone's relief, no attack came from behind or below, and soon they were standing once again on dry land.

"So, we have it. The Tear of the Dragon," Rangvald said, letting it finally sink in. "Now we must hurry back before it's too late for the kingdom of Vestmor."

"I'm afraid it already is, Rangvald," the craftsman said sadly. "This deed has taken us all day."

"No! But we've come so far. And we got it. We actually got the tear!" Rangvald lamented.

"I'm sorry," Dvalinn said softly.

"Wait! The Witch Queen won't attack early in the night. She will have to come back from the northern lands, and that will take hours."

"It has already been night there for some time. And think about it, Rangvald. I know your sense of time is confused here, but you know what things we must traverse to return—the three goblin armies, still locked in battle, the valley of slumber, the forest of the spiders, and all of the leagues in between."

"So what was any of this for? It's meaningless!" Rangvald cried.

"No; you can still take the Dragon's Tear back and defeat the evil queen, but now, instead of saving your friends, you will be avenging them. You will also be saving the next kingdom that she would have destroyed."

"I feel just as empty as when the dragon took Hefring's kiss from me."

"Come, Trufflesbane. We still have a long way to go and many challenges to face to make it back to the gates of Nifl," the craftsman said, and she set off at a trot. They had only traveled a short distance when they came to the other path, the one that led to the tunnel with the almost deafening roar spilling out of it. Again, Dvalinn paid it no heed.

"What is that?" Rangvald asked, having to fairly bellow to be heard.

"That must be the roaring cauldron Hvergelmir, where the rivers come from," Dvalinn bellowed back.

"The river? You mean Ellvagar, the river we have seen along our journey?"

"No, not river. Rivers! All the rivers that exist anywhere in the world," the dwarf corrected, shouting even louder as they passed closest to the tunnel.

As Trufflesbane hurried along and the sound began to fade into the distance, the craftsman shouted, "Wait!"

"What is it?" Rangvald asked, startled.

"There is a chance. A crazy, potentially suicidal chance. But a chance nonetheless."

"A chance for what? What do you mean?"

"If you are right and the Witch Queen cannot attack until later in the night, we may be able to get there in time."

"What? I don't care how crazy it is; let's try it!" Rangvald cried, daring to hope again.

"All right, back to the cauldron," the craftsman said, and Trufflesbane turned and ran back toward the sound. "When I tried to tell you that all the rivers flow from there, and you thought I meant just the river Ellvagar, that gave me the answer."

"I understand!" Rangvald said. "If all the rivers in the world flow from there, then the river Ellvagar flows from there too, and it runs swiftly back to the gates and beyond!"

"Yes, with chunks of ice drifting along its length!" Dvalinn added excitedly.

They had to dismount to make it down the narrow tunnel. With each step, the noise became more and more painful to the ear. Rangvald felt as if his brain were splitting down the middle. The three stopped where the tunnel opened onto a large chamber and stood gaping at what lay within. A massive swirling whirlpool inhabited the center and, just as the craftsman had said, all of the rivers were emanating from it. But that was where their frame of reference ended.

The place seemed to reject the laws of nature. Some of the rivers ran off into the distance along the ground, but others came from the cauldron, flowing up into the air at all angles. The rivers had no banks, no beds to contain them—they were torrents of flowing water that floated, suspended on nothing, as they rushed off into the dark. Stepping further in, Rangvald felt a sensation he had not felt since arriving in the underworld: heat. It was warm here.

Dvalinn waved for them to follow him and began making his way amongst the strange rivers, crawling first under one, then jumping over another very close to the edge of the swirling cauldron where their streams were still narrow. Rangvald was terrified of the screaming cauldron. If they slipped into it, its chaotic waters would rend them to pieces in less than a heartbeat. He forced himself to stop looking at it and stared instead at the craftsman's back. Sometimes the dwarf would stop and stand alongside one of the rivers and close his eyes. Then, with a shake of his head, he would move on to the next one, searching with his magical sense of direction. At last, he pointed excitedly at a river that was rushing out along the ground, and they all hurried to follow it.

Rangvald held up the glowing rod strung around his neck to light their way, and in no time, the sound of the cauldron began to fade. To Rangvald's disappointment, so did the glorious warmth they had enjoyed. As it disappeared, the freezing cold seemed far more miserable than it ever had before.

"Hurry, now, keep going!" Dvalinn urged.

Rangvald noted that the dwarf's voice sounded muffled by a lingering hum in his ears but he could hear him and he obeyed. As they jogged along, he observed that the river had become a normal river now. It appeared just as they had seen it on their way across the Niflheim, raging along its snowy banks. They trudged along, slowing to a careful walk as the icy riverside grew treacherous beneath their feet. The slippery bank narrowed more and more until they came to a point where the river disappeared down a tunnel where there was no place for them to walk.

"End of the line," the craftsman said disappointedly. "Well, it was worth a try anyway."

"Can Trufflesbane try to swim it?" Rangvald asked doubtfully, eyeing the raging waters.

"No. The water of the Corpse Fjord is much warmer and calmer than these waters. Even if she could carry us down it without us all being smashed to pieces and drowned, the cold would take her."

"Speaking of cold, where are the broken sheets of floating ice we saw before?" Rangvald asked.

"I had hoped we would have encountered them by now, but still the river flows with no ice. We best start back the way we came," Dvalinn said sadly.

"Why? Why is there no ice?" Rangvald said miserably, unwilling to give up.

Why don't you make some like you did before? Trufflesbane thought to him.

"What's that, Trufflesbane?" he said, turning to the boar.

Why don't you make ice, like you did when the flying things were attacking us?

"No, that won't work," he said. "I no longer have the power of the goddess strengthening my magic. Without Hefring's kiss, the most I could do is make a small blast of ice that could freeze a man. Nothing that could freeze a flowing river."

"Wait, the kiss of a goddess is not the only thing which can enhance the strength of a magic user," the craftsman said excitedly, overhearing Rangvald's side of the conversation.

"I don't understand. What else could make my magic stronger?"

"The Dragon's Tear. The whole reason why we came here!" Dvalinn explained. "It isn't just a charm that can ward off magic directed at its owner. It is a vessel that can capture magic, and that magic can be used by the one who wields it. I assure you that without the Dragon's Tear, the Witch Queen's necromancy would never be strong enough for her to control hundreds of spirits at a time."

"I do recall her saying that drinking up the essence of the wizards made her stronger, but I don't see how that helps us here and now. Unless there is a wizard other than me present that you are proposing I murder with the Dragon's Tear."

"No one said that the magic has to come from a living source. It can be drained from magical items as well. I can see at least two items you have that are imbued with magic."

"Oh, yes, I see!" Rangvald exclaimed, catching on. "I have my glowing rod and the vambrace master Val gave to me."

"What else do you have?" the dwarf asked, unimpressed.

Rangvald dug into his purse and produced a small assortment of charmed items, each with simple magics such as his seeing stone or direction rod or distaff used for divination. Dvalinn shook his head and said, "I have a few items, like my armor, that also have small charms placed on them, but even all together, they will not amount to much magic at all. Certainly not enough to help you accomplish the feat you are after."

"So what can we do?" Rangvald asked.

"We must use your enchanted sword. Only it contains enough magic to aid you in this," the craftsman declared.

"Enchanted sword?" Rangvald said with surprise, drawing the blade and looking at it with new appreciation. "She said that it was special and would aid me when I most needed it," he said, remembering Hefring's words when she had presented it to him in the waters of the mere. He fished out the purple stone for which he had unwittingly traded her blessing. "Tell me what I must do."

"We must first find a way for you to wield it safely. You must not touch the stone as you command it to drain the magic," the craftsman said, stroking his long beard as he thought. "Ah, yes, I have it!" He reached into one of the saddlebags and withdrew a long coil of rope that was tied all along its length with knots. The dwarf cut a short piece off and tied the Dragon's Tear so it could be dangled like a pendulum. "Lay the sword in the snow and hang the stone above it. Then simply command it to take the magic that it finds before it into itself."

Rangvald did as he was instructed. The entire tunnel brightened as the pale beam of light washed over the sword. A single fluttering shadow traveled up the shaft of light, and Rangvald could feel something inhabiting the giant sapphire which before had simply felt like a lifeless lump of stone. "It worked; I can feel it," he breathed as the pale light ceased.

"Indeed it did," Dvalinn agreed, lifting the sword. It was now a dull and dingy gray, where before it had been a gleaming silver. He slid it back into the wizard's scabbard. "You will find that it is still an excellent sword, although it will not allow its wielder to fight without ever tiring as it did before."

"Now what?" Rangvald asked, still holding the stone by its rope.

"I don't imagine that the magic from the sword will come anywhere near to equaling the power of the goddess, but it may be enough to make us an ice raft. If it does, then we still will have to decide if we want to use it."

"Why wouldn't we?" the wizard asked, confused.

"A couple of reasons that I can think of. What if you do produce a raft? Should we climb aboard and trust that it won't simply fall to pieces beneath us? What if it holds, and then just ahead in the dark we find that the river flows down into the ground and travels beneath the earth?"

Rangvald considered these scenarios for a few moments. "I will try it. I said before that I don't care if it's crazy—it's better that we try."

"That's what I was hoping you would say," Dvalinn laughed. "Give me one moment." He reached into the saddlebag once more and produced an iron hook, which he tied to the coil of rope. "All right, I'm ready when you are."

"No time like the present," Rangvald said, taking out his spellbook and finding the page for battle ice. "If this works, there will only be a matter of seconds from when the ice finishes issuing from my hand for us to make our final decision and either climb aboard or let the ice rush away in the current." Memorizing the words, he stowed the book, then crouched down and thrust one hand into the river. Holding up the dangling Dragon's Tear, he called upon the magic within and spoke the spell aloud.

As ice shot forth from his hand into the water, there was no hum of magic coursing through his chest, no blessing from the goddess filling his core, but still, he heeded the lesson taught to him by Val of Kattegat. He performed the spell with complete conviction. The surface of the river solidified into a sheet of ice in a circle, spreading out from his hand, becoming a raft just barely large enough for the three to fit on. In that brief moment that he had warned them would come, just as the magic ceased and the ice began to float away, they clearly saw that the raft was nothing to put confidence in. Nonetheless, without a word, all three clambered aboard and went whipping down the rolling river into the dark. Almost at once, the sheet of ice began to crack and fail beneath them, but they simply clung to one another and held on for dear life. After a few minutes, a gray circle of light appeared ahead, giving them a point in the darkness to yearn for. The circle grew larger as they hurtled down the river.

Emerging from beneath the tunneling roots of Yggdrasil, they found themselves in the frosty gray winter's twilight once again, surrounded on both sides by the frozen tundra of hard-packed snow. The raft of ice was falling apart at the edges. They began casting their eyes about, seeking a means of escape, but the banks were too far away and flying by far too rapidly. Rangvald screamed in fear when, without warning, they slammed to a halt and went tumbling forward off of the capsizing raft. They braced themselves for the inevitable splash of frigid water. Instead, they landed, bruised and battered, on the unforgiving surface of solid ice.

"The river is frozen solid here! We slammed right into it!" Rangvald moaned in a daze.

"Come, let's go along the bank," Dvalinn said, rising and making his way off the frozen river with Trufflesbane trotting behind.

"What's the point? We were finally making progress on the ice raft!" Rangvald lamented.

"Keep going!" the craftsman ordered. "We know it flows again; we've seen it."

Rangvald hurried to catch up. After just a few minutes of walking, the river turned and headed out to the west, or maybe it was the east. Just like his sense of time, his sense of direction was completely confused here.

"This is good even ground. Let's ride," Dvalinn said, mounting up. Rangvald climbed up behind him, and Trufflesbane took off, loping alongside the frozen waterway.

Rangvald held on tightly as they coursed ahead, squinting his eyes against the icy gusts, trying to see where they were going."What's that?" he shouted through the wind, pointing straight ahead at the wall of pitch-black they were swiftly approaching.

"Something I was hoping to avoid altogether," the craftsman shouted back.

Rangvald had noted on several occasions along the day's journey that the horizons were dark in every direction he had looked. It had appeared to be simply a product of the poor visibility in the gloomy, winter-like conditions, but now it appeared that they were riding straight for a wall of black. It reminded him of the realm of fire he had beheld on arrival. The blackness seemed to be obeying some type of invisible border.

When they finally reached it, Trufflesbane came to a stop before the wall of darkness and they dismounted. An uneasy vibration seemed to reach out from the dark, and all three of them shivered as one.

"Most of the Niflheim is like this. A drowning darkness where the goddess Hel buries souls to be forgotten forever," the craftsman explained.

"Do we have to go in there?" Rangvald asked, staring into the void and seeing nothing.

"Yes. Look, this is where the river starts to flow again," Dvalinn said, pointing to the spot where the river became unfrozen again. It was the exact place where the unwholesome vibration had begun to touch them. Rangvald watched as a chunk of ice broke free from the frozen sheet and rushed down the river, disappearing into the dark. "Is it safe?" Rangvald asked.

"Oh, goodness, no," Dvalinn said with a laugh. "Once we enter, I do not know if we will ever be permitted to leave."

Rangvald stood squinting at the impenetrable black for a few moments, then he laughed too. "Well, what are we waiting for?"

"That's the spirit!" the craftsman said jovially. "Now, let's make ourselves an ice raft big enough for three this time."

The dwarf directed Rangvald onto the iced river. Trufflesbane got on next, followed by the craftsman himself. Again, he reached into the saddlebags and pulled out the long length of rope bearing the iron hook affixed to its end.

"Why is it you are holding that when we ride the rafts?" Rangvald asked.

"The forest of the spiders with its many trees will be where I use this. It is just inside the gates. I must try to hook a tree to arrest our motion. If I miss, we will all be dead, for the river flows right out of the gates and into the fires of Muspell. Now both of you, get down low and hold on for dear life." With that, Dvalinn took a hammer and made a series of precise, chipping blows along the ice behind them. Then he quickly huddled next to Trufflesbane.

For a few moments, it seemed to Rangvald that the dwarf had left the job unfinished, but then, there was a sudden lurch forward, and in a blink, they were plunged into darkness. Rangvald opened and closed his eyes, trying to make them work, but all was black. He lifted his glow rod before his eyes. He could see it was glowing, but its light did not cast away from its surface. Even the fingers with which he held it were not illuminated. Just like in the chamber of the roaring cauldron, it seemed as if the laws of nature were being disregarded. The raft bumped and tossed along the water as they went, and he held onto Trufflesbane, feeling sick with terror. The wild ride would have been frightening in any circumstances, but to endure it in complete blindness was far worse.

A movement within the blackness caught the corner of his eye, and he turned his head, desperate to see if something was actually visible. Yes, something was there —some *things,* in fact. They were keeping pace alongside the raft, watching its occupants' progress, and he realized that he recognized them. They were the same little fireflies that had come bursting out of the Witch Queen's ghouls each time he had used his magic to destroy the dead bodies they inhabited. Just like his glow rod, they were not shining or twinkling the way they did outside the darkness. Here, they were more like moving, colored dots, but he knew them for what they were.

Looking around, he saw that they were surrounded by them to every side. He looked up and found that they were even hovering overhead. Then, all at once, the spirits flew away, and Rangvald felt the tingling vibration increase. He was still looking up as the spirits disappeared, and he saw what appeared to be a rainbow, high, high above. Then the ice raft came to a jarring halt. If it weren't for Trufflesbane's sturdy bulk, he would surely have been flung forward again and tumbled off into the darkness.

"What happened? Are we stuck on something?" he asked, but no one answered. Presently, he became aware of a strange odor, like that of decaying flesh mingled with roses. The wretched vibration pressed down on them from above, and he became aware of a presence. Rangvald's already-queasy stomach clenched as the thought of an eternity trapped in this darkness invaded his mind. Then, as quickly as it had come, the unseen presence was gone, and with a lurch, the raft passed from darkness into light. "What just happened?" Rangvald shouted in relief.

"Well, I'll be. She let us go," Dvalinn replied in surprise.

The raging river did not allow them a chance to rejoice their freedom from the dark for very long, as it now took a turn and began rushing down a fierce decline that eddied and churned furiously, trying to throw them off into the savage waters. The raft dropped out from under them as they hit an even steeper decline, and as they crashed back down, part of the ice on the craftsman's side cracked and fell away. Dvalinn was swiftly following it into the water when Trufflesbane caught him by the neck of his shirt of scales and hauled him back on. He had just settled back onto their narrowing raft when he shouted in a panic, "Hold your breath!"

A second later, the decline leveled off as they crossed the floor of the valley of slumber. Blindly, they rushed through the treacherous fog. Rangvald had not had sufficient time to take a deep breath, and his lungs were just reaching the point of bursting when, mercifully, they exited the valley and entered a gorge carved between the icy rocks. The river once again began to rise.

Another piece of ice broke away in front of them as they were tossed out into the open. Rangvald was still trying to catch his wind when Dvalinn got precariously to his knees on their dwindling ice raft. Rangvald looked up and saw that they had been traveling so quickly that they had already reached the forest of the spiders. The raft bucked beneath them as the craftsmen threw the iron hook. It failed to catch any trees. Rangvald realized that there would only be time for one more throw traveling at this pace. Then, just as the craftsmen had warned, they would be plunged into the realm of fire in mere moments. Dvalinn swiftly pulled back the hook and threw again. This time, the raft did not shift beneath him, and the hook caught a sturdy-looking tree. The raft spun around as he hauled on the rope, fighting the mighty current. A chunk of ice broke away from the rear, and Dvalinn pitched forward toward the water. Again, Trufflesbane grabbed his armored shirt in her tusks and held on.

"Get ready to jump!" the dwarf yelled, holding tightly to the rope as the current pushed Rangvald's side of the raft against the bank. "Go! Hurry!" Rangvald jumped, rolling onto the snow, his spellbook falling from his satchel and his sword sliding halfway out of its scabbard before he could arrest his momentum. He stowed his gear back in its place as Dvalinn shouted, "You, too, Trufflesbane, I've got it!"

Trufflesbane released his shirt and leaped for the shore. Rangvald watched helplessly as her shifting weight cracked the raft in half. As she touched down safely, the craftsmen disappeared beneath the raging waters. Trufflesbane rushed past Rangvald, nearly trampling him in her haste, and grabbed the knotted rope in her jaws. Moving back step by step, she pulled the rope up from the water. After a few moments, the craftsmen came flopping up to the surface, the coppery scales of his armor making him look like a strange fish had been caught. Rangvald jumped up and ran to the riverbank, grabbed the dwarf, and fell backward, dragging him up onto dry land.

The craftsman with ice crystals forming in his wet beard sprang up at once, wasting no time. "We are almost there; let's go," he said, grabbing the hook and rope and starting towards the gate.

Rangvald stood up and looked at the dwarf, then pure reflex took over. He read the runes on his vambrace and cast a fireball directly above the craftsman. His magic was far less powerful than it had been with the kiss of Hefring or when he had called upon the Dragon's Tear, but it was still more than potent enough to blast the giant spider that was flying, fangs drawn, onto the craftsman from behind.

"Run!" Dvalinn yelled, glancing back and seeing the army of arachnids in the distance following behind the first attacker.

In a sprint, they passed the trees. They were only a hundred paces from the tumbled-down wall which marked the boundary of the realm.

"Rangvald, get the apple out; we won't have much time once we are outside," Dvalinn called. Rangvald opened his satchel while he ran and reached for the apple. He stumbled to a halt, then turned and, looking back, saw exactly what he knew he would. There on the bank of the river where he had sprawled when jumping from the raft, the bright red apple peeked out of the dingy snow. He ran toward it. "The apple! It fell out!"

A second later, a blur of reddish fur passed him. *You go. I will get it,* Trufflesbane thought to him as she thundered back toward the approaching spiders.

"Come! Only she is fast enough," Dvalinn said, dragging the young wizard over the crumbled wall.

"I'm so sorry! It fell out when I leaped from the raft!" Rangvald cried.

"It's all right," the dwarf said soothingly.

Trufflesbane smashed through the spiders just as she had done before and came to a halt at the apple. Scooping it up, she turned to start back, but then squealed in anguish as a spider landed on her back and sunk its venomous fangs into her flesh. With a massive buck, she sent it tumbling, then ran drunkenly with the screeching monsters hot on her heels.

"Get ready to run," the craftsman said, pushing Rangvald back from the wall. A few moments later, Trufflesbane leaped over it, a thousand furry bodies in pursuit. She bit the apple, then tossed her head, throwing the rest of it through the air. An instant later, she was covered in a blanket of spiders. Dvalinn plucked the flying apple from the air. "Run!"

Rangvald saw him bite the apple as well then toss it his way before he, too, was buried by spiders. Rangvald ran as fast as he could. Biting into the apple, he felt the poisoned fangs stabbing into his back again and again.

◆ ◆ ◆

Rangvald screamed and writhed with pain.

"Rangvald. Rangvald, stop," Idunn said, laying her hands on his back and holding him still. Rangvald rolled over slowly and found himself back in the cottage. He looked from Idunn to the craftsman and Trufflesbane, who were getting up from the floor.

"But the spiders?" he asked in confusion.

"Look in your hand, Rangvald," Dvalinn said.

Rangvald lifted his hand and found the apple, which was little more than a core now. "The apples of Idunn. They grant the gods their health and their long lives," he said, understanding.

"That's right. Now give me the tear; there isn't any time to lose!" Dvalinn said, reaching out a hand. Rangvald scrambled to his feet, and fishing out the rope and stone, placed it in the dwarf's hand.

"Come, everyone. To the workshop. I have something I can mount the stone to. It will take but a moment, and it will allow you to safely wield it," the craftsman said, striding out the cottage door into the hallway beyond.

"Walk with me, Rangvald," Idunn said, linking arms as they followed quickly behind her brother. "Before you left, I told you that our destinies were intertwined, and that if you returned, I would ask something of you."

"Yes, I remember."

"What I ask of you is this. That you go and teach wizardry at the same school that you studied at. And while there that you do me a favor."

"I am a bit young to be a teacher," Rangvald told her.

"Oh, you needn't go now. The favor I ask will not be needed for another two hundred and seventy-four winters."

"What? It is true that wizards often live very long lives. But I have already reached twenty-five. I will be nearly three hundred years old by then. Wizards don't live that long!"

"Wizards who have eaten twice of the apples of the gods do," she replied.

"Oh. Oh, yes, I see. What is it that you wish me to do for you?"

"Simply this. There will one day be a boy who comes to learn from you the art of wizardry. The ravens of Odin will come and perch upon his windowsill and sing a dream into his mind as he sleeps, just as they did to you when you were in your bed not even a week ago. He will be frightened to heed these visions, just as you were, and he will need someone to guide him to his destiny. You will be that someone for him."

"How will I know him? Will he be the strongest wizard I ever teach?"

Idunn shook her head. "No, he will be the weakest. Even his body will be twisted and feeble. But his heart will be the purest. They will call him Asmund."

"I will do as you ask," Rangvald said softly.

"I have a favor I would ask of you as well," the craftsman said as they entered the workshop and found him already hunched over a workbench, preparing the Dragon's Tear.

"What is it?" Rangvald asked.

"The sword that you wear, the one that saved us with its magic. The sword that was forged for Alver the Just, who passed it to Voll Ironfist, who lost it to Halder Helmbreaker. It is named Scattersoul, and it was forged by our father Ivaldi."

"Say no more," Rangvald said, pulling sword and scabbard free from his belt and stepping forward. "It was given to me by the goddess Hefring, daughter of Ran. She told me it would serve me well, and it has."

The craftsman nodded and, bending once more to his work, finished his task. "There. It's not a perfect fit, but it will suffice." He presented Rangvald with a black metal bar terminating in what looked like a rendering of a human hand, the cold iron fingers of which he had bent to hold the Dragon's Tear. They exchanged weapons, and the craftsman said, “Now go as fast as you can.”

“How do I get back?”

“Go to the wall. You will find that the opening is there again.”

“Wait, take this,” Idunn said, holding out the rope and hook which had saved them in the Niflheim.

Rangvald accepted it without question, then ran across the workshop and slipped through the opening into the kingdom of Vestmor.

CHAPTER SIXTEEN

"All right now, lift him up. That's it, turn him like he is searching the horizon. Now pull him down quickly, as if he were afraid to be seen for too long," Eirik said.

Revna stood watching the grotesque puppetry as her brother directed his two remaining warriors to hoist the body of the archer she had killed using the Hand of Fate up above the wall. They had dressed him in Eirik's helmet and shirt of mail to look the part.

"Now push him up again over here. Yes, that's it." When nothing happened, he ordered them to bring him down. "Well, it seems like all of the archers took part in the doomed raid. Either that or they are simply not falling for our little ruse," Eirik declared, taking his helmet off of the dead man.

"Can I borrow that?" one of the five remaining elderly volunteers, the last man of the group asked, reaching out for the helmet. Eirik handed it to him. Putting it on, the old man struggled up onto the fragment of statue and stood looking out over the wall, fully exposed. When no arrows came, he carefully climbed back down and handed the helmet back. "There are no more archers, My King."

"Thank you, grandfather," Eirik replied with respect.

"So what do we do with this information?" Revna asked.

"We could flee," Leif suggested.

Eirik looked back at the people who were filling the great hall. They were milling around, getting some fresh air and light before night fell and they were again forced to retreat to the deeper chambers. With no battle having been waged the night before and the magic bread filling their stomachs, they seemed in slightly better spirits, but Eirik suspected that could not last for long. "No, we cannot flee, Leif. We have over five hundred women children, and what's left of our elders, the ones who were too weak to fight and die. The walkway is buried, and we have but one rope fashioned from harness leather."

Revna nodded her agreement. "Even if they could reach the ground safely, where would we go? We set the horses and oxen free so they could graze, and the wagons are only a memory now. It will be night in another hour, then the Witch Queen will make her return. She would love to find us out in the darkness on foot."

"So the archers being gone doesn't help us much at all," Leif said dejectedly.

Eirik thought for a moment. "Well, when the witch returns with her army, they will still need to scale the wall with ladders or throw some grappling lines. If we are not in danger from the archers, we can push their ladders down and cut the ropes."

"What if they have another siege engine?" Leif countered.

"I don't believe they will. But if they do, they have to funnel up a few at a time. That means our small force can hold them."

Leif looked around at the tiny band of defenders. "Do you really think that ten of us—"

"It doesn't matter," Eirik said, cutting him off. "Every time we fought her, it should have been our last. But every time, she has been driven back. We will fight her again, and if it really is the end, then so be it. Every one of us must die some time. We will die fighting for those we love."

Taking heart, Leif stood up straighter and nodded. "If they do have a siege engine, I could perhaps light it with flaming arrows," he suggested.

"They soaked the last one with water in anticipation of that tactic," Eirik said dismissively.

"We have some lanterns still with oil in them. Many a house has met its end from a broken lantern," Revna said.

"Yes, that's true!" Eirik agreed.

"If there is no siege engine, we can throw the lanterns down on the dead warriors and burn them up," Leif said excitedly, garnering nods all around.

"There are the stone tables and stools left by the dwarfs. We could throw them down and crush the warriors below," Revna added.

"They certainly would crush them. They are very heavy. A little too heavy, unfortunately. I don't believe we could get them up and over the wall of the landing." Eirik told her. After a moment of thought, he added, "That doesn't mean they can't be useful, however. Anything that can be moved, we will drag into the doorway leading to the water basin and the chambers beyond. If we cannot fight them at the landing any longer, we will fall back behind the barricade there. There won't be enough to block the path completely, but it will slow them down while we make our stand." Without hesitation, he hurried to the stone table across the room and grabbed an edge as others joined him. "Come, Revna, lend us a hand."

"But I'm just a—" She stopped mid-sentence and corrected herself. "I forgot, I'm not such a little girl now," she said with a laugh and hurried over.

It took nearly two hours, but they moved everything they could budge into the entranceway connecting the great hall to the deeper chambers.

"This will slow them down," Eirik said, jabbing a spear over the top of the makeshift barrier experimentally. "Stab out their eyes if you are able. They can't attack what they can't see."

"If there are enough of them, they will push this aside," Leif said, patting one of the blocky stone stools.

"If we are still alive when the barricade falls, then we defend the three rooms as long as we can," Eirik replied.

The young king looked at the weary faces around him and knew that he should say something to give them heart. He tried to think of something his father or Amazigh would say, but nothing came. He considered drawing his sword, holding it aloft and shouting something, anything, but he knew it would seem false and do more harm than good. Instead, he knelt and began to pray.

Hail to the day!
Hail to the sons of day!

Hail night and her sister!

With kind eyes look upon us here and bring us victory!

Hail the gods!

Hail the goddesses!

Hail the fertile earth!

If you will not bring us victory, then remember us! Remember the way we lived! The way we died!

When he rose, the faces around him no longer wore the same weariness. "Luck in battle, warriors of Vestmor," he said, then turned and strode toward the landing.

Falling in behind the king, the ten defenders followed him. "Luck in battle, Princess Revna," Leif said.

"I love you too," she replied.

They had gone a few more strides when he froze in his tracks. "Wait, what did you say?"

Turning back, she laughed. "I said I love you too."

"Oh," he said, thunderstruck, which caused her to laugh again.

"Come on now," she said, holding out a hand, and they hurried to catch up.

◆ ◆ ◆

The hours passed slowly by while they kept watch, seeing no sign of the enemy. "Perhaps there will be no attack again tonight," Leif said hopefully.

"You may be right," Revna agreed. "She may still be hunting the deer herders. They do not build towns as we do. They tend to move their encampments around following the food."

"Do not get your hopes up yet," Eirik cautioned. "It may be that she is traveling toward us right now and simply has not arrived yet."

"Yes, it wouldn't be wise to let our guard down, but

I still think that we may not see her tonight," Revna argued. "We don't know how long it takes her to perform her necromancy, and it seems reasonable to think that she will need to build long ladders or find ropes to scale the wall. All of that will take time."

"That is true," Eirik said, swayed by her arguments. "Maybe she won't attack tonight."

"Wizard!" The Witch Queen screamed from the darkness outside, instantly contradicting him. "Wizard, come out and face me!"

Leif, Revna, and Eirik crowded onto the statue fragment and looked out into the darkness. What they saw there defied all expectation. There was no sign of the queen and her army of the dead. Instead, they saw a giant, standing fifty or sixty feet tall, its outline clearly visible in the moonlight.

"Does she command the body of a dead giant?" Eirik asked Revna in shock. Before she could muster her wits to answer, the witch screamed again.

"Where are you, Rangvald of the Oaken Stump? I am ready for you to come and do battle with me!"

Revna drew Deathwhisper and commanded its blade to glow. The three gave a collective gasp as the true nature of the giant was revealed.

"It's horrible!" Revna cried, staring at the hundreds of bodies whose limbs were intertwining to form the body of the giant. At the center of its chest was the wretched pale queen herself, being held by the hands of the possessed corpses she controlled while her own hands held out the glowing stone set in her gnarled scepter.

"My stone protects my body. This is my body, all connected as one with my dark magics. Come out and try to hurt me, Rangvald," the Queen taunted.

"She is immune to the magic of wizards, but what about the magic of the gods? Eirik, hold my sword," Revna said, relinquishing the blade so she could reach into her purse and withdraw the Hand of Fate.

"I grow impatient, Wizard," the queen crowed. "Is that you with the glowing blade, you coward?" The giant stepped forward, and Leif and Eirik realized that what they had thought was a safe distance was but a single stride for the huge legs of the corpse giant.

"Run for the barricade!" Eirik screamed. Revna, who had been looking down into her bag and had not seen the danger, was gathered up into Leif's arms. He leaped down and ran, racing the giant arm that was reaching into the cave after them. He didn't stop until they had reached the stone tables. Turning around, they saw the arm withdrawing, now engulfed in flames as the four remaining grandmothers were throwing the last of the lanterns into it. When the burning arm disappeared back outside, the women turned and ran as fast as their aging bodies would allow. But then the second arm quickly entered in place of the burning one and swept them away like ants before rushing back towards the barricade.

"No!" Leif screamed as the women were crushed and broken. Revna grabbed his shoulder, and together they scrambled over the barricade and joined the other survivors.

The queen's voice called out, "Where are you, Wizard?"

"Look, she can't reach us!" Revna exclaimed, seeing the arm come up short. The grotesque amalgam of clinging bodies appeared to be trying to stretch itself in their direction.

The giant's body hunched forward, and the witch's face peered in at them. "I see you hiding back there. Come out and face me!"

Leif moved as fast as he could, leaping up onto the barricade and loosing an arrow at the queen. The giant's other hand shot up into the arrow's path still smoldering from the flames which had engulfed it. Leif crouched down, trying to get another shot, and saw the many hands of the corpses passing the queen's body down the front of the giant torso and out of sight. When she spoke again, her voice came from somewhere out in the night. "You will pay for your audacity," she wailed.

"Move, Leif," Revna shouted. As he jumped back down, the Hand of Fate came up in her hand. Pointing at the giant arm, she spoke the words. One of the bodies went limp and hung from the arm, still entwined by one of its legs, and a little red spark exited the corpse and went flying out of the cave. The princess pointed the hand to repeat the process, but then half of the arm fell apart.

"What happened?" Leif yelled.

"Get ready! They're coming!" Eirik shouted as the fallen bodies began to disentangle themselves and stand up. "Keep them from getting to Revna. She is our only chance!"

The dead began arriving in ones and twos and threes. Revna moved the Hand of Fate back and forth, her lips murmuring ceaselessly, and a pile of bodies began to form in front of them. As warriors began to arrive en masse, her five remaining companions fought with all of their might, knocking them back while she dispatched them. A torrent of tiny spirit lights poured from the mouth of the Nordhule and whizzed away to the north with a chorus of hollow screams.

Sweat poured down Revna's brow as she banished the wretched souls to Hel. When there were no more warriors attacking the barricade, she pointed the hand at the body of the giant and continued her work, causing another eight or ten bodies to fall away from the torso.

Again, they heard the Witch Queen's voice screaming in rage from the darkness. The giant backed off from the cave and moved away.

"Is that it? Did we defeat her?" Leif asked excitedly.

Eirik surveyed the carnage, then shook his head. "I think Revna killed maybe sixty men. There are hundreds more in that giant. She is probably just changing tactics." As if to confirm his suspicion, a loud crash came from outside the cave.

"What was that?" Revna asked, startled.

"I do not know," Eirik replied, crawling over the tables and heading cautiously to the entrance with the other defenders trailing behind him. Standing on the fragment of statuary, he lifted Revna's glowing sword and peered out into the night, seeing nothing. Then, off to his left, he heard a loud scrape, followed by a rumble and then a crash. "The giant is clearing the broken statues from the walkway!" he shouted.

Revna scrambled up beside him, but she could not see past the massive broken head of the dwarf statue. "Help me onto the wall," she yelled, and Eirik boosted her up. Standing up, she saw the giant moving a chunk of granite. She instantly went to work on the longer of its two arms, pointing the Hand of Fate and whispering as fast as she could. She again caused a torrent of souls to go screaming to the north.

Suddenly, she froze, and looking down at Leif and

her brother, she said, "Do not grieve. I chose this end."

Eirik and Leif watched helplessly as the pale light with a legion of fluttering moth wings in it reduced her to a withered husk that fell lifeless into the dark beyond.

The Witch Queen's evil cackle rang out in the dark. Eirik stood immobilized in shock as the image of his sister's wasted face, falling into darkness, etched itself forever into his memory.

With an anguished howl, Leif knocked the king aside, then leaped to the spot Revna had been only a moment before. His keen huntsman's ears tracked the sound of laughing, and his sharp eye caught a hint of moonlight glinting off a purple stone. The queen's laughter became a scream of agony as Leif's arrow pierced her shoulder.

The giant reached her in two strides and, lifting her from the ground, began to carry her from the field. Leif fired again and again, trying to finish her off, but the giant cradled her to its chest and turned away, causing Leif's arrows to lodge harmlessly in its back. Leif began to scream his rage and frustration, but he fell silent as the wizard Rangvald appeared beside him on the wall, affixed a hook, and descended a rope to the ground below.

◆ ◆ ◆

Rangvald raced across the field as fast as he could with his eyes fixed to the back of the fleeing giant. In the space of a minute, it had become little more than a faint outline in the distance. After a minute more, it was gone. Every one of the giant's strides was so long and carried it so far that he knew he could never catch up. As he ran on through the dark his breathing came in massive gusts, his sides were splitting with pain, and sweat stung his eyes, but he kept going. "Not again!" he wailed. "She always escapes!"

Rangvald went on until his heart was nearly bursting and he could hardly breathe. Finally, he stopped running. He knew that it was useless. "No!" he panted in despair. Then he fell silent. Now that he was quiet, he could hear something pounding up behind him in the dark. Spinning around, he lifted the glowing rod tied around his neck, expecting to see the giant bursting from some hiding place he had blundered past. What he saw instead was an even bigger surprise.

"Plowbreaker!" he shouted with joy.

All of the other horses went away, but I stayed. I didn't want to leave you! Plowbreaker thought to him. *Now climb up and hold on with all of your might.*

"Thank you, Plowbreaker. I am so glad to see you!" Rangvald said, mounting and holding the glowing rod up as Plowbreaker took off at a speed that would threaten to throw him even if there had been a saddle and reigns, but somehow, he clung on. Speeding through the night, he was certain that some unseen obstacle hiding in the gloom would trip them and send them sprawling, but Plowbreaker's steps were true, and in only a few minutes, the back of the giant came back into view.

"Turn and face us!" Rangvald bellowed as they drew near.

The witch was startled at the sound of his voice, and the hundreds of ghouls making up the giant received mixed signals, some stepping forward while others tried to turn and look. The queen was thrown free and landed sprawling on hands and knees as the giant came crashing down.

Plowbreaker galloped past and, digging in his hind legs, skidded to a halt. Rangvald dismounted and pulled the wand holding the Dragon's Tear from his belt.

"You!" the queen screeched, standing up. Then her eyes fell on what he held. "No! No! It isn't possible!" She tried to point her own wand, but Rangvald was quicker. The pale light leaped from his stone as he commanded it to drain the magic that it found before it. His light had no tiny wings fluttering within. It was simply pure light. The witch thrust her staff forward, and to Rangvald's surprise, his shaft of light affixed, not to her, but to the Dragon's Tear that topped her wand.

Now his beam danced with fluttering, ghostly moths. As soon as it ceased, he could feel them, the magical souls of wizards trapped within the sapphire tear. It brought with it a spike of profound sorrow as he realized there were hundreds of them. In this moment of distraction, Rangvald did not see the giant rise to its knees, lift the longer of its two arms high above its head and bring it crashing down towards him.

He only lifted his eyes as a golden-colored streak flew past him on thundering hooves. He watched as Plowbreaker slammed into the center of the giant with his head down like a battering ram. Everything seemed to happen at once after that. The giant fell to pieces, the bodies of the entwined ghouls smashed apart as Plowbreaker's neck snapped like thunder and he fell and lay motionless among them.

The wizard and the queen rushed forward, both of them pointing their Dragon's Tears at the other, and both reflexively grabbing the other's weapon and holding it away from themselves. The Witch Queen tugged at Rangvald's staff and was shocked by how easily she pulled it from his grasp, almost as if he had simply let go. This thought barely had time to form in her mind before he reached in and, grasping the broken shaft of the arrow jutting from her shoulder, pulled it free with a searing jolt of pain. Both scepters fell from her hands as he plunged the arrowhead back into her once, twice, and a third time.

"Why?" he wept as she fell to the ground and looked up at him in shock. "You killed everyone!" he wailed. "Farmers and women and children! Why? What reason could you possibly have for being so evil?"

The queen laughed wetly as blood gurgled from her lips. "We are what we are... All of us," she replied.

"You're filth. That's what you are," Rangvald spat, reaching down and picking up his wand. As he straightened, his ears were assailed by a myriad of tiny screams, and his face was covered in a swarm of tiny fireflies, all different colors, clustering in his face, dazzling his vision and rendering him blind. "No, not this time!" he shouted, breaking into a run and leaving the tiny spirits scrambling to catch up to blind him once more.

He saw her ahead. She had almost made it to the cover of the trees when he aimed and the fluttering light engulfed her from behind. "No, please," she screamed in terror. Then she shriveled away and died. Instantly, the spirits she had been marshaling to attack him fluttered away, and he felt her presence in the stone. Her massive power over the dead was locked away now within the prison of the Dragon's Tear.

Still weeping, Rangvald staggered away, searching for Plowbreaker's corpse. He was determined to do nothing but lie down next to him and never move again. All around him, the tiny spirit lights were leaving the bodies of the dead, no longer under the command of the queen. They lingered for a few moments, then floated off to the dark corners of the world they had come from. Kneeling down beside his friend, he cried, "Oh Plowbreaker."

Yes Rangvald? Plowbreaker replied.

You're alive! Rangvald thought back in shock. *Are you in pain?*

I feel nothing. But I can't move, Rangvald, and I can barely breathe.

The wizard watched the horse's side and could detect only short, shallow movement there. *Your bones are so big and your body so different from mine—I don't think I could ever be strong enough to heal you. The blessing of the goddess is gone. I'm not powerful now,* Rangvald thought to him as fresh tears ran down his face.

That's all right. I was the best horse I knew how to be. Now it's time to go.

"No!" Rangvald cried, taking out his book and reading the spell. He laid his hands on Plowbreaker's neck, but nothing happened. "I don't have the power! I traded it for the Dragon's Tear, and in the end, the wounds of the arrowhead probably would have done for her. I didn't even need the worthless Dragon's Tear," he sobbed.

Quiet, Rangvald. You did it. You saved the women and children. Now say goodbye. I must go, Plowbreaker said, his thoughts sounding fainter in Rangvald's head.

You're right. I'm sorry I couldn't save you. I'm sorry I traded my power for this worthless... Rangvald stood up suddenly. "The Dragon's Tear!" he shouted, lifting the wand and staring into the stone. "I feel you, my brothers and sisters! I feel your power bound within. I feel you, wretched queen, and your command of the dead. I call upon your powers. Lend me your essence!" The stone began to glow brightly. Rangvald turned in a circle, seeing now with a second vision. Looking out into the darkness, he called, "I see you. Those who still linger nearby, watching and mourning your fallen queen. You will heed my voice now as you heeded hers."

Rangvald lifted the glowing sapphire on high, and tendrils of light reached out and snared the ghostly lights that huddled in the darkness and brought them back to him. At his command, they shot into the corpses lying around Plowbreaker, and slowly, they began to stand. "What is your bidding, master?" one of the ghouls asked.

Rangvald did not need to speak his desires aloud. He simply thought it, directing them with his mind as the witch had done. Again, the bodies of the dead entwined, just as they had when forming the giant. Some of their hands rested on Plowbreaker's neck, while others clung to Rangvald himself. He joined in an unnatural communion with the dead, and together, they became one. He picked up his spellbook. "Hear me, oh prisoners of the stone, be you wizards of light or wizards of darkness. I call upon your powers!" Then he thrust the glowing gem toward the sky and read the spell. The night winds swirled around him as one by one, the spines of the ghouls cracked in half, and their nerves and tendons popped and split, causing the bodies to contort in a gruesome dance of ruin.

Plowbreaker gulped in air with a deep, full breath and lurched to his hooves, then lifted his head and whinnied at the sky. Rangvald ran to him and hugged him tightly, never wanting to let go.

"We will need new bodies if we are to serve you, master," the same ghoulish voice as before spoke. Rangvald looked at them lying now at unnatural angles with arms and legs still clinging to one another. "No. There will be no more possessing the dead for you. You may go now. I release you."

Instantly the corpses' mouths yawned, expelling the colored motes of light, and he saw them flee into the night. This time, none of them stopped and lingered nearby.

He regarded the glowing stone. "You may also go. I break this prison and set you free!" he yelled, holding the staff above his head. One last time, the pale beam of light shot out from the Dragon's Tear, filled with its fluttering torrent. The beam continued for a moment more after all the shadowy wings had left it, and again, the light was clean and pure, stretching up into the night sky. Then at last it was gone.

CHAPTER SEVENTEEN

Revna opened her eyes and saw a clear, cloudless sky above her. Sitting up, she found herself surrounded by a strange assembly of ghostly forms. They were standing or sitting or lying in different positions. Looking down at her own legs, she found the same ghostly, translucent appearance she observed in the people around her. But as she watched, she saw and felt herself becoming solid.

"Princess, is that you?"

Revna turned her head and watched her elderly teacher, Val of Kattegat, also finishing the process of becoming corporeal.

"Yes, it's me," she answered, getting up and embracing him.

"Master!" a voice cried, and they turned to see Val's

apprentice Ulfhild rushing up and joining their embrace.

"My, you've grown, Princess," Ulfhild said once they separated.

"Have I?" Revna looked down at her hands. "Yes, I think that happened today," she said, then frowned at how strange her own words sounded.

"Where are we?" Val asked, looking around.

"Look, there are other wizards here," Ulfhild said, pointing at some of the other people who had just become solid as well. Revna and Val looked around and instantly agreed with her assessment. Many wore garments they recognized as wizards' robes, and others, whose dress was strange to them, wore clothing adorned with magical symbols of various types. Most of these wizards were walking toward a massive gate that was guarded by a hound of exaggerated size who was dripping with blood. The trio found that they, too, had started walking in that direction, though none of them remembered deciding to do so.

"I know where we are!" Val declared. "This is where we enter to take the road to the afterlife. Either to Hel or the realms of Asgard, depending on how we died. That is Garmr, the guardian of the land of the dead."

"I believe I will go to sit by the side of Freya or Odin. I believe I remember falling in battle with King Gorm near the western shores," Ulfhild said.

"Yes, I think I fell in battle too. On the western road with the new king," Val of Kattegat said.

"I fell at the Nordhule, defending the mothers and children," Revna added. "How is it, then, that we wake here in the afterlife on the same day, when we died at different times?" Revna asked.

"You were imprisoned by Asling of the Bog," the

giant dog's voice rumbled in reply, causing all of the wizards to stop and stare in wonder.

"The Witch Queen of Pretania imprisoned our souls with her magic stone, didn't she?" Val said, seizing the scrap of a memory.

"That's right," the Hound of Hel confirmed. "Your magical souls were harnessed inside a prison formed when the blood of Yggdrasil was made solid inside the very body of evil itself. With it, her humble necromancy grew strong enough to control thousands of the dead. She has been roaming around collecting your souls for a very long time. Some of you wizards have stood as shadows in this field for hundreds of years, unable to enter through these gates until this very day."

"How is it that we were finally freed?" Revna asked.

"Why don't you ask your jailer yourself, Princess Revna?" the dog's deep voice rumbled in reply, then lifted its dripping head and looked toward the back of the crowd of wizards. Everyone turned and, following his gaze, beheld the Witch Queen herself. She stood defiantly, hands on her hips and chin held high. She had all the bearing of a queen, but now, without her army, without her iron litter festooned with shriveled wizards' heads, she cut a pitiful figure. She was nothing more than a thin, grubby slip of a woman.

"Why don't you explain to them how they came to be free?" Garmr urged.

"Rangvald Gunderson, the Wizard of the Oaken Stump, slew me, and instead of keeping the power of nearly three hundred enslaved wizards for himself, as anyone else would do, he released them."

"Do you know why he did this, Asling?" Garmr asked.

The Witch Queen seemed to consider it for a few moments, then nodded. "Yes. It is the last thing I told him before I died. It is because we are who we are. All of us. Is that what you wanted to hear?"

Garmr nodded his huge gore-stained head once.

"Why am I here? Why am I not in Tir Fo Thuinn with my ancestors?" she demanded.

"Because the king and queen of Asgard will it otherwise," Garmr replied, rising and walking through the assembly toward her.

"I am the Witch Queen of Pretania, and I order you —"

"Tell that to the serpent Nidhug as it sucks the flesh from your bones every day until I call forth Ragnarok," Garmr growled, cutting her off.

The witch was poised to launch some new protest, but before she could, the dog's massive jowls snapped, picking her up like a discarded shoe. She hung limply as he turned, entered the gates, and carried her to the blackest pit of the underworld.

As soon they were gone from view, the wizards started forward again, walking with a vague purpose, knowing they had somewhere to be. Some were destined for the ocean ruled over by Queen Ran. Others were off to proclaim themselves at the foot of the Bifrost and be admitted to Odin's table. Almost without noticing, Revna, Val, and Ulfhild joined a contingency of fellow wizards, left the road, and made their way through a veil of mists, emerging at the other side on a green sunlit field that stretched on forever.

Revna smiled at Val and he laughed for joy. She knew him, even though she had never seen him with long, dark braids cascading over broad shoulders before.

All around her, several of their companions had been transformed and were also laughing for joy.

Across the field, parties were coming out to meet them, and wizards rushed ahead to have their reunions. Straight ahead, a royal band was led by Revna's parents and grandparents, the Kings and Queens of Vestmor. Behind them, she saw Signe, Trygve, Halfdan, and all those who had fought and died at her side to save those they loved. Revna recognized them all, even though they had grown young once more. She saw no sign of Amazigh, the giant man with the beautiful brown skin, but she knew without having to ask that his spirit was even now watching over the deserts of his birth.

"Hail to the heroes of Vestmor!" Signe called, and the host cheered as the newcomers embraced everyone and were embraced in return.

"Come, let us feast!" declared King Gorm, and another cheer rang out.

Then, as they were turning to go, a thing which had never happened here before occurred. From behind them in the mists there blew a strange wind. It was both sweet and foul, as if it carried the mingling of roses and rotting flesh.

As one, the fallen of Vestmor turned, and at the edge of the barrier, where the mists grew thin they beheld a giantess striding toward them—a giantess who was divided down her center. One half was flush and blooming with youth, while the other was dead and decaying.

In the twinkling before the giant stepped from the mist, it vanished, and in its place, out stepped a little girl cloaked all in black. As she was approaching, she became a young woman, then further on, a woman of middle-age. When she arrived before them, she had become a crone, bent with age.

"To what do we owe the honor of your visit, granddaughter?"

The assembly turned to see who had spoken and watched Freya, queen of the gods, girded in her gleaming armor, step down from her chariot, which had appeared seemingly from nowhere.

"I have come for Revna, the Princess of Vestmor," the figure answered, now a little girl once more.

"But you are mistaken, my dear. Revna has fallen in battle. Odin and I share the souls of those who die in battle, but I have the right of first choosing. The land of Vestmor is dear to me, and its warriors come here to Folkvang. They dine with me at my table in Sessrumnir. What makes you believe that she would belong to you in Helheim, where those who die not in battle dwell?"

"I would not change where she dwells, only when," the strange figure said, transforming into a young woman again.

"I see. This, I will allow. But it is not for me or you to decide. Revna must say for herself," Freya decreed.

"I do not understand," Revna said. "This is where I belong; with those I love! I have never felt happiness such as this before!"

"Just hear me, child," the cloaked figure said as her visage shifted and her voice changed yet again. "I am the goddess Hel. You used my gift, the Hand of Fate. Each time you spoke the words, you were not speaking a simple spell of magic where you aligned the forces of nature to your will. You were speaking a prayer directly to me, asking me to accept each errant soul you found in your way. The first time you prayed to me, you became my adherent. With each new prayer, you grew higher in my priesthood and higher in my esteem. You were performing great deeds on my behalf. Of all the wizards who have possessed my gift, you have stopped the most lost souls from wreaking havoc in the land of the living and banished them to their rightful place. You have helped me, and I have returned the favor, even when you did not know I was doing it. It was I who allowed your companion Rangvald to pass through the darkest abyss of Nifl with the Tear of the Dragon, a place where none may pass, so that he could return and vanquish your nemesis. You are my greatest servant."

"Is that why you want me to join you in Helheim?"

"That is not what I desire. Just as Freya has said, you have died a warrior's death, and here among your brave ancestors, you have taken your rightful place. I have come to offer you a different bargain. Will you hear it?"

◆ ◆ ◆

Leif sat weeping at the foot of the wall, cradling the husk that had been Revna in his arms.

"Dry your tears, Leif. She asked us not to mourn," Eirik said, kneeling beside him.

"I am sorry, but I am not like you or Revna, My King. I cannot be strong all the time," Leif wept.

"I understand," the king said, placing his hand on the younger boy's shoulder. Then, at the snapping of a twig somewhere in the dark, Eirik was up, sword in hand, searching for danger. He relaxed as Plowbreaker emerged from the shadows and plodded forward.

Wearily, Rangvald threw the withered head of the Witch Queen. It landed at Eirik's feet. The young king looked at it, but he felt no triumph, no hint of vengeance fulfilled. She was simply dead, and now hundreds of women and children were safe in the caves behind him.

Rangvald dismounted, and they both stood looking down into her vacant face. "She's the only person I've ever killed," Rangvald said. "I swept the dead warriors from the field with my magic, but she was the only living person. I don't like it. I never want to do it again."

"You did what you had to. We all did," Eirik said, looking down at his sword, then letting it drop from his fingers. "It is done. Now I can let myself cry." He turned and walked back to Leif.

The wizard and the warrior king knelt down beside the huntsman, and their tears fell freely over the body of the dead princess.

"I thought I told you not to grieve for me," Revna said, opening her eyes.

"Princess!" Leif cried, hugging her to his chest tightly, while Eirik kissed her hand and cried even harder.

"How?" was the only word Rangvald could manage.

Once Leif was no longer smothering her in his arms and she could speak, she explained. "The queen of death has sent me back. But it must be my lifelong vocation to seek out and banish the lost souls who wander where they do not belong."

"It is a worthy occupation, Princess," Rangvald replied.

"One that I am not yet equipped for. My wizard's training is far from complete, Master Rangvald."

"Master?" he repeated in surprise. Then he remembered his oath to the goddess Idunn. "Yes, it is, in fact, my destiny to be a teacher of wizards. And it would be an honor if you would be my first student. But first, I must take some time and visit the sea," he said, closing his eyes. "There is someone waiting for me there. I can feel it."

"Sister, you must have been overjoyed when you learned you could come back," Eirik laughed, wiping tears with the back of his hands.

"Oh, no, brother. You do not understand. I did not want to. I could never describe to you the feeling of joy and contentment I felt there. At first, I refused. I did not think that anything in all the world could make me return. But then I remembered, and something stronger drew me back here."

"What was it?" Leif asked, still cradling her in his arms. In reply, Revna reached up drew his face closer, and kissed him with a love that had defied eternity.

◆ ◆ ◆

Thank you for reading *The Wizard and the Warrior King*, the second book in *The Nordheim Sagas*. Will you take a moment to leave a review? Word of mouth plays a huge role in a book's success, and you can help with just a sentence or two.

- Review on Amazon -

Thank you so much!

Joel Newlon

The Immortal Trilogy

Meet Mike. He's just a regular guy trying to make his way in the world. The only difference is, he's been doing it for five hundred years.

Well, that, and he has a habit of killing every murderer, rapist, and child molester that crosses his path.

- See *The Immortal* on Amazon -

ACKNOWLEDGEMENTS

To the staff of Silver Eel Publishing, I am eternally indebted, especially to Ashleigh and Michelle for editing and proofreading and everything else it takes to turn a manuscript into a novel.

Special thanks to Kevin, the artist in Brazil who did an amazing job bringing Rangvald to life on the cover.

I also thank my parents for a lifetime of love and support. My father, who hadn't read fiction for years (certainly not fantasy), began in his 80s to read my books. My mother, who reads voraciously, but thrillers and mysteries, not fantasy, reads everything I write. I am very fortunate to have been raised by such wonderful people.

Lastly, I thank my amazing wife, without whom my dream of being a writer would never have become a reality.

ABOUT THE AUTHOR

Joel Newlon

Joel Newlon is from the United States. Over the years, he has wowed audiences as a stuntman, brought them laughter as a comedy writer, and saved lives as a police officer. But his biggest passion in life has always been writing. He specializes in tales of fantasy and adventure that provide an escape from the everyday world. He lives on a small, secluded farm with his wife, Ashleigh, and two children: Pyewacket the cat and Laika the dog.

Made in the USA
Columbia, SC
24 February 2025

54288049R00164